THE GIRL
and the
GOLDEN LEAF

A Novel

JUNE N. FOSTER

BALBOA
PRESS

A DIVISION OF HAY HOUSE

Balboa Press books may be ordered through booksellers or by contacting:

Balboa Press
A Division of Hay House
1663 Liberty Drive
Bloomington, IN 47403
www.balboapress.com
1 (877) 407-4847

Stock imagery by Hein Nouwens/Shutterstock.com and Alen Kost/Shutterstock.com

Library of Congress Control Number: 2018913944

Print information available on the last page.

ISBN: 978-1-9822-1699-3 (sc)
ISBN: 978-1-9822-1698-6 (hc)
ISBN: 978-1-9822-1700-6 (e)

First Edition: January 2019

Balboa Press rev. date: 12/12/2018

CONTENTS

DEDICATION

To our blessed children around the world who are hungry, frightened, oppressed, abandoned, or brutalized: may you find peace, love, hope, prosperity, and happiness.

And to my precious papa, Timothy L. Foster, who will forever and always be in my heart, thoughts, and prayers.

CHAPTER 1

The Dirt Cell

Present Day

I slowly regained consciousness realizing two things: My head was throbbing in pain, and I smelled dirt. As I cautiously opened my eyes, I saw nothing but dark gloom, but I could hear moaning. I sat up slowly, trying to focus, with nothing much to see. The agony in my skull nearly made me pass out again, so I propped myself into a sitting position with my back against a wall. It was a rough wall, like it was made of uneven wood. I could just barely see the outlines of several bodies; whether they were dead or not was impossible to tell, but at least one was groaning.

Come on, Tia: focus.

The pain seemed to slowly drain out of my head, but it only made me realize how much I hurt everywhere else. I allowed my fingers to gingerly touch my throbbing scalp, and I discovered a thick patch of crusted blood at the hairline.

As my eyes adjusted to the gloom, my nose took in the stench: body odor, human waste, decay, vomit, and maybe decomposition. I shuddered as I tried to recall how and why I got here.

I hoped Finn was okay. He was not only my twin brother, he was my closest friend. Wherever he was, I prayed he was okay. As I lay on the dirt floor, I closed my eyes and tried to control a wave of nausea. The faces of my family came easily. Our time together felt like a distant dream, a time gone by, never to be experienced again. My thoughts drifted to a particular thunderstorm that caught Finn and me by surprise as we kayaked down the New River.

I wrapped my hand around my golden leaf pendant and replayed the day in my head. If I tried hard enough, I was convinced I could smell the spicy, resinous scent of the pine trees whispering overhead.

Last Year

I felt less in control than usual, as the unpredictable winds wreaked havoc on the rapids.

I got this!

I had been down the gorge a thousand times, even though the Class III whitewater felt like a Class VI: much more jarring. I looked up briefly and gasped, seeing the coal-black clouds and feeling the streamlined winds that whipped mercilessly across the bow of my kayak.

Earlier that morning, the sweet kisses of the sun had danced upon the lush autumn foliage blanketing the steep mountains on both sides of the New River. The storm caught us by surprise, and to be honest, I felt powerless as the lightning bolts hit their mark just a few feet away on the shore. Torrential rain pounded upon my helmet like a relentless woodpecker desperately drumming for hibernating ants. I could see Finn shouting at me, but the thunder was deafening as it bounced off the canyon walls.

"Get in front of me! I can't see you; get in front of me!" Finn shouted.

This time, I heard him.

I mustered my strength to try and pass him, but the gale whipped me toward the most dangerous part of the rapids. I held on by the skin of my teeth.

Finn was quartering the water as best he could, but a squall took control, lifting his kayak and capsizing him under the unstable eddy.

I pictured him gasping for air and trying to recover his kayak.

"Finn; *Finn!*" I screamed, my voice probably lost in the howling wind and roar of water. I'm not even sure I heard it.

For a fleeting moment, I imagined a world without my twin brother. We had turned sixteen a few months earlier, and I couldn't think of him not being there.

And then, as soon as it came, the thought was gone. I saw the top of Finn's helmet bobbing on the surface several yards away.

I careened through the rapids, avoiding the dangerous eddy. "Finn, pull out ahead!"

He raised his head and wearily looked my way, and we managed to navigate to a makeshift takeout.

Out of breath and visibly dazed, Finn pulled his kayak out of the rushing water; he removed his helmet and life jacket, and tucked them into the cockpit.

I followed as the rain continued to pour down, a crash of thunder rolling around us.

"Let's go to Tackett's Cave!" I yelled, and he nodded.

Lifting our kayaks above our heads, we navigated through the dense trees, uphill on the slippery ground. After a half a mile, it leveled out a bit, and we entered the cave, setting down the kayaks and collapsing on the ground, exhausted and sopping wet.

The cave was relatively deep, and wide enough to hold at least thirty people. There were old drawings of running deer, fire, and stick people wearing feathers carved into the rock near the back. We were never sure if the carvings were authentic Indian markings from a time gone by or carved as a joke by some drunken teenagers. Either way, I felt comfortable.

I turned to Finn. "What the hell were you thinking going straight down the meat grinder in this storm?"

"Guess I lost track of where I was. I was trying to keep an eye on you," he said.

"Well, you scared the crap out of me. Don't ever do that again." *I don't know what I'd do without you,* I almost said.

"Yeah, yeah," Finn said, smirking.

We spent a few minutes in silence. I was still a little out of breath from the rapids, the scare in the water, and hiking up the hill to the cave.

I watched Finn as he squeezed the rainwater from his long hair; it was incredible how much we look alike. Even as babies, it was difficult to tell us apart. We were Irish through and through, and shared the same blue eyes with little speckles of green, and long strawberry blonde hair with loose, unmanageable curls. While he was as tall as a light pole, I somehow got the short end of the stick, coming in just shy of five feet, four inches.

Teagan and Fionn were our given names, but ever since we were young'uns, our folks simply called us Tia and Finn. Well, that is, until we got caught red-handed in the middle of some sort of mischief. In those moments, Teagan and Fionn were highly exaggerated and fully pronounced, and in those moments, we would burn the wind and scatter like buckshot.

He was a big guy for his age, and his rippled physique were the subject of dreamy looks from hopeful girls in their class and the envy of rival boys. Me, on the other hand, well, I was on the "lean side," as Papa used to say. To be painfully honest, my physique failed to attract much attention in general from the boys in town, who were undoubtedly looking for a softer place to lie.

Finn had always been animated and high-spirited. I usually envied his tenacity and self-confidence, though his reckless actions resulted in many broken bones along the way, starting with shattering his left ankle at the age of four when he'd tried to mimic the way his hero, Tarzan, swung from the trees.

"What?" he said.

It was my turn to smirk. "I was just wondering what's up with you and Miss Tinker Bell."

"Molly. Molly Tinder, not Tinker Bell!" he said, his face turning red. "Wish you'd stop calling her that."

"Well, she's such a tiny little thing. I get confused," I said, smiling. "Really, though, is it serious, or what?"

"No. Not really. We have fun," Finn said with a grin. "What about you? Sean's had a crush on you forever, says you're as cute as a button. Why don't y'all go out sometime?"

"Cause he's a creep." Truth was, Sean wasn't really a creep, just not my type. Whatever that was.

"Well, there are other guys out there who aren't creeps. It's like you're avoidin' life. There's more than just headin' home after school, writin' in that journal, and keepin' your head buried in books."

"If you recall, we just went down the river; if that isn't getting out, I don't know what is." I paused. "Honestly, ever since you and Miss Tinker—I mean Molly—hooked up … Well, you and me used to hang out all the time, until lately, anyway."

Finn sighed. "You've got friends, Tia. You may not do much with them, but maybe you should start. I think it would be good for you to hang out with someone other than me. I mean, I know how awesome I am, but …"

I punched him in the arm. "I just don't feel comfortable with them. I have nothing to say, and we have nothing in common. All they want to do is talk about boys or clothes, or fix their hair, or do their nails. And spending time with guys; well, boys are boys. It's boring."

"Okay, thanks for the compliment, but I get it. They're shallow and you're … what's the word? Multidimensional. You may not find friends that are exactly to your likin', but it's better than nothin'. Like I said, I think you'd have fun; take a chance sometime. You've just been mopin' about since Mama and Papa died."

I shot him a look. What was I supposed to do? I missed them. Trying to make friends seemed like a sad, thin replacement. I'd always been shy and much preferred the solitude of the forest. I'd rather sit on a stump and watch a squirrel than talk about clothes or which boy had a better butt. Truth is, I'd rather be hanging out with family.

But there was less family now.

Feeling self-conscious and a little hurt, I changed the subject. "I'm cold and kind of hungry."

Finn looked at his watch. "Once the rain lets up, how about we mosey up to the ol' cabin and break out the nuts and raisins? That'll hold us till we get home."

"Sure, sounds good."

Just then, my stomach let out a loud growl—*eeeewwwwwrrrrrrllll*—that made us both burst into laughter.

I led us through the thickets. We hadn't been inside the old house since Mama and Papa had died five months earlier, but we'd visit the graves on the outskirts of the property every month. The land and cabin still belonged to our family, but there hadn't been any reason to go inside. Not anymore.

The cabin was tucked in the middle of the dense forest and surrounded by a cluster of trees. Young saplings and fallen leaves had overtaken the once-worn paths; only by accident would someone ever happen upon it. Great-Grandpa Thomas had built it many years ago, and while it didn't have electricity, Papa had rigged up the plumbing so Mama could draw water from the well directly into the sinks and tub.

We set our kayaks down and walked up to the rickety porch made of old railroad ties. The house itself was built out of pine logs and plywood. Every now and again, Papa would replace the old logs and boards with new ones, clambering up onto the roof to patch any holes and reinforce soft spots.

I ran the palm of my hand down one of the saturated black and gray planks. The months of neglect had taken a heavier toll than I expected.

"We could fix it up, me and you. One day, I want to move back here."

Finn smiled and nodded.

"Hey, Tia! There's the ol' tub." He laughed and pointed to the old-fashioned tin container propped along the far end of the porch.

I thought about Mama gently scrubbing my shoulders with a soft cloth. I loved that feeling. It was like the softest massage ever. Sometimes Mama would put dish soap in the water to make it extra bubbly, and that made it seem even more luxurious.

I twisted the front door's worn wooden handle, pushing it open to expose the darkened room beyond. I normally loved the way the cabin smelled: a deep piney scent from the logs mixed with the aroma of supper coming from the big cooking pot in the fireplace, which spit and hissed among the flames.

But now the cabin just smelled damp and stale, unused and unloved.

"Thought this place was bigger," Finn muttered to himself as he walked around the living room, taking it all in. "Look! Mama's rocking chair is still here. It's worn and faded, but still sturdy."

I made my way to the back bedroom, where the kids used to sleep. The bunk beds were in the trailer home, where we now lived with our younger brothers. All that remained in the bedroom were some scrap pieces of paper, an empty closet, and one old white tube sock with blue stitching around the top.

"I miss them so much," I said, hanging onto the doorframe as if my legs might buckle at any moment. "Mama read to us in here every night."

"Yeah, those were great times," Finn said.

Then he headed back through the living room.

I joined Finn beside the fireplace, where he unearthed a plastic bag filled with nuts and raisins. I took a handful, and we sat in silence, munching on the snacks.

We were at school when our parents had been heading to Mannington for the day. Bright yellow, diamond-shaped road signs that read "FALLING ROCK" peppered the sides of the narrow and twisting roads along the Appalachian Mountain Range, but the hundreds of times we'd been down that route, I had never seen a falling rock. On that particular day, a boulder barreled down the side of the mountain and crashed into the car, killing Mama and Papa.

Finn and I would be turning sixteen in a few months, and our brothers, Wes and Paddy, were even younger. I guess there's never a good age to receive bad news, but fifteen, eleven, and eight are, well, particularly hard.

I knew something was wrong when the county sheriff had shown up in my classroom and escorted me to the principal's office. The worst I thought was maybe Paddy had gotten into trouble, talking back or writing notes.

My heart sank when I saw Father Harold, Papa's older brother, sitting on the long couch between Wes and Paddy. Like most days, Uncle Harold was wearing his short-sleeve black clerical shirt with the white Roman collar, black slacks, and heavy black shoes. When he saw me, he immediately came over, held me tight, and kissed my forehead. His light blue eyes were puffy and bloodshot. Then he led me to a chair next to Finn, who looked like a ghost.

"What's going on?" I asked.

"I'm sorry, Tia," Father Harold said.

After we'd left school, Father Harold took us to a dinged and worn old trailer parked behind the church rectory.

"This is your home now, at least for a little while," he said.

The trailer was long and narrow, complete with electricity, running water, two bedrooms, a small, discolored kitchenette, and a sitting area covered in dark brown carpet that would always look dirty, no matter how often I vacuumed it.

The bathroom had a tiny shower with a sliding door and a toilet that squatted close to the ground. The whole place was dirty and dusty, having sat idle for many years.

We cleaned for two solid days; after that, it smelled strongly of Pine-Sol but was finally livable. It still didn't feel like home, but at least every nook and corner reminded me of Mama and Papa.

While the boys were out for lunch, I sat at the kitchenette table and slowly peeled back the lid of a box labeled "FRAGILE." My hands shook as I pulled out two delicate teacups: Mama's treasured items, having been passed down from one generation to the next.

I held the teacups close to my chest before placing them down with care. Then I pulled out my journal and, without forethought or hesitation, began to scribble:

You can't take it with you
echoes in my ear.
You can't take it with you,
so why hold the cup so dear?
My Mama left me on a cloudy afternoon.
No warning, no whistle, gone too soon.
Here, my dear, teacups for you.
Cherish them deeply; they were meant for us two.
Please, I cannot; I cannot bear the pain.
I want to hold my mama, her tiny, tiny frame.
Teacups and stuff hold no value.
You can't take it with you, only feels shallow.
Mama, I miss you; it's hard to get up.
My heart is broken; please share my cup.

Finn's voice startled me back to the present.

"We used to cook squirrel and rabbit in this fireplace," he said. "Do you remember that?"

"Yeah. Of course I remember."

"I've still got that ol' shotgun Papa gave me when I was eight," he said.

I looked around and smiled, thinking about how the family would gather every evening after dinner to tell stories, sometimes even sing and dance. I stared down at the old plywood floor. "I got so many splinters from this floor."

"Yeah, we should have worn shoes. Bottoms of my feet are as soft as a baby's butt these days."

"Finn, were we really *this* poor? This desperate? Why didn't we care?"

Finn's eyebrows shot up and his eyes widened. "Sissy, we're *still* this poor and desperate. Difference is we can turn on the light to see how poor we are." He then lifted both arms and flexed his well-toned muscles. "Don't worry, we'll rebuild it and make it good as new."

"Real funny, but seriously, it's like there's a hole in my heart, and I can't patch it up. It's like we shouldn't be here. It just doesn't feel right anymore."

I could usually push my feelings back to the deepest part of my heart and bury them, but on that day, in that moment, there were too many memories to ignore. They rushed upon me like a tidal wave crashing against a rocky shore.

I stood up, wiped my cheeks, and tried to smile.

"I'm going on a walk; I'll be back soon," I said, heading out the front door before he could protest.

The scent of the damp pine trees was intoxicating. I tilted my head back and felt the warmth of the sun caress my face. I closed my eyes, longing to touch Mama's soft cheek and see Papa's gentle smile.

I walked down a familiar path to a fork in the road that had made Papa's eyes light up every time they crossed it. Papa had known that the hills contained special mementoes dropped by soldiers during the Civil War days, and "by gosh and by golly," he'd always been determined to find something. When Mama brought home a used metal detector from the church flea market, it'd been an exciting day for everyone.

He loved sweeping that machine back and forth across the hard-packed dirt until it found its mark. He would shout "Wahoo!" every time the machine began bleating its tinny-sounding beeps, signaling a find. When that happened, Papa would kneel down on the ground and pull out the soup spoon from his pants pocket. His ritual was to make a large circle around the target with the end of his spoon, and then, ever so carefully, he'd start scraping the dirt from left to right, layer by layer. He was as giddy as a schoolboy.

One time after thirty minutes of painstaking skimming along that fork in the road, Papa's spoon had met an object that gave off the smallest of "tings." He unearthed a cap box, canteen, and bayonet from the soil. His prized find, though, had been a medical bleeder. He laughed at the contraption, finding it to be the most ridiculous gadget ever invented. It wasn't a common bleeder, either, but an elaborate tool with a cover made of mother-of-pearl and two steel blades that were still sharp to the touch.

I picked my way through the forest, finding a rock that was mostly dry. I sat on it, wrapping my arms around my knees.

There were no squirrels, but a couple of birds flitted about now that the rain had stopped.

"Why, Lord?" I asked, hunching over. "Why'd you take them from me?"

There was no answer, which was how it always went.

I hadn't experienced any sort of communication or sign from God since I was a child. Maybe I never would again.

Each Sunday at Mass, I would snuggle close to Mama and gently rub my thumb against the top of her small, suntanned hand, back and forth, over one prominently raised vein.

One day, as service was about to end, a miracle happened. My eyes were fixed on the crucifix on the wall. It was a beautiful carving of Jesus, one I found particularly soft and gentle, unlike some in picture books where Jesus's face was brutally twisted, contorted, drenched in pain and blood.

On that Sunday, without notice or warning, Jesus had somehow released himself from the cross and floated ever so gently toward me, looking at me with an expression full of love and care. I know it sounds ... well, crazy, but Jesus—or the image of Him—didn't say anything, but I felt filled with an insurmountable amount of reverence and peace.

I looked to Mama, Papa, and my brothers, but no one seemed to see what I had seen.

As we walked home from church, I asked my family if they

had seen the vision. They had not, but Mama squeezed my hand in quiet acknowledgment.

I pulled a leaf from a tree and blew my nose, wiping at my tears. I pushed off the rock and continued walking, staring up at the slivers of blue sky through the cloud cover.

I refocused my eyes along each side of the trail, kicking away the fallen leaves and sticks: a little ritual I had started many years ago during my daily hikes.

"Lord, please help me to care for my brothers. Help me to find a job that pays well. Help me find my Golden Ticket."

I know it might sound silly, but I always included the Golden Ticket in my prayers since watching *Willy Wonka & the Chocolate Factory* at Sara Bell's house when I was in sixth grade. Even though I was older—and hopefully wiser now—a small part of me still prayed for a Golden Ticket.

Maybe my Golden Ticket would be a lost diamond, an antiquity worth millions, or even a map to a hidden treasure buried in the hills. I didn't know what would be revealed, but if I prayed hard enough and looked long enough, my special Golden Ticket would save us from poverty and hopelessness.

I knew deep down that it was a silly, unsubstantiated ritual to endlessly search, turning over rocks and fallen branches, praying for that Golden Ticket. But it gave me hope.

I made it back to the cabin and saw Finn standing on the porch, smiling, holding a small tin.

"Why are you smiling?" I asked.

"You're not going to believe this," he said.

"Oh yeah? What?"

"I was checking out the old fireplace and saw a few weird-shaped bricks. They looked loose and out of place. When I nudged the corner of the first brick, it slid out, and then two more slid out. And check this out: behind the bricks, I found this tin." He handed it to me.

I looked down at the blue and green paint on the lid.

"Someone must've hidden it for all these years … but why?" Finn asked. "The hole went down a lot farther, but I couldn't reach. There could be something else in there."

"That's plumb crazy," I said. "I wonder if there's anything else in there."

"It's hard to say. We'll have to look next time we're here," Finn said.

Before heading out, we walked about a half-mile to the eastern edge of the property, and our family's burial place.

"One day when I get some money," I said, looking at the plots where our parents, grandparents, and great-grandparents were laid to rest, "I'm going to buy them all beautiful headstones with little angels on top."

We spent a few minutes pulling weeds from the gravestones and quietly praying.

It was getting late, and I knew our brothers would be worried, so we hurried back to the river and began the descent down the gorge. It was a turbulent ride down the rapids, but the rain had stopped, and we safely made it to the takeout.

We pulled our kayaks out of the water and headed for the old Ford truck that had belonged to Papa. I got into the front seat while Finn pulled the kayaks into the bed of the truck.

As we drove to the trailer, I opened the tin, pulling the contents out one by one: a marriage certificate and a birth certificate from their ancestors, an intricate green brooch, a black-and-white photo, letters, and other odds and ends.

I stared at the photo, faces staring back, faces so much like my own. There was my pointed chin on the face of our great-aunt and the curly wildness of my hair atop great-grandmother's head. I was so consumed by the tin that I didn't even notice it was dark by the time we returned home, the sky an inky black, the moon a rising orb of whiteness that lit up the starkness of the night.

CHAPTER 2

Deep in the Appalachians

Present Day

As I lay on the dirt floor, I saw a door at the far end of the room and felt an instantaneous urge to run, followed by a horrible jolt of fear when I saw a tall, slender man in the corner. He was holding a rifle and wore a wide-brimmed cap that covered his eyes, his mouth set in a hardened, expressionless line.

I tried to take in a deep breath, but the air was thick, the stench overpowering. I redirected my eyes to identify the source of the foul odor. A swarm of flies danced upon a pile of human waste a few feet behind me.

I held a hand against my mouth, stifling the vomit that wanted to come up. Adding to the horrible effect was what tasted like a thick layer of fungus coating my tongue, and my gums throbbed inside my bone-dry mouth.

The gun-toting man watched me as I propped myself up on my hands and knees; I crawled to the farthest corner of room, found a small opening between a skinny girl and boy, and collapsed onto to the floor once more in exhaustion.

I counted the outlines of at least ten sleeping figures.

While the room was stuffy and hot, I couldn't stop shivering. I wrapped my arms tightly around my legs, resting my cheek against my knees. It took a few minutes, but the pounding in my chest slowed to a normal rate.

I peered down at the young girl sleeping next to me and took a deep breath. It was one thing to be held captive, but another to see the pain in others. I resisted the urge to brush the hair away from her face and instead bit my lower lip in anguish.

How the hell am I going to survive in here?

Oh, God, why can't I be more like Finn? Lord knows he would have scratched gravel by now.

Growing up, we were poor as church mice, and I think somewhere along the way, our hardships gave us thicker skin. But now, as I looked at the dire faces around me, nothing in my past had come remotely close to preparing me for this place. I felt vulnerable and physically weak, unable to protect myself, let alone the young'uns around me.

Thinking Back

Believe it or not, Finn and I didn't discover we were poor until one morning during third grade math class. I'm not even sure I knew what "poor" meant.

Miss Watson stretched out her roll of white paper and cut a fifteen-foot strip. Then she secured it to the back wall with masking tape and pulled out a big box of Crayola markers, causing everyone to bounce up and down in their seats in anticipation of a coloring game.

"Today, you're going to learn about line graphs," Miss Watson said. "I've given each of you some numbers, and I want you to plot them on a line graph. These numbers represent how much money people earn."

The kids jumped up and had a lot of fun drawing the bright, bold lines and plotting the green, blue, red, purple, and orange numbers on it. Miss Watson then drew more lines to separate the graph into three parts and labeled the parts as "poor," "middle-class," and "wealthy."

"Okay, class, now I want you to glue pictures that I cut out from magazines and add them to your chart. There are photos of homes, fashion, cars, and vacation destinations. I want you to guess where each photo should go. Should they be glued below the poverty line, in the middle-class area, or in the wealthy section?"

Jessica giggled and held up a picture of a small home. "A shack!" She plastered it in the lower section.

My heart sank. *That was my home: a shack.*

I glanced over to Finn, his usually rosy cheeks suddenly devoid of color.

While we'd always known we might've been less fortunate than some of the kids who lived in the two-story red brick houses around town, I honestly never took notice of the haves and have-nots. Our friends Simon and Jody didn't have electricity, either. I had always loved our little cabin and couldn't understand what all the fuss was about.

Something changed that day for the kids, however. Classmates began eyeing each other. Small groups formed, and within an hour, Miss Watson had effectively stripped the kids of their rose-colored glasses. Finn and I had become painfully aware that we were poor as dirt.

Then we noticed how Mama wore the same faded jeans and plaid shirt every day and the same worn, thin nightgown every night. Papa's brown sweater was threadbare at both elbows. We saw how every spare penny was used to buy food for the kids instead of Mama buying herself a pretty new dress or a fancy purse like the other ladies had when they attended church. I felt pity—and I know Finn did too—not for ourselves, but for our parents and two younger brothers.

I would fantasize about how one day I would quit school, find a job, and get lots and lots of money to buy Mama pretty clothes and help Papa with the bills.

To make matters worse, our classmates relentlessly teased us about our hand-me-down clothes purchased from the thrift shop or donated by the church. They laughed at our shoes that always seemed to have a hole in the canvas big enough for a toe or two to peek out of.

Then the teasing and bullying really began around fifth grade, when Finn and I were given the nickname "Tango Foxtrot." One of the boys had learned the military phonetic alphabet from his father. He replaced "Tia" with "Tango" and "Finn" with "Foxtrot." That meant they could gossip about us without the teachers knowing who they were talking about.

In the beginning, the words stung like a thousand bees, but as the years passed, we let it slide like water off a duck's back. One day, I remember Father Harold saying, "Listen, young'uns, you only have one pair of feet. Therefore, you only need one pair of shoes." Hearing these simple words, well, things just seemed to make sense after that.

By tenth grade, Tango Foxtrot was no longer a disparaging secret phrase but an endearing term used by classmates and teachers alike. Truth be told, we actually felt special when someone yelled out "Tango Foxtrot." I remember one time, Finn was late for the biggest basketball game of the year, and I raced behind him into the gymnasium.

Coach Thompson was madder than a wet hen. He threw down his hat and hollered, "Tango Foxtrot! Get your sorry asses in here! We need you."

I felt proud as a peacock.

When we turned fifteen, Finn and I began working as rafting guides for the Wild White Water Rapids Company, also known as 3WR. Working there was a natural fit, as Papa was a master guide who had worked for 3WR for many years. We were too young to be officially certified, but since we looked older than we were and had been whitewater rafting since the age of five, the owner made an exception, as long as we promised not to reveal our real age. And, of course, we wouldn't.

To top it off, the owner capitalized on the Tango Foxtrot team in his marketing campaigns, and our faces were splashed across entertainment and travel venues as the team to go with for the "adventure of a lifetime." Soon, visitors and thrill seekers from across the United States—and even abroad—were requesting the Tango Foxtrot team to guide them down the rapids.

Present Day

I was somewhere in Latin America, but where? I squeezed my eyes shut, searching for any crumb of memory. *Brazil? Uruguay? Colombia? We had been driven for hours, it seems. Too bad I didn't pay closer attention in geography class.*

The frail bodies that lined the edges of this small dirt cell were sound asleep, and I wished I could do the same. It was still pitch-black outside, and the slender armed thug in the corner was still watching every move I made. Time was excruciatingly slow as an imaginary tick, tick, tick of a nonexistent clock tolled in my brain. A voice, any voice, would perhaps reassure me I wasn't in hell after all.

CHAPTER 3

Last Year

As the truck pulled up to the trailer behind the rectory, I looked up to see eleven-year-old Wes and eight-year-old Paddy running up to greet us.

"Where y'all been? I was 'bout to send out the sheriff and his hound to track y'all down," Wes said as he pushed his long blond hair away from his eyes.

Probably time for a haircut, I thought, though that was not a battle worth fighting.

Finn got out and pulled a kayak from the truck bed. "Sorry, guys, the thunderstorm took us by surprise. Didn't mean to be gone for so long."

"Well, that was stupid of y'all," Wes said, frowning. "All you had to do was look up at the sky. Even a blind man on a galloping horse could see it. Really stupid."

He always had a keen sense of injustice, even as a toddler.

"Sorry, sweetie. Didn't mean to worry you." I knelt down and hugged him.

"We're starvin' here," Paddy said, his coal-black hair in need of a haircut as bad as his brother.

"You and your stomach; you're big enough to cook your own meals, you know. There's no need for you to wait on us. So why don't y'all empty the back of the truck and then wash the grimy Joe's off your hands. Wes, it's your turn to set the table. Paddy and Finn, you can get the coals started. I'll get the venison going; should be thawed by now."

I entered the trailer and could still smell it. No matter how much I cleaned, nothing seemed to get rid of that damp, musty odor, like a moldy dish sponge or stacks of wet newspapers.

There was a little sitting room to the left of the kitchen, with a small couch and a couple of beat-up armchairs. I thought it would be fun to put a TV in there one day, but in the meantime, I flipped the knob on the little radio. Wes and I sang along with George Strait's "All My Ex's Live in Texas."

I opened the door to see if Finn had started the grill—he did—and noticed Paddy tinkering with the bike he'd rebuilt.

"Paddy, quit your piddlin' and get to work."

"Talk to the hand!" Paddy said, briefly holding up one palm.

I tried not to smile, but I wasn't too successful.

Paddy's real name was Patrick, named after an ancestor who

came to America from Ireland in 1880 and then settled in West Virginia to work the coal mines.

Paddy was short and stocky like Papa, but he had Mama's long, curly coal-black hair and sparkling blue eyes. Kids at school always commented on how jealous they were of Paddy's long dark eyelashes. The girls loved him, as he was always playing the role of class clown, the one student who could always make the grumpiest of teachers lose their composure and laugh out loud.

He already seemed a decade older than eight due to his dry, sarcastic sense of humor. Ever since he was knee-high to a grasshopper, Paddy had an endless curiosity and was never content with the answer, "Because I said so." He was a natural tinkerer, always having to explore, take something apart or put it together, or meet up with his friends in town to play a game of ball or build a fort in the trees. He would be gone for hours in the day, and sometimes in the summertime, he wouldn't return home until the sun was low in the sky and it was time for bed.

I shut the door and returned to slicing up the onions, carrots, and celery. "Paddy's always goofing off," I murmured. "He really needs to learn how to cook and help out around here."

"Yep," Wes said. "He's 'bout as useful as a screen door on a submarine."

I glanced over at Wes and smiled. How different my little brothers were. Where Paddy was spontaneous, curious, and loud, Wes was gentle and quiet, with deep bluish-green eyes and blond curly hair that skimmed his shoulders. He stood a full head taller than Paddy, but due to their age difference, that was to be expected.

Wes's true passion was drawing, and he spent hours down by the river, daydreaming and sketching the way the light fell on the water, with the frogs hiding in the long grass along the riverbank. He much preferred the quiet and was content just listening to the gentle thud of his own heartbeat.

After saying grace, Finn began telling Paddy and Wes about our day and the tin box he'd found. They were excited to see what was inside, so after dinner, I brought it out.

"Holy smokes; this is plumb crazy," Paddy said, examining the brooch and turning it over in his hands. "Do you think it's worth anything?"

"I wouldn't want to sell it, but we can bring it to the jewelers to see if they can tell us anything about it."

"Look at these skinny gold bands. Probably wedding rings," Finn said.

"Can we open the letters now?" Paddy asked, jumping up and down in his seat.

"I actually have a better idea," Finn said, tucking the letters deeper into the tin. "Why don't we mosey up to the old house next weekend and read them up there? Bring some blankets and sit on the floor like old times? You two haven't been in the cabin since Mama and Papa died."

"Yeah, okay," Wes said, while Paddy nodded in agreement.

I glanced up at the clock. "Jeez Louise; it's already nine. Why don't y'all skedaddle off to bed? And don't forget, Finn and I are headin' out early in the mornin', takin' a raftin' group out for the weekend. We won't be back till Sunday evening. Oh, and Father Harold wants you to check in with him tomorrow morning when you get up. He'll keep an eye on you."

Finn got up from his chair. "Actually, I'm heading into town to see Molly. I'll be back in a few."

He was gone before I could think of the words to respond.

"Hey! 'Bout time y'all showed up," Travis shouted when we arrived at the docks the next morning, even though we weren't late.

"Take a chill pill, ol' man," Finn said. "We're here for you."

Travis had been Papa's best friend. He was short and robust with weathered, tanned skin. He was in his early forties, with two broken front teeth from a bar fight. Travis said he'd never gotten them fixed because they made him appear more rugged, but I suspected it was because he couldn't afford to.

"It's gonna be a full party of westerners this weekend," Travis said as he and Finn inspected the two-man rafts we'd be using.

I gathered the helmets and paddles from the storage shed and placed them by the rafts. "Who's signed up?"

"A group from California, newbies. Never been out on the river. Don't know if they can even swim," Travis said.

The big blue bus with "3WR! Wild White Water Rapids" splashed across the side pulled up, and fifteen people stepped out.

I did a double-take.

Except for one guy, all the adults were wearing similar shirts with a horse's head stitched on the breast, colorful jackets wrapped around their shoulders with the jacket arms tied in the front, athletic shorts, and docksiders. They must have sat for hours thinking about what they would wear.

The one gorgeous guy, with his brown hair slicked back and beautiful green eyes, wore a simple pair of board shorts, a T-shirt, and gray running shoes. He looked like a guy in a US Marines poster, except for the dimples.

As the group made their way over to the rafts, Finn chuckled. "They're all gussied up; you'd think they were headin' to a beauty contest."

Normally, folks wore clothes they didn't mind getting wet, dirty, or torn. But I liked them right away. They all had huge smiles on their faces, always a good start.

"Over here, everyone!" Finn shouted to the small crowd. "Can't hear a lick with all this hoopla."

Everyone formed a semicircle around the three of us.

"Welcome to our home, y'all," he said. "Beautiful West Virginia and the New River. Raise your hand if you've ever been whitewater rafting before."

No one raised their hands, but several of the guests laughed nervously.

"No one? Well, that's okay, because you're all in for the adventure of a lifetime. Next question, who here can swim?" Finn asked.

Thankfully, all fifteen hands shot up.

"That's a relief," Travis said. "I'm Travis Houlihan, and I grew up on this here river and have been a master guide for many years. You already met Finn, and his twin sister Tia is also one of our guides. These two are also known as the Tango Foxtrot team. Now, they may *look* young, but they've been going down the rapids since they were shittin' yellow in diapers."

"Thanks for the touching intro, Travis," Finn said, rolling his eyes.

"Here's what this weekend will look like," Travis continued. "Over the next two days, we'll travel over thirty miles down the river. The first day will get you warmed up, and you'll be in a two-man raft floating around most of the day. Every now and again, you'll experience a few Class I to Class II rapids, although yesterday, it rained like a cow pissin' on a flat rock, so you'll see some Class IIIs today. Once we make it to Dowdy Creek Falls, there'll be tents set up for you and a supper'll be waitin'. On Sunday after breakfast, we'll pack everything up again and head out for some rougher water on our eight-man rafts. Y'all will be zippin' down the river like a hot knife through butter. We'll end the trip down at the New River Gorge Bridge. Now, is there a leader of this group?"

A tall man toward the back raised his hand. "Guess that'd be me. Mikael Rossi."

To me, he looked like a forty-year-old businessman who was probably more comfortable in a suit jacket than khaki shorts and long-sleeved baby-blue polo shirt.

"This is my wife, Katrina," he said, "and our two daughters, Sophie and Maddie."

Mikael introduced their group, but I tuned most of it out. And then, Mikael pointed to a young man named Boyko, who turned to me and gently took my hand.

"I'm very happy to meet you," he said in a smooth European accent before he kissed the back of my hand, causing me to blush about twenty shades of red.

He was in his early twenties, with big green eyes, brown hair parted to the side, and a gentle face with high cheekbones, dimples, and a square jawline. I remember all that because I couldn't look away from his penetrating stare for a solid three seconds. When I finally did, it was to gawk at his muscular body, his biceps bulging from the confines of the clean white T-shirt.

"I've never known Tia to be speechless before," Finn joked, handing Boyko a helmet.

After a safety briefing, the group was split into twos, and everyone began casually drifting down the New River. The day went by quickly, and by late afternoon, we were greeted by the other 3WR crewmembers at Dowdy Creek Falls.

The tents had been erected, and the campfire was going strong. 3WR's cook, Lillian, was busy preparing her homemade peach cobbler for dessert.

I glanced over to the young girls, who were removing their helmets, exposing their mussed-up sandy blonde hair. "Sophie and Maddie, do y'all want to check out the waterfall?"

"Sure," Sophie said. "Now maybe we can finally jump in the water."

It didn't take long until Mikael, Katrina, Phil, and Greg joined us.

"This is paradise," Mikael said, looking up at the cathedral of trees surrounding us.

And it *was* paradise. There was a sweet scent in the air from the damp forest, and the tantalizing mist from the falls settled on our faces and shoulders in a refreshing spray.

Greg took off his T-shirt and carefully picked his way across the moss-covered boulders. "Last one in's a rotten egg," he called back.

Greg and Phil seemed to fit perfectly together. I hadn't met anyone who was gay, but it was obvious these two had a love for one another.

Eventually, we returned to the campsite, and I know my belly was rumbling. The intoxicating aroma from the grill didn't help.

After the swimmers changed into dry clothes, we sat around the table and stared at a meal we rarely had at home: sirloin steaks, grilled chicken, potato salad, coleslaw, baked beans, rolls slathered in melted butter, watermelon, and slices of fresh cantaloupe.

Mikael raised a hand. "Hey all, before we dig in, I wanted to say a few words." He held his glass of beer up high. "I know I gave you a bunch of grief when we were trying to decide where to go on our team outing. I was pretty sure you all wanted to head to Vegas. But I was overruled—and pretty surprised—when everyone wanted to come here. If memory serves me, I think I grumbled for a least a month."

"Maybe two!" one of the men said, laughing.

"Well, I'm not often wrong, but I have to admit that this has been the most fun I've had in years, not to mention one of the most beautiful places I've ever been. I'd like to thank Travis, Finn, and Tia for a fantastic day and the crew for this feast in front of us. So … here's to wild and beautiful West Virginia and conquering the wild rapids."

The group lifted their drinks in the air, shouting and hollering.

"Phil and I also wanted to give a special thank you to our team. Over the past three years, all of you have worked tirelessly to get us ready for the upcoming shoot. Each one of you brought your creativity, flexibility, expertise, and love to our production, and I am confident it will be a success! Here's to *Wolfgang's Treasure*!"

I leaned toward Finn. "Shoot? Production? What's *Wolfgang's Treasure*?"

"They're heading to South America to film a movie."

I raised my eyebrows. As nice as these folks were, they didn't seem like movie types, except maybe Boyko. I could picture him up on the silver screen.

After dessert, a thoughtful silence fell as we watched the beauty of a West Virginian sunset. Silhouettes of the maples seemed to melt into the night sky as the gentle patter of the waterfall echoed nearby.

Once it was completely dark, Finn said, "Go ahead and change into some warmer clothes, grab your flashlights, and we'll meet back here around the campfire."

I went to my tent and flipped on the battery-powered lamp. After changing into Levis and an old sweatshirt, I grabbed my guitar and went next door to Finn's tent. "Is it music time?"

"I believe it is," he said, coming out with his guitar.

We headed to the campfire and took our seats as the others joined the circle. We strummed and got our fingers loosened up. I glanced at Finn, and he looked at me, and in a silent cue, we began playing *Sweet Home Alabama*.

The group let out a combined "Wow!" and started clapping their hands and singing along. While I am terribly shy, I couldn't help but come out of my shell any time I was singing and playing guitar.

We played several traditional campfire songs, ending the set with Papa's favorite, John Denver's *Take Me Home, Country Roads*. A lump formed in my throat, remembering him singing, the way his eyes had always sought me out in the final chorus.

"I've got to say," Mikael commented "you've got some talent."

"They're plumb good at everything," Travis said. "It's sort of annoying, but they're good kids, not like some of the briggity young'uns in town."

"Where's your family from originally?" Mikael asked.

"We're Irish," I said. "How about you? Have you always lived in California?"

"Well, my ancestors are European, mostly Italian and German. But I was born and raised in Dallas and went to the University of Texas." Mikael pointed his thumb toward Phil. "This guy was my roommate and frat brother, and we've been best friends ever since. My first job out of school was an internship with a Hollywood production company, and my career took off from there. Ten years after I moved to California, Phil came out and we started our own company, Open Borders Studio."

He took a sip of beer.

"Then, I met this beautiful lady, and we got married six months later. The rest—including our two girls—is history."

Finn set his guitar aside. "Phil, how'd you and Greg meet?"

Phil placed his hand on top of Greg's hand, and laughed. "I'd love to retell how we met. Let's see, when I moved to California, Greg was my Realtor. I wanted to find an apartment close to the studios, but Greg kept showing me flats around Newport Beach, not very close. After the third outing, I confronted him on why he was showing me these homes in Orange County. He gave me a goofy smile and said he wanted me to live closer to where he was so that he could see me more often."

Phil paused and smiled at Greg. "Well, since that time, we've been together ever since."

Greg laughed. "Goofy smile," he said. "Yeah, I guess that's about right."

"How about you, Boyko?" I asked. "How'd you make your way to California?"

Boyko looked up from his s'more; his green eyes seemed to sparkle in the firelight. "Ah, it's a great story, actually. I was born in a little town not too far from Sofia, Bulgaria, and I studied theater in school. I graduated a year ago and was invited to Cannes for the film festival. I was introduced to Mikael and Phil at a party, and we just hit it off right away. They said I had the look they'd been searching for, and now I'm the lead actor in their upcoming movie."

I melted at the sound of his European accent.

"You never know what life is going to bring, huh?" Travis said as he stoked the embers of the dying fire.

I looked around. The fresh air and long day had caught up to the group, and there were a lot of half-stifled yawns, with eyes blinking, trying to stay awake.

"Well, we've got an early start tomorrow," Travis said. "Off to bed with y'all."

The campground quickly went dark, the only sounds being the peeping of distant frogs and leaves rustling overhead.

I had camped out in the forest hundreds of times, but that night, I felt spooked. I found myself hurrying to my tent; I crawled in and zipped up the flap. I had no idea why I felt the surge of inexplicable dread, a fear that slowly crept up from my stomach, radiating out through my limbs, with a heaviness that almost paralyzed me.

From the tingles creeping over my hands and feet, and the sick, queasy feeling in my stomach, I knew something was on its way. But what?

CHAPTER 4

The Golden Maple Leaf

The next morning, droplets of dew dotted the grass, and billowy white clouds hung low between the maples. The air was cool and damp, and the leaves seemed to have magnified overnight to clearly display their radiant orange, red, and yellow highlights. I loved my morning hike, and nature didn't let me down.

I came to a small stream full of brilliantly colored stones, and the sun was just beginning to peek through the treetops when a shiny object caught my eye. I bent down and picked up an old pocketknife peeking out from a fallen leaf, and my heart might have stopped. I immediately recognized it as Papa's. *Papa's!*

It was a simple knife with one blade and a pair of scissors, but just holding it made my chest throb with hurt. I woke so happy and optimistic that morning, and suddenly this one memory plunged me back to reality.

"Why, God? Why'd you take them from me?"

Anxiety rushed through me at the responsibility that had been laid on my shoulders: caring for two younger brothers with no money, little food, and cramped housing.

I held the small knife and felt warm tears spilling down my cheeks.

"Please, Lord, help me find my Golden Ticket—any treasure, anything, really—just to get us to a better place."

I felt panicked. I forcefully kicked at fallen leaves and sticks, trying to uncover the Golden Ticket I'd been praying for, a sign from God that he'd give me the strength to keep going. I was certain if I looked long enough, *hard* enough—turning over fallen trees, sticks, leaves, and rocks—I'd find it. I wondered if I was slowly going insane, especially when I caught myself searching inside darkened tree holes that had been formed by forest animals.

I'm losing my freakin' mind!

As I rounded the bend toward the far end of the stream, a warm gust of wind swept through the valley and rushed across my face. I looked up and gasped.

Hundreds upon hundreds of bright golden leaves cascaded down around me, flying this way and that, left to right, and right to left. It was an amazing sight, because the tree branches kept holding fast to their vibrant red and orange leaves; only the golden maple leaves were falling. I couldn't break my stare; I was in total awe. It was the most magnificent sight I had ever seen.

Dozens of leaves fell on my head, and I stretched my arms out, peering up into the sky. One perfectly formed golden maple leaf swirled down and landed on my open palm. At that very moment, in that very instant, I felt a rush of overwhelming love and peace. All of my cares, my worries, my concerns, and my sadness were gone: evaporated in a heartbeat, and replaced with a feeling of absolute tranquility.

I clung to the maple leaf, pressing its satiny smoothness to my cheek as I whispered a prayer of thanks.

How was I so blind?

I let out a heavy sigh. All of this time, throughout so many searches, I'd been looking down at the ground, searching over miles and miles for the Golden Ticket. And here it was, in my palm. I knew the beautiful yellow maple leaf was a sign from the Lord that both lightened my heart and filled me with hope.

I returned to the tent with a sense of peacefulness and placed the maple leaf between two pages in my journal, smoothing out the contours of the leaf with my fingers before closing the book.

I came out of my tent and saw Finn packing up his bags.

"Morning, Sis. You've got quite a glow about you."

All I could do was smile.

"Remember what I told you in the safety briefing," Travis said as the group ate breakfast. "There are many large boulders that we'll have to navigate around, so it's important that you *always* listen to your guide. We'll split into two groups, with Finn taking one and me taking the other. Tia will set the course in her kayak at the front."

Soon, we were all in our watercrafts, navigating the river. Each rapid was more exhilarating than the last, and there were loud hollers of excitement from the group. It didn't seem to take long until we could see the New River Gorge Bridge, where the other 3WR crewmembers were waiting on the shore to help the group unload.

As Travis got out of his raft, he pointed to the bridge. "This was built in 1977 and is the third-highest bridge in the United States. The third Saturday of October is known as Bridge Day, and there's a festival with great home-style food and music. Folks come in from everywhere just to BASE jump and rappel off the bridge. Great time to come back, y'all."

Sophie's eyes seemed to widen to three times their normal size. "I want to jump off the bridge," she squealed. "Can we, Daddy?"

"Maybe when you're a bit older," Mikael chuckled as he lifted her off the raft and helped her onto the shore.

As Finn and I began shaking hands with the guests, thanking them for their participation, Mikael approached us.

"I was wondering if I might have a word with you."

"Sure," Finn said. "What's up?"

Mikael smiled. "Phil and I were talking last night after you both turned in, and we believe you two have great talent. You're good-looking, charismatic, and you both sing beautifully. We'd like to consider you for roles in our movie."

I looked at Mikael. *He was offering us a job,* I thought. *Me! An actress, no less.*

"Good Lord," Finn said, his eyes sparkling with excitement. "I'm not sure what to say. We're open to hearing more, right, Sis?"

I smiled, not quite sure how to respond, my tongue all at once stuck to the roof my mouth, which had gone dry.

"I'll be staying in town the next few days," Mikael said. "Would you like to meet at the diner around ten tomorrow morning?"

"That works for us," Finn said.

Mikael handed Finn some bills. "We had a fantastic time this weekend. Here's just a little something to show our appreciation."

"Holy cow!" Finn said as he fanned out five $100 bills.

"This is too generous," I said. "We can't accept this." Though we *really* needed the money. And there it was, clutched in Finn's hand. Wes and Paddy needed new shoes and clothes, and this extra cash would make our lives easier for a spell. Frankly, it was a gift impossible to refuse.

"I insist," Mikael said, smiling. "I look forward to seeing you both tomorrow."

"Jeez Louise!" Finn said as we began loading our truck. "This is crazy."

"I'm excited to hear more," I said. "Maybe this is the break we've been hoping for."

The golden maple leaf popped into my mind, and I wondered whether pursuing the movie deal might just be the path God wanted me to take.

"Just think," I said. "We could get enough money together to rebuild the old cabin, get angel headstones for Mama and Papa, and who knows? Maybe, just maybe, we could start our own rafting company."

"That'd be awesome," Finn said. "I don't know anything about acting or movies or whatever, but it can't be that hard to do, right?"

"Right," I said, climbing back into the truck. "Let's not jinx it by telling the boys yet, okay?"

"Good idea," Finn said, revving the engine.

"Are you ready?" Finn yelled from the front door the next morning. "You're takin' your own sweet time."

"Can you wait a cotton pickin' minute? Just trying to do something with my hair," I yelled back, looking in the mirror and sighing with exasperation before giving up entirely on trying to braid the unruly curls. I jogged out to the truck.

"Your hair looks the same," Finn teased as they drove to the diner in town.

"Hah! So does yours," I said, laughing.

"Maybe we can get a telephone for the trailer," I said as we pulled into the parking lot of the diner.

"We'll have to if we're leaving the boys for a while," Finn said as he found an open spot to park.

Mikael, Phil, and Boyko were already sitting at a large corner booth when we walked in. It was an old diner, built in the early 1900s by the Owen family. It was full of worn red leather booths, the linoleum scuffed by the tread of so many pairs of feet over the years. The place had been passed down from generation to generation and was loved by the community for its authentic home-style cooking. The meatloaf plate with homemade mashed potatoes and gravy was awesome, and the cherry pie with crumb topping was my favorite.

The guys stood up when we approached the table, wide smiles on their faces.

"Good to see you again," Mikael said. "Did you eat yet? Can I get you something to drink?"

I noticed they all dressed the same again: polo shirts, tan khaki pants, and docksiders.

Boyko scooted back into the booth and offered me to sit next to him, allowing enough room for Finn to sit on the end.

"Thanks," I said, "but we ate a little while ago. I'll take a cola, though."

"A cola would be great," Finn said as he took his seat.

After ordering the drinks, Mikael said, "I bet you have a thousand questions, so maybe it would be easier if we started from the beginning. I mentioned at the campout that Phil and I are movie producers out of Hollywood. Our company is relatively new compared to Warner Brothers, Paramount, and Universal, for example, but luck, timing, and talent broke all odds, and we've become number ten internationally. Phil, could you fill them in on our little movie?"

Phil set down his cup of coffee and leaned forward. "It's about an eccentric young adventurer born in Bulgaria and raised in France."

That sounds familiar, I thought. It sounded like Boyko and his background.

Phil said, "In the original script, Boyko's character found a journal containing a map from the mid-1800s that belonged to an explorer named Wolfgang Steiner. Wolfgang was a valued member of the Royal Geographical Society and had been commissioned to explore the treasures of Brazil and the animals of the Amazon. After three years in Brazil, Wolfgang found a few dozen emeralds during his travels and kept them stored in a large metal box. He was never interested in the wealth for himself; his dream was to start a local geographical society close to the Amazon. Sadly, local thieves caught wind of Wolfgang's precious stones and targeted him, so he retreated deep into the rain forest and hid the box, marking on the map exactly where it was buried. He returned to England with plans of going back within the year to begin his foundation, but he contracted tuberculosis and died. Years later, while rummaging through old books at an antique market in Frankfurt, Germany, Boyko discovered Wolfgang's journal."

"And now he's on a quest to discover the lost emeralds," Finn said, smiling from ear to ear.

"Exactly," Phil said.

"Look," Mikael said, "you two are amazing young people. Not only are you excellent whitewater rapid guides, you're attractive, you sing, we love your accent. You've got the whole package. Exactly what our audience wants today. We believe the audience will connect with you, so much so that we'd rewrite portions of the script with you in mind. Phil shared with you the original storyline, but after meeting you, we thought of a way to heighten the excitement as well as draw a greater interest from adventurous viewers worldwide."

Phil leaned forward. "Boyko is an avid adventurer and recently discovered the excitement of whitewater rafting. After meeting you—the Tango Foxtrot team—on an excursion, he's commissioned you to meet him in Chile to raft down the Río Futaleufú. Once you conquer the rapids, Boyko then invites you to Brazil to spend a few days with him traveling down the Amazon River. You two jump at the opportunity, and after a few days on the river, you return home while Boyko continues on his search for Wolfgang's hidden treasure."

I glanced at Finn, wishing I could read his thoughts. He had a thoughtful look with a hint of a smile, perhaps his best poker face. I, however, couldn't contain my excitement.

"It sounds fantastic," I said. "How long would we be gone for?"

"In all, about two to three months at the most, depending upon the final production schedule. In April, we'd like to bring you to California for a few weeks. Then, we'll head down to Chile for the rafting scenes and then onto the Brazilian rain forest, where you'll spend a couple of days with us. You'll fly home from Brazil."

"It sounds like an amazing opportunity," Finn said. "But I ... we ... well, we don't know a thing about acting."

Mikael shifted in his seat. "We realize that, but we'll help you. From now until April, we'll have an acting coach visit you here in West Virginia. Caroline will help you review the script and give you acting lessons."

"When we get back to California," Phil said, "I'll have

Jonathan, our composer, begin writing an original song for you to sing while in Chile. As soon as he finishes, I'll send it over for you."

I let out a deep breath. "Mikael, we're blown away at your offer, more than we could have ever imagined. But two to three months is a long time to be away from our little brothers. It would just be so hard for us to really consider it."

"I don't think Father Harold would mind," Finn said, "and Wes will be twelve by then. They both can take care of Paddy just fine."

"Who is Father Harold?" Mikael asked.

"Oh, he's our uncle. He looks after us," I said. I turned to Finn. "What about school? It lets out the first week in May, so we'd miss three or four weeks. I doubt they're going to just let us go."

"Well, it's only September now," Mikael said, "so maybe you can talk with your uncle and your teachers and somehow work extra hard during the year so you can finish up before April. Just a thought; our student actors have to do this all the time. The other option is for us to bring a qualified person on set that would take you through the lessons and then submit them for credit to your school. We've got some options here."

I smiled. "That sounds pretty good. But be warned: Father Harold's going to want to meet you. He'll probably do a background check."

"I'm sure he would," Phil said. "We'd be happy to give him anything he needs. I want to make sure he knows you'll be in good hands. So do you live with Father Harold? Where are your parents?"

"Our parents died a few months ago," Finn said. "Father Harold is letting us live in the mobile home out back of the church. It's just down yonder if you want to meet him. He's the priest at St. Mary's Catholic Church."

Mikael reached out his hands and placed one on top of each of ours. "I'm so sorry to hear this. Losing a loved one, especially both your parents, is such a tragic loss. Yes, I would love to meet your uncle before we head back to California."

"Thanks," Finn said. "It's been a tough few months for sure."

"We're flying home on Thursday morning," Mikael said. "How about we come around Wednesday after school? That will give you some time to think everything over and talk with your uncle." He let go of our hands, pulled a card out of his shirt pocket, and handed it to Finn. "Here's my number; just give me a call and let me know if four o'clock is good for everyone. We can meet at the church."

"We really appreciate the chance to do this, Mikael," Finn said, "but it's a lot to think about. Can you tell us how much we'd be getting paid?"

I shot him a glance. *I'm glad he asked, but wow; he's so bold.*

"Great question," Mikael said, smiling. "We know it's a hardship to leave your little brothers, your school, and your home while placing your trust in total strangers. The company's prepared to offer you two hundred thousand dollars each for your work. You'll get half when you come to California and the balance once we've completed the Brazil shoot. Also, you'll be entitled to 2 percent of all monies generated from the release of the film as well as ongoing residuals."

I wasn't sure I heard him right, and then I could barely breathe. I clasped my hands under the table so they wouldn't see how much they were shaking.

"That's a lot of money," Finn said. "You're really taking a chance on two kids who've never acted before."

"Just be yourselves, and the camera will love you. Caroline and the team will make sure you're more than prepared."

My head was spinning so much, I felt like I'd been strapped on a carnival ride for too long. Everyone began to scoot out of the booth.

"Well, guys, thanks for coming in this morning," Phil said. "Best be getting off to school."

"Yeah, we better be off. Thanks, y'all," Finn said as he shook everyone's hand.

"Bye, and thanks so much," I said, giving everyone a hug.

"Great," Phil said. "Oh, and by the way, if you do decide to join us, bring your IDs, Social Security cards, and birth certificates when we meet with Uncle Harold on Wednesday. We'll need to get the paperwork going as soon as possible for passports and visas."

When we got into the truck, I leaned my head against the seat in a daze, thoughts as cloudy as if I'd just awoken from a dream.

"I can't believe this," I said, wiping my sweaty palms on my jeans.

"We've gotta talk about this with the others," Finn said.

"Well, Wes and Paddy get out of school in a few hours. How

about we pick up some supplies, get our sleeping bags, order a couple of pizzas, and camp out at the old house tonight?"

"Can't miss another day of school," he objected. "I don't think Father Harold would like that too much."

"We won't," I promised. "We'll get up super early and make it to school on time tomorrow morning. I think we need this time together tonight; it'll give us some time to explain everything."

"Yeah, okay. When are we going to tell Father Harold?"

"How's tomorrow after school sound?" I suggested.

"Okay. I'm kinda afraid he'll say no," Finn said.

"We'll figure out how to tell him," I said, sounding more confident than I felt. "The way I see it, except for us missing each other for a couple of months, there is no downside."

CHAPTER 5

Selling the Plan

After loading up the truck, we went to Sammy's Pizza and picked up two large pepperoni pies and four bottles of Coke. We headed to the school parking lot, arriving just as the bell rang and a rush of kids came running out.

We watched as Paddy and Wes jumped on their bikes and started for the road.

Finn honked three short bursts from the horn. They turned and saw us, puzzled looks on their faces. They quickly peddled to the truck, racing each other.

Wes skidded to a halt, with Paddy nearly crashing into him.

"What y'all doing here?" Paddy asked as Finn got out of the truck. "Is something wrong?"

"Let's put your bikes in the back," he replied, "We're goin' for a ride."

I watched as they wiggled into the back seat of the cab and buckled themselves in.

"We thought y'all might want to go to the old house tonight," I said. "We've loaded up the truck with sleeping bags, snacks, and pizzas. Sound good?"

Wes squinted suspiciously. "Yeah, sounds great," he said. "But why? I mean, why now?"

I smiled. To me, with his baby-soft cheeks and wide eyes, Wes seemed as innocent as a toddler.

"We thought it would be fun to hang out together," I said as Finn got behind the wheel. "Plus, we have some exciting news we want to share."

"Uh oh," Wes said.

"Put a cork in it," Paddy said, laughing. "We've got snacks and pizza."

Once at the cabin, we unloaded the truck and then sent the boys to collect firewood, Finn following. I headed for the small kitchen and placed the pizza and pop bottles on the wooden kitchen table. I glanced out the window and smiled, watching Finn loading Wes and Paddy's small arms with firewood. It looked like they were having one of their contests to see who could carry the most.

The sun was setting, and soon the old home would be dark as coal. I flipped on five battery-operated lanterns and placed them randomly around the kitchen and the living room.

Soon, Finn had the fireplace alive and dancing with flames,

and we were sitting in a circle and passing around a bag of caramel corn.

"Do you think we'll ever move back here?" Wes asked quietly as he stared solemnly at the curl and sway of the fire.

"One day, little man," Finn said. "No doubt."

"I almost forgot," I said, digging around in my backpack for the silver tin Finn had found on our last trip. "Who wants to read the letters?"

I pulled the tin out, admiring it. An old Irish biscuit box with a beautiful woman wearing a emerald-colored skirt and matching green scarf tied around her dark brown hair. Rolling green landscapes and the sparkling blue streams of Ireland covered the top and sides. With my thumb, I gently opened the lid and pulled out a marriage certificate, a rosary made out of blue twine with a wooden cross, a green stone brooch, and a black-and-white photo of a family standing on a porch. The man in the photo held a long hunting rifle, and there was a straggly dog asleep at his feet. The girls wore little white dresses that fell just below their knees. I set the items carefully on the floor.

I turned it over and read the caption: "The McSherry's, 1910." I handed the picture to Paddy, and he stared at it.

I pulled out a stack of musty yellowed envelopes bound in twine.

"There's quite a few letters here, so let's just read a couple for now." I selected one from the stack. "Let's start with this one."

"'March 1880. Sara, my dear little daughter.'" I smiled. "Sara was your great-great-grandpa Patrick's oldest daughter. And 1880 is the year they came to America from Ireland."

"Wow," Wes said.

The rest of the letter read:

> This is to you this Sunday and I am very sad and it seems like a long day and I am very lonesome for you. I can't take you up on my nee and say little birdy on a tree singing chic a dee chic a dee like I ust to do last summer. Tell mama that I want her to give John one bushel of my oats that I stored before I left. Thars 10 bushels there and thare will be 9 bushels left for mama to sell them and get you a nice dress for the winter and for her to make it in a dress and not a Mother Hubbard. But a regular dress, and if she does not do so, I will make it pretty lively for her. Tell mama that dress will be for that nice Sunday dance. I want you to be a good girl and be mannerly, for I think it is so nice to be mannerly and good. Goodbye Sara, from your most affectionate Papa.

"They talked so funny back then," Paddy said.

"Yeah, and it seems that he spelled the words liked they sounded." I passed the letter to Paddy.

"My English teacher would go nuts," Paddy said.

"Read the next one. What happens next?" Wes asked.

"Okay. This one's written in July 1880."

I cleared my throat.

> Dear Eliza, wilst try and send you a few lines in answer to your most kind and welcome letter.

Blessed to hear that you and Sara are well. Work is grusom in the mines, spendin twelve hours a day deep underground. Reckon to have enough dollars to you short of a few months so we can be together. My appetite has been sorely poor, and hard to keep morsels down. I've worked on until yesterday but I had to give up; could not go any more. I lost over forty pounds in flesh. You asked how the water was, and it is practically undrinkable in these here parts. If you knew how many times I wished that I could go down to our old spring at home and get a good drink ... Corn and potatoes are plentiful, but that is all thar is so I'm tired of them. No hay nor grain. Give my love to Sara and ask her to pray out loud so that God will bless her all the days of her life. Your most affectionate husband, Patrick.

Everyone was quiet for several moments.

"They were so poor back then," Wes said.

Finn said, "Way I see it, if it wasn't for their courage to venture all this way, we wouldn't be here now."

I stood up and asked, "Who's ready for some pizza?"

"Me!" Wes and Paddy both shouted, raising their hands.

I replaced the letters in their worn envelopes, and as I reorganized the contents of the tin, I noticed something: a large yellow maple leaf pressed between two sheets of wax paper.

"That's *really* strange," I said under my breath as goose bumps rolled up my arm.

What are the chances that just a few days ago, my golden ticket, a golden maple leaf, floated down into my hands, and now, in this hundred-year-old tin, one of my ancestors kept a golden maple leaf. Why?

I studied the leaf for a few more moments before putting it back in the tin.

After stoking the fire, Finn cleared his throat. "Hey, y'all, listen up. There's something really important that Tia and I need to talk to you about."

"We're ready," Wes said around a mouthful of pizza. "What's up?"

Finn looked at me with uncertainty. "Well, remember we went on the weekend rafting trip? The group we took down the rapids came here from Hollywood. Turns out, they make movies, and ... well ... Tia?"

I smiled and nodded. "They offered us a role in their upcoming movie. We're going to be actors playing a part, kind of like when we were in the Christmas play last year, but this time, it will be in a movie."

"Freakin' awesome," Paddy said. "When does this all happen?"

"Not till the spring. There's an acting coach who will visit us this winter, and we have to learn a new song, but we won't leave until April."

I noticed Wes was as quiet as a mouse peeing on cotton. Finally, he asked, "What do you mean by *leave*?"

I crawled over and sat next to him, pushing his long blond hair behind his ears. I glanced at Finn, who nodded.

"We'll be gone for about two to three months. They'll fly us to California for a few weeks in April, and then we go to Chile. You see, Finn and I will be playing rafting guides, just like we do here. We'll be going down one of the rapids in Chile, and then we'll spend a few days along the Amazon River in Brazil."

The words coming out of my mouth were still unbelievable but exhilarating.

California. Chile. Brazil!

I had never even been on a plane; none of us had.

I felt Wes's hand tighten, and he placed his head on my shoulder.

"Just don't reckon you should go," he said. "It don't feel right. We just lost Mama and Papa; don't want to lose y'all too."

Finn crawled over to Wes and took him in his arms. "Hey, buddy, nothin's gonna happen. I'll take care of Sissy. We'll be fine and back here before you know it."

"Ah, and here's the best news of all," I said, trying to get a smile on Wes's face. "We're going to be rich. They'll pay us two hundred thousand dollars *each*."

Their mouths both fell open, and I had to laugh at the astonishment on their faces.

"So does that mean you're cool with us being gone for a few months?" Finn asked.

"We're going to be filthy rich," Paddy screeched.

"It will feel like it," I said. "We'll definitely be much better off. Just think, we could have enough money to rebuild this cabin."

"What do you think, buddy?" Finn asked Wes.

"I don't know, but it's not till April, so I've got a lot of time to talk you out of it." He was trying not to smile. "If you do end up going, though, it'd be awesome to rebuild this place and move home. So, yeah, I guess it's okay."

"Oh, thanks for granting permission," I said, reaching over and ruffling his hair.

"That's it for now," Finn said. "We'll talk to Father Harold after school tomorrow, okay? If you happen to see him, don't say a word. We have to break it to him gently."

The boys nodded and crawled into their sleeping bag.

"Now get some shut-eye," Finn said as he turned off the lanterns.

The next day passed by slowly, as my head was in the clouds, daydreaming about the movie, traveling to unknown lands, and all the money. It still seemed too good to be true.

Once the boys got home from school, Finn and I headed over to the rectory. We passed through the back door and made our way through the dimly lit hallways, passing a few small rooms furnished with office desks and chairs. We found our uncle sitting at the small kitchen table, with a glass of iced milk and a plate of ginger snaps.

"Hi, Father Harold," I said, bending down to kiss him on the top of his shiny head. He was almost bald, with a tuft of white hair combed along the lower half of his head. He was tall and fit, his baby blue eyes sparkled, and his smile radiated enough to reach every member of his congregation at Mass. He was pure and gentle, through and through. If one were to imagine an angel on earth, it would be Father Harold, and in many ways, he'd been our guardian angel. Although he was our uncle, we had always called him Father Harold for reasons I couldn't quite explain. Maybe it was as simple as the fact that it seemed impossible to separate the man from the priest.

"Hey," Father Harold said. "Whatcha up to?"

We sat down, and Finn leaned forward.

"There's something we need to talk with you about," Finn began, "and need your blessin' on."

I sat quietly as Finn recounted the entire story and proposal.

When Finn had finished, he took a deep breath and let it out slowly.

At first, Father Harold had no reaction. He just lifted his index finger and laid it across his lips with his thumb under his chin, thinking. He had a look of deep concern right before he closed his eyes.

The room was quiet, except for the clock ticking in the corner and the slight rustle of the wind outside.

Minutes went by before Father Harold finally opened his eyes.

"Well, that's a lot to take in from out of nowhere," he said, smiling with his mouth, but I saw it didn't touch his eyes. "To be honest, it sounds shady to me. Who in their right mind would take two young'uns from a small town in West Virginia and make them movie stars? Something's not … kosher. Just pick up a newspaper. Every day there's another young'un, your age, getting kidnapped and killed. Other things too … too horrible for y'all to imagine."

I sat up and reached for a ginger snap, turning the cookie over in my hand, more for something to do than anything else. "I know it's gotta sound off the wall, but Mikael, you should have seen him with us this weekend. He was there with his wife and his two children, a real family man. And Phil, he's a great guy. And Boyko, the lead actor, believed in them so much he left his home in Bulgaria and moved to California to work with them. Maybe, well, if you just meet them tomorrow, I think you'll change your mind."

"You're not convincing me; still sounds shady," Father Harold said, pursing his lips in a way that let me know that his approval, if it came, would be hard won.

I reached across and placed my hand on his. "It does sound unbelievable to me, even now, but I think they're the real thing. It doesn't sound like they would lie about something like this and come all the way to West Virginia just to find two suckers. But, yeah, I want to make sure it's all legit too."

Father Harold paused and let out a deep sigh. "I tell you what. I'll make some calls. I want to be prepared. I know a few priests out in the Los Angeles area; they'll give me the honest answers I'm looking for. Maybe one of them can stop by their offices and meet with Mikael. I just don't want anything bad to happen to you. You understand, right?" Father Harold looked directly into my eyes.

I nodded.

"What time are they coming around tomorrow?" he asked.

"About four o'clock, right after school," Finn said.

"Okay, I'll be here. What about your schoolwork though? School doesn't get out until May or so."

"We've already thought about that," Finn said. "School gets out the first week in May, so we'd be missing about three weeks. Tia and I are meeting with our teachers and the principal next week to see if we can finish all our work ahead of time. If not, we'll take it with us, I guess."

"Like I said, we'll see," Father Harold said.

"So if it all does pan out, would you take care of Wes and Paddy while we're gone?" I asked.

"You're putting the cart in front of the horse. Of course, I'll always be here for y'all, you know that," Harold said.

Finn and I stood up.

"Great. Thanks, Father Harold," I said as I hugged him.

Four o'clock Wednesday finally came. Finn and I were nervously pacing the floor in the front room of the rectory.

There was a knock on the door, and Finn greeted Mikael and Phil and led them to a small sitting area adorned with furniture we knew well: two golden-hued love seats separated by a mahogany coffee table with elegantly shaped legs. To the right of the farthest love seat was my favorite piece: an ornate high-backed chair with open sides in a rich shade of dark blue and gold. During the harsh winter months, I would curl up and turn the chair ever so slightly to face the warmth of the fireplace while enjoying a good book.

The stained-glass lamps threw a warm glow upon the walls and highlighted the numerous oil paintings with gilded gold frames.

I poured the guests a cup of coffee as they waited. After a few minutes, Father Harold entered the room, and Mikael and Phil stood and shook his hand.

"Hi, Father Harold. I'm Mikael Rossi, and this is Phil Jenkins. We're co-owners of Open Borders Studio, an independent motion picture distribution and production company."

"Please, have a seat," Father Harold said. "So I hear you want to take my two gems away for a while. Have to say, I'm quite skeptical about it all."

Mikael leaned slightly forward. "Yes, I don't blame you. We're looking at about two to three months over the summer."

"Well, tell me who you are and what your plans are," Father Harold said. "In detail."

While our uncle had always been a gentle soul, he was a fierce lion when it came to protecting his kin or community members. He kept a poker face as Mikael related their company's history, successes, and their upcoming moving production itinerary schedule.

"You mentioned you have made other movies," Father Harold said. "Would I have heard of them?"

Phil opened his briefcase and pulled out some magazines and newspapers. "Maybe this will help explain who we are."

I got up and stood behind the love seat, staring at the magazine covers.

"Well, look at that. Is that you two standing there on the red carpet?" Father Harold asked. "You're all dolled up in fancy suits."

Phil smiled. "Yes, that's Mikael and me. It was taken last year during the Academy Awards. We won best picture that year."

Phil pointed to a *Fortune* article. "Here we are again."

"You seem to be doing quite well," Father Harold said. "Now that I know a bit more about you, I can't imagine why you'd want to bring Tia and Finn along with you. Can't you find two young'uns in Los Angeles for this movie of yours?"

"Before coming on this rafting trip," Mikael said, "our script was complete. To be honest, we didn't realize until we met Tia and Finn what potential they could bring to our movie. Their roles will not only widen our audience but also bring a heightened sense of adventure and excitement to the movie. We now feel the movie just wouldn't be complete without the new scenes with them in it."

Father Harold nodded his head slowly. "This morning, I made a phone call to a friend of mine from the Los Angeles archdiocese. He was very familiar with your company, as well as your generosity to the community. He scolded me a bit for not knowing your movies and told me I needed to get out more." Father Harold laughed. "I suppose I should."

I glanced at Finn and smiled. *So far, so good.*

"Listen, y'all, I need to head to evening Mass," he said, standing up and straightening his collar, "but what I've heard so far passes muster. I'll give it some more thought and pray on it a bit, need to talk to a few more folks. I'll give you a call in a few weeks. Sound fair?"

Mikael and Phil stood up, nodding in agreement.

"It was great to meet you, Father Harold. We'll take good care of Finn and Tia," Mikael said as he shook their uncle's hand.

"So long for now," Father Harold said before leaving through the side door.

CHAPTER 6

Decisions

A week after meeting with Mikael and Phil, Father Harold knocked on the trailer door.

"Hey," I said. "I was just going to start dinner. Want to join us?"

He frowned. "Maybe. There's something I need to talk with you and Finn about."

I blinked a few times. "You made a decision?"

His frown didn't go away. "Is Finn here?"

"Yeah, he's working on the truck." My heart was sinking.

"Why don't you two come on over? Let's talk."

"Okay," I said. My stomach went queasy.

Uncle Harold nodded once and then turned and walked back to the rectory.

My mouth went bone-dry.

I was uncomfortable as Finn and I sat on the far side of Father Harold's desk. I trusted our uncle completely; he always did what was best for us and looked out for our family. I tried to convince myself that his opposition was for our own good, and he would have excellent reasons why this movie adventure was a bad idea.

Father Harold pulled the phone close to him and picked up a white card. I guessed it was Mikael's business card.

"Can't you just tell us yes or no?" Finn asked. "The suspense is killing me."

"It will just take a moment," he said, picking up the receiver and dialing carefully.

I crossed my legs and uncrossed them. I tried to slow my heartbeat, but it didn't work.

"Mikael?" Father Harold asked into the phone. "This is Father Harold McSherry. How are you doing?"

After some pleasantries, he got down to business. I felt light-headed.

"I'm calling about your proposal for Finn and Tia. Yes, and I appreciate your patience. So my initial reaction to the whole thing is to decline. And I'm still leaning that way, but I've put considerable prayer into this. I must admit I have not received a clear indication which way to go, so I am relying more on my research and background checks—as well as intuition—to come to this decision."

There was a long pause as Father Harold listened to whatever Mikael was saying. Every so often, he nodded and smiled.

"I understand. So my thought is to decline ..."

Another pause as our uncle looked from Finn to me and then down at the desk.

"... unless these conditions are met."

I can't prove it, but I'm sure my heart stopped at that moment.

Father Harold then outlined his conditions, which I have to admit sounded reasonable. The first was that cell phones would be supplied to both Finn and I so we could contact him and the boys when we wanted. The second was to have a contract drawn up with all the provisions listed out, including one that let us leave if we felt it was too dangerous. Also, all expenses would be paid over and above the $200,000 salaries we would each receive.

Harold listened to Mikael and nodded. "Good," Father Harold said. "Then it sounds like we have a deal. I will let Finn and Tia know, and I look forward to hearing from you."

He hung up the phone and looked at both of us somberly.

"I guess you're going to California in the spring."

I almost flung myself over the desk to give Uncle Harold a hug but instead ran around the desk. Finn was not far behind.

Mikael followed up as promised, with the contracts and cell phones arriving just a couple of weeks later. The fall and winter months flew by.

Caroline, the acting coach, showed up in January and put us through our paces. She had us memorize the script and made us rehearse repeatedly until it began to sound natural. By the end of March, Finn and I felt confident about our lines and abilities. We weren't Chris Pratt or Amy Adams, but we felt like it.

Then several pages of sheet music arrived in the mail, and we had to call Mikael to admit we couldn't read the notes. He promised to send us recordings from the composer so we could learn the songs. Once the recordings arrived, we listened to the music and picked it up easily; the songs were written especially for us.

We turned in the last of our homework assignments we'd be missing and received approval to leave school at the beginning of April.

To celebrate, I cooked a special meal of wild turkey, baby potatoes, and green beans in the rectory's kitchen. I could hear Paddy in the adjacent room, performing one of his stand-up comedic acts, followed by Wes and Finn roaring in laughter. I stood in the doorway watching them, not a care in the world. I loved those moments.

Soon, Father Harold joined us around the small dining room table.

"Let's bow our heads and pray," he said as we joined hands. "Jeremiah 29:11: 'For I know the plans I have for you, declares the Lord, plans for welfare and not for evil, to give you future and a hope.' Remember, dear ones, that God's plans for us are so much bigger and better than we can imagine. Sometimes, those plans involve things that make our stomachs flip. But we can rest assured that if we are following His plan, there's nothing to fear. Our hope is in Him, and that guarantees our safety. Before you know it, we'll all be right back here together."

I felt the hairs on my arms stand up as if the air itself had suddenly become electric. I squeezed my eyes shut and prayed for the family's safety.

The next morning, Father Harold drove us to a small airport for private planes; Phil and Mikael had arranged a special ride out to California.

I knelt down and wrapped my arms around my little brothers.

"I love you a bushel and a peck," I said, smothering them in kisses. "Paddy, don't forget to help out around the house, and Wes, I'll expect to see a magnificent piece of art when I return; keep your head out of the clouds. I'll try to call every day from LA, but I don't know how often I can call from South America. I'll try though."

"Hey, Phil's down yonder," Finn said, pointing toward a white jet.

We gave one last hug to our uncle and brothers and carried our luggage toward the plane.

"Hi, guys!" Phil said at the base of the stairs. "Head on up."

We climbed aboard and took seats on the luxurious jet, the leather soft and cool as butter under my fingertips.

As the doors closed and the engine started with a low roar, I clasped Finn's hand.

"It's okay, Sis," Finn said with a squeeze.

Looking out the window, I felt my insides turn upside down as the jet raced down the runway and lift into the sky, the ground falling away like a safety blanket. I watched the vast, craggy peaks of the Appalachian Mountains and winding rivers below grow smaller and smaller. I wrapped my arms around myself, hugging my shoulders, a steady wave of unease moving through me for reasons I couldn't quite discern.

I felt so small and vulnerable in this little can of metal taking us up above the clouds, like if it suddenly broke apart, I might just float away.

I soaked up the sun's warmth at the plane door's exit. Excitement flushed through me as I walked down the narrow staircase onto the tarmac. Phil escorted us to a long white limousine and held the door open.

"I feel like a princess," I said, peering around the immaculate car. "Not that I have any idea what a princess feels like, but this must be pretty close."

There were two long seats facing each other, with a black mini refrigerator, a telephone, and a sunroof that was partially open.

"You deserve it," Phil said, offering us bottles of water from the fridge. Then he pulled out his cell phone and called Mikael, letting him know we had landed and were on our way to the hotel.

"Get a load of these tall buildings, Tia," Finn said as we drove by a cluster of skyscrapers gleaming in the warm California sun.

"Back at home, the tallest building is our town bank … just three stories tall. Crazy."

"Yeah, and check out all these fancy cars; they're driving so fast and so close to each other," I said. "Is it like this all the time?"

"Pretty much," Phil said. "Actually, today isn't too bad. It can take us up to an hour sometimes just to drive ten miles. It's the only annoying thing about Los Angeles as a city, really: the traffic."

The limo pulled up to the Ritz-Carlton; the steel and glass façade glinted in the light.

"Wow, I've read about elegant hotels," I said, "but this looks like something else. Look at how tall it is."

"It's got to be at least thirty stories," Finn said.

"You'll have to check out the heated swimming pool on the twenty-sixth floor," Phil said. "There's an amazing view of the city up there."

As we rode the glass elevator to the twenty-fifth floor, my ears popped like they did on the plane. After getting out of the elevator, we made our way to the end of the long carpeted hallway. There were tables in the hall adorned with large vases of white lilies; their spicy, exotic scent hung in the air like rich perfume.

Phil removed the key from his pocket to let us in. I nearly squealed in delight as I took in the room.

"This is bigger than our whole house," I said, going from room to room, checking everything out. The living area had two plush curved couches and chairs upholstered in deep navy blue velvet, and the dining room boasted a long glass table and eight high-backed chairs swathed in white fabric. There were two queen-sized beds in a large bedroom, both with puffy, white down comforters on top and at least five pillows each. The bathroom had inlaid white- and gray-veined marble, a huge walk-in shower with mounted body jets, and a large soaking tub that stood in one corner that seemed to beckon me closer with its sparkling chrome fixtures.

We looked out the floor-to-ceiling windows in disbelief at the busy city below and the far-off Hollywood sign glowing white in the distance.

Finn collapsed in one of the plush oversized wingback chairs and shook his head slightly, seeming confused. "This is all too uppity; I feel out of place staying at a joint like this."

"This is nothing," Phil said, walking over to the minibar and peering inside. "We want you to enjoy your time out here and feel comfortable. So eat whatever you like; heck, order room service if you want." He closed the minibar door and straightened up, a broad smile on his face. "Get some rest this weekend; we begin rehearsals on Monday. If you want to go to the beach or explore LA, just call this number, and one of our drivers will pick you up."

Phil handed Finn a business card.

"Oh, by the way, Mikael wants you to get some new clothes and has a family friend who offered to take you shopping. Her name is Melanie, and she's about your age. Would that be okay?"

I nodded. "Yeah, but I'm not sure how much I'll be able to afford."

Phil smiled and opened his leather briefcase, pulling out two notebooks. He handed one to each of us.

"These books contain the schedule for the next few weeks and all the important phone numbers you'll need while you're here. Take a look at it when you can. And don't worry about the clothes; it's all covered. Melanie knows the city inside and out, all the best shopping spots. She'll come around tomorrow morning at eleven and pick you up in the lobby. You'll like her. She's the daughter of one of our writers."

I opened my notebook and found an envelope with a stack of cash inside.

Finn's eyes grew wide as he pulled a thick stack of bills from his envelope.

I'm sure I had a look of disbelief.

"What's this?" Finn asked.

"Some spending money. Should be two grand each. It'll come in handy over the next few weeks," Phil said, as if gifting envelopes full of cash was an everyday occurrence. "Oh, and one more thing before I forget." He stood up and walked to the hallway closet, pulling out two acoustic guitars.

Finn and I bounced out of our chairs and gently took the guitars. They were brand-new Gibsons, models we could only have dreamed about back home.

Finn strummed a few chords. "Wow, I'm speechless. Thank you, Phil."

"Yeah, it's beautiful," I said. "The sound is as warm as my ol' feather blanket; it's just too much." I put the guitar down carefully and gave him a big hug.

"It's our pleasure," he said, pulling his cell phone out of his pocket and checking the time. "Listen, I gotta run, but have fun tomorrow with Melanie. Call me if you need anything. Otherwise, I'll see you both on Monday."

After Phil left, I looked at Finn.

"I don't know what to do first," I said. "Should we eat, go swimming, or check out the Hollywood Walk of Fame?"

Before Finn could answer, his stomach growled. "I gotta feed this beast," he said, rolling his palm across his stomach.

"I don't want to go anywhere too fancy though," I said. "I don't have the right clothes."

We unpacked our suitcases, washed up, and headed down into the city below.

The nightlife was energizing, and we made our way around hundreds of people of all shapes, sizes, and nationalities.

A few blocks from the hotel, I spotted a small restaurant offering spaghetti and meatballs as their nightly special.

"That sounds perfect," Finn said as he opened the restaurant door.

Antique paintings and decorations reminiscent of old Italy adorned the dimly lit restaurant. As the waiter led us to our seats, the rich smell of savory tomato sauce and roasted garlic made my mouth water.

"I didn't think I was so hungry," I said as I tore off a hunk of soft Italian bread. "Aren't you going to miss going to prom this year?"

"Me in a clown suit? It'll take more than a prom to get me all fancied up. What 'bout you? I heard Jessie wanted to ask you."

My face flushed red. "Yeah, he did ask a few weeks ago, but I had this trip for an excuse. He's kinda cute though. Maybe when we get back, I'll swing by to see him."

Finn nodded. "Good for you, Sis. Glad to see you opening up a bit."

"Well, ever since you started dating Molly, and then Rachel, and then Sandi; is it still Sandi this week?"

"No, she got too possessive, stalking me everywhere. I had to let her go. But I did take out that new girl from Michigan last week, Erin. She's pretty cool."

"Sheesh, is there anyone at the school you haven't gone out with?"

"Yeah, one or two, maybe," he said before stuffing another piece of bread in his mouth.

I paused. "Anyway, I thought I should try to get out more, and who knows? By the time I graduate, I might finally be sociably adept." I decided to change the subject. "Hey, while we're waiting, there's something I've been wanting to tell you. Just wanted to find the right time."

"Go for it."

So I recounted the story of my Golden Ticket, how for so many years on my hiking trips, I prayed, wished, and hoped to find just one ticket, scrounging under fallen logs, stones, and leaves to find anything of value.

Every once in a while, I caught Finn smiling, probably visualizing me romping through the dense forest in search of the ticket that would lead us out of poverty.

When I got to the part where a thousand maple leaves floated down, this way and that, and how one brightly colored golden maple leaf fell into my hand, Finn's face turned serious and thoughtful. He leaned forward on the table, resting his chin in his hands.

"Wow, Tia," he said. "All that time you were searching the ground, when all you had to do was look up to God."

I smiled and nodded. "Every time I think about that morning, I feel like God has blessed me, blessed us all. And here's another crazy twist to it all: There was a golden maple leaf at the bottom of that tin we found. I keep wondering why."

I paused, still amazed by the coincidence.

"Why would someone take the time to press a maple leaf between two sheets of paper, place it in a tin with other valuables, and then hide it behind a fireplace? It's uncanny."

After a moment of silence, Finn shrugged. "Remember how Mama used to say that we don't understand the reasons for things until many years later? I think this might be one of those times."

CHAPTER 7

Javier's Bench

We got up early, worked out, went back to the room, and ordered room service.

As we waited for breakfast, Finn opened one of the dresser drawers and pulled out the cash.

"Let's put most of this in the safe and bring a thousand today for shopping." He stuffed the money in the safe, closed the door, and punched a passcode in.

"I don't think we'll even spend that," I said, stuffing the remaining wad of bills in my wallet.

After breakfast and showers, we walked to the lobby and spotted a young woman wearing a pink and white sundress. She was beautiful. I thought she looked like a movie star, with her flawless makeup and upswept hair.

"Bet you a hundred bucks that's Melanie," Finn said just as the girl began waving and walking over.

"Hi there," she said. "You must be Tia and Finn. My dad said you were twins, but I didn't realize just *how* alike you'd look. I'd kill for eyes that color." She casually looked Finn up and down. "You know, you both could be models; you have the look. And Finn, with your height, I could introduce you to some runway agents who would love to have you."

"Ha," he said, laughing. "Can you picture me getting all gussied up and walkin' down some runway with a bunch of highfalutin' guys? I'd never hear the end of it."

"Back home, maybe," she replied, "but here, they'd eat it up."

"Let's get out of here, y'all. I want to see some of this Los Angeles in the daylight," he said as we walked toward the exit.

Melanie's cheeks turned pink. "I love your accent. It's got a great twang to it."

I rolled my eyes. I was used to seeing girls react this way to Finn; they were always falling all over him. I was never sure he knew they were flirting, but I think he knew Melanie was.

"My driver's waiting," Melanie said as we stepped into the sunshine, "and there's an indoor shopping mall not too far from here." She held up a black piece of plastic. "My dad gave me the company card and said we could spend up to two thousand."

"On clothes? Are the shirts encrusted with diamonds?" Finn said, sending Melanie into a fit of giggles as she slid into the back seat of the car.

We climbed in beside her.

◊

The shopping trip was a success, and we both found a lot of nice things that weren't too overpriced. As we headed back to the car, Melanie asked what we would like to do.

"Oh, gosh," I said. "What can we do that we don't have back home?"

"Just about anything," Finn said, laughing. "Hollywood, the beach, clubs …"

"There's a spring fling festival in Old Town Pasadena if you want to go," Melanie said. "There will be live bands and international food carts; I always head for the Chinese venues. They make the best lettuce wraps."

"Sounds like fun," I said.

As we made our way on the freeway to Pasadena, I watched the scenery pass by. Something that seemed out of place caught my eye. *Mattresses and shopping carts?* "Melanie, why are there mattresses under the bridge over there?"

Melanie shrugged as she applied a fresh coat of pink lipstick. "There are a lot of homeless people here, and they sleep under the bridges sometimes."

"Wow. That's really sad," I said, thinking about my newly purchased clothes. "I don't think they'd make it through a West Virginia winter."

"Probably not," Melanie said, not sounding very concerned.

When we reached Old Town Pasadena, the driver dropped us off on Colorado Boulevard. "Thanks, Andrew. I'll give you a call about eight o'clock," Melanie said, stepping out of the limo with us right behind her.

The plaza was filled with people, food trucks, and many folks dancing to loud music in the street.

"Good Lord," I said, watching a couple dance sensually nearby, staring deeply into each other's eyes. "This is a *lot* different than Fayetteville."

After exploring the shops and then eating Chinese lettuce wraps and lo mein noodles, we continued to explore, finding a park nearby. Night was falling, and the air turned cool. I looked up toward the sky. The moon was almost full and shone down on the earth. The sounds of music and laughter from the festival faded away, becoming faint and distant.

For a brief moment, I wished I was home, nestled underneath my sleeping bag, staring at the big West Virginia sky, stars sprinkled through the darkness like confetti. Here, the stars were barely visible.

The park was dimly lit, but I noticed a man wrapped in a blanket lying down on a bench.

Finn saw him too and pointed in the man's direction. "Is he wasted or something?"

"He's homeless," Melanie said. "That's probably where he's living right now. Come on, let's get back to the car." She pulled out her phone and called the driver.

I frowned. "Melanie, I don't really understand. This is California. So many rich people live here. How can there be people living out on the street? Aren't there any resources for people who need help?"

"Yes, Andrew, the same place you dropped us off," Melanie

said into the phone before hanging up. "Sorry, what? Resources? You don't get out enough, Tia darling."

I felt a heavy pang in my heart. "Just hold on a sec; he needs help," I said as I turned and walked toward the man.

"Listen, Tia, I feel bad too," Melanie said from behind me, "but it's not safe to go over there. Tia, stop."

I ignored her as I unzipped my purse.

"Tia, wait for me at least," Finn yelled, jogging up to me.

I tried to make my steps louder so the man would know we were approaching and not sneaking up on him. I felt so guilty staying at the Ritz-Carlton, knowing this man and so many others were sleeping outside on benches and under bridges.

As we walked up, I could see he was wearing worn black combat boots and a knit cap, the rest of him covered up in a dirty blanket that smelled like body odor.

The man suddenly sat up.

"Who's that?" he shouted, throwing off his blanket and raising his fists as if to fight.

I gave a little gasp and jumped back, while Finn stepped in front of me.

The man stood up; he was a giant, almost as broad as he was tall. His complexion was dark and pock-marked, and as he removed his knit cap, I saw his dark brown hair was plastered to his head. His fists were the size of two of Finn's put together; I'd never seen anyone with such large hands before.

"Please don't be mad at us, sir," I said. "I just wanted to give you some money for a hotel room and a hot meal."

The man stared at me, working his jaw back and forth and slowly lowering his hands as he realized we weren't a threat.

"My name's Tia," I said, "and this is my brother Finn. What's your name?"

He paused and licked his lips. "Javier," he said with a Spanish accent.

I stepped away from Finn. "Hi, Javier. I'm sorry for scaring you. Why are you out here on a bench?"

"Tia," Finn said. "That's not our business."

"I came here four months back to look for my brother," Javier said in broken English. "I, eh, was robbed when I got here. I waiting for money to be sent so I can go back home."

"And where is home?" I asked.

"Argentina."

"How much do you need to get back there?"

"Um …" Javier looked at the ground. "I not sure, hard to say. I tried to do some jobs, but no one hire me for more than a few dollars."

Finn grabbed my arm before I could continue. "Tia, *wait*," he hissed.

"Would a thousand dollars be enough?" I asked, not looking at my brother.

Javier stepped back, staring around the park in fear, his eyes darting about as if he might bolt at any moment.

"What? Are you police?" he asked, his eyes narrowing.

"No, no, I'm not," I said, reaching into my bag to pull out the envelope of cash. "Here. Please take it. Maybe it's enough to get you home."

Javier's eyes continued to roam around, but he eventually reached out one hand tentatively and took the envelope. He opened it and checked. Then he looked at me.

"Why? Why?" he asked in disbelief, his eyes filling with tears.

"Because we all need a little help sometimes," I said. "God bless you, okay?"

"Th-thank you," Javier said, wiping his eyes as we turned to rejoin Melanie on the outskirts of the park.

"You know," Melanie said, "that money won't be replaced."

I nodded, smiling. "I know. I didn't think it would."

⸾

I was happy to return to the hotel and decided to take a long hot bath, pouring so much bubble bath in that the white froth almost cascaded over the side. It was luxurious, and I felt so relaxed.

I knew Melanie and Finn weren't happy with me, but I felt a warm glow, believing that Javier might just make it home to his family.

When I was fully soaked and nearly a prune, I dried off and put on my robe. Finn was already asleep, so I rummaged around for my journal.

Where do I even begin? So much has happened, so much to tell. Such a different world here; so crowded, but so diverse and full of life.

I kept writing until I could barely keep my eyes open. I flipped off the light and lay back against the soft, cool sheets.

⸾

The next morning, we went for a swim in the hotel pool. From the rooftop, Los Angeles stretched out endlessly in a blur of steel and glass that twinkled and sparkled in the bright sunlight.

At lunch, I asked Finn if we could go to Newport Beach, since Phil had said it had some of the prettiest views of the coast.

"Sure, call for the car," he said. "It's crazy to think this will be the first time we see an ocean."

"Yeah, I'm super excited."

It took about an hour on the concrete freeways to make it there. As we stepped out of the car, I was immediately struck by the cool, clean sea breeze. There was a boardwalk as far as the eye could see, and the homes were colorful and inviting, painted in pastel hues that reflected the coastal vibe of the city. People were walking, biking, running, and roller-skating.

I looked out on the vast ocean and white sands. Sunlight sparked off the water, and hundreds of people were lying on the sand, soaking up the rays, playing volleyball, swimming, and making sandcastles. Families were sprawled out on large, brightly colored beach towels.

"Last one in," Finn said as he slipped off his shoes and ran toward the water's edge.

Squealing, I ran close behind, my feet digging into the sand.

Finn stepped into the water like it was quicksand.

"Water's freezing," he said as he gingerly inched his way farther into the water. He paused to roll up his shorts, exposing his pale knees.

"It's gorgeous." I splashed water toward him, hitting him in the face.

"Okay," he said. "You asked for it."

That started a splashing war that got us both wet until we gave up and eased our way in, only daring to go as far as our knees.

After a while, we made our way back to the boardwalk, admiring the beautiful homes that lined the walkway. Each was unique, trimmed with little gardens, decorative artwork, and balconies with cozy little sitting areas. For a brief moment, I imagined myself living in one of the quaint little homes and waking up to the magnificent ocean views.

I pointed down a street. "Hey, there are some restaurants and shops. Let's go check it out."

As we walked along the narrow street, I saw a store with an elegant façade featuring sparkling diamond necklaces in the window, draped over heaps of red velvet, and ropes of lustrous-looking pearls.

"Milano's Fine Jewelry," the sign read in fancy gilt lettering. I paused.

"I wish I brought the green pendant. I bet they could tell us where it came from. Can we go in and talk to them?" I asked.

Finn nodded and opened the door. A little chime went off.

Unlike the other souvenir shops with harsh florescent lighting, brightly colored souvenirs displayed from ceiling to floor, and jammed packed with curious tourists; this store had a naturally warm, almost museum-like feeling with a lavender scent in the air. The walls were covered in antique Italian paintings rendered in soft colors of romantic waterways with gondolas, masterful sculptures, and historical monuments.

We made our way over to a long glass counter filled with

bracelets, rings, and necklaces adorned with every color stone imaginable, sparkling under the display lights.

An older gentleman with silver hair and wire-rimmed glasses stood behind the counter, smiling.

"Hello. My name is Joseph Milano. What can I do for you today?" I noticed his Italian accent.

"Hi," I said. "I'm Tia, and this is my brother Finn. Can I ask you a question?"

"Certainly," he said, his eyes crinkling at the corners. "How can I help?"

I did my best to describe the green brooch we'd found in the tin and explained some of our background.

"Hmm …" he said. "I would have to see it in person to know the stone's classification and history. It may be an emerald, and if your ancestors brought it from Ireland in the 1800s, it might be quite old and valuable. Next time you are in town, come back. I would be honored to help."

I understood how difficult this request had been, but I was still disappointed. I looked down and noticed some beautiful necklaces in the glass cabinet.

"Oh, these are gorgeous," I said, bending down to take a closer look.

"Thank you. I make them all by hand," Mr. Milano said.

"They're amazing," Finn said. "I've never seen anything like them before. How long have you been doing this?"

"My family has been making jewelry for many generations, and I started learning when I was still a child. We came to

America when I was fifteen, and my father opened this little store shortly after."

My eyes lit up as I had an idea. "Can you make jewelry based on requests? Like, could you design a custom piece?"

"I can make almost anything," Mr. Milano said. "What did you have in mind?"

I told him the story of how a thousand golden maple leaves floated down from the trees during my hike and how one had made its way into my palm. I described how the golden maple leaf had five thick veins running through the middle that seemed to mirror the shape of my hand.

"In my own way, well, I think it was somehow a gift from God. Do you think you can make a pendant like that for me?" I asked, studying his face for a reaction.

Mr. Milano smiled. "That is a beautiful story, Miss Tia. I would be honored to bring it to life. Let me draw something up, and you can approve it before I begin."

"Can you tell me about how much they would cost? I'd like one for me and one for my brother." I looked over at Finn. "We can wear them on our trip for good luck."

"Thanks, Sis," Finn said, smiling.

Mr. Milano nodded. "The cost will depend on what material you want to use. As I consider your golden leaf, I am thinking gold with a lining of silver around the edges."

My eyes were dancing as I pictured the pendant in my mind, sparkling in the light. "Yes, yes! It sounds perfect," I said.

"Also, there is the choice of the chain, but the design and creation of the leaf will be …"

He paused as he thought about it.

I thought I saw a hint of compassion and understanding coming from his warm brown eyes as he bit his bottom lip.

"… four hundred dollars each, which includes the chain. Does that sound okay?" Mr. Milano asked.

I glanced at Finn and he nodded.

"Sounds good," I said, my stomach churning with guilt over spending what was a small fortune on a necklace.

"Come back in two weeks, and they'll be ready."

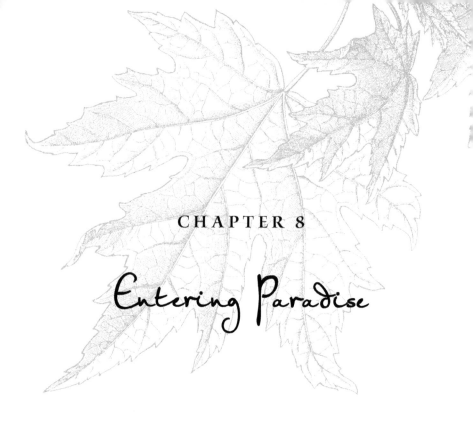

CHAPTER 8

Entering Paradise

On Monday morning, I stared into the closet, trying to decide what to wear for our first day of rehearsals. I finally settled on a dress with a blue and gold pattern, with thin spaghetti strap sleeves that left my shoulders bare and flowed freely to my knees.

Finn walked in wearing his new blue shirt and a pair of khaki slacks. His long hair was pulled back in a ponytail.

"Ready to blow this popsicle stand?" he said.

"I reckon," I said, glancing in the mirror one last time.

We went down to the lobby, where Phil was waiting for us.

"You two look great," he said. "Melanie sure knows what she's doing."

As I looked out the car window, I was mesmerized by the people walking along the sidewalk. In my small town, most folks felt comfortable in a baggy shirt and a loose pair of blue jeans. Here, the city folk looked so picture perfect with their well-tailored suits, manicured nails, upswept hair, and flawless makeup. I fidgeted, feeling like an awkward teenager. I glanced over at Finn. He always seemed so self-assured. Sometimes, it was hard to believe we were even related.

As we approached the studio, the car passed through an open gate; a security guard waved us through. We then went by a series of long buildings until arriving at the back of one with a large number 27 on the front.

Mikael was standing just inside the door and greeted us with hugs. He wore a dark blue polo shirt with tan slacks, and his hair seemed grayer than the last time I saw him. Was it my imagination, or did he have a few more worry lines around his eyes?

"Great to see you kids," he said. "How was your weekend? Do you have everything you need?"

"Yes," I said. "Thank you so much for everything. It's been great."

"Let me introduce you to the team," he said, ushering us inside.

I recognized several people from the rafting trip, and more hugs were exchanged all around.

I felt my heart skip a beat as Boyko approached, smiling broadly. He was even cuter than I remembered, dressed in faded jeans, a tight-fitting gray sweater that highlighted his well-developed pecs, and stylish brown shoes. I hate to admit it, but my knees went a little weak.

"Tia! Finn," he said, as both dimples appeared.

He leaned in to give me a kiss on both cheeks, his two-day beard feeling scratchy. I didn't mind it at all; I also liked the musky scent of his cologne.

Am I supposed to kiss him back now? I wondered.

"I wanted to see you both before I left," he said. "My sister's getting married next weekend, and I'm flying out in a few hours."

"Well, congratulations to her," I said, feeling myself blush when I looked into his green eyes, holding his gaze for as long as I dared before looking away.

"Safe travels," Finn said, "and see you in Chile."

His interruptions were usually annoying, but this time, I welcomed it.

Over the next few weeks, we rehearsed our lines with Caroline, and while we didn't have a huge part in the movie, we perfected our lines and practiced the song over and over again, with a stand-in actor pretending to be Boyko. Mikael commented on how natural we were.

The day before we were scheduled to fly to Chile, I received a call from Mr. Milano, letting me know the pendants were ready. I bugged Finn about taking a drive down to Newport Beach, and he finally agreed, maybe because he needed a break too.

When we arrived, Mr. Milano greeted us and pulled a blue velvet box from a drawer.

"I'm so excited," I said.

As Mr. Milano opened the box lid, I felt a kind of calming

awe settle on me. The pendant had five veins and a stem, as well as a translucent radiant golden hue with a thin beading of silver around the edges. I thought it glittered in the light like hope itself.

Finn gently picked one up and held it to the light. "It's so thin you can see through it," he said. "Hold it up to the light. It seems to glow somehow."

I was touched beyond words and felt my eyes welling up with tears. "It's the most beautiful thing I've ever seen."

Mr. Milano smiled and nodded his head. "Well, I was inspired. Let's pick out a chain."

Finn and I each picked out gold necklaces and put them on each other before paying Mr. Milano. I walked over to a small mirror on the counter.

"This means so much to me. I'll never take it off," I said, my voice shaky.

That night before dinner, as we did every evening, we called the boys back home. Wes was quiet. I brought up the ideas we had on renovating the house, about buying the necklaces, and the work on our lines, but he just didn't seem to want to respond.

"What's wrong?" I asked.

There was a long pause, but finally, he said in a somber voice, "Just be careful; that's all I wanted to say. Just be careful out there. Here's Paddy."

Before I could say anything to reassure him, he handed the phone to Paddy.

"Hey," he said. "See any movie stars yet?"

"Same as yesterday," I said. "Not yet."

"I got a B on my math test," Paddy said.

I could picture him in the living room, fidgeting restlessly as he spoke.

"I'm so proud of you," I said. "But do me a favor and try to cheer Wes up. Tell him everything's going to be okay. We'll call as soon as we can, okay? I love you and miss you both."

"I love you too."

"Bye for now," I said, handing the phone to Finn.

"We'll be back there before you know it," Finn said as I played with the golden leaf pendant around my neck.

We'll be back before you know it.

Mama's face popped into my mind.

Those were Mama's last words, the words she spoke to them right before closing the car door and heading to Mannington with Papa. If I had only known that was the last time I would see them, I wouldn't have let them go. If I had only known these were Mama's last words, I wouldn't have stopped the conversation.

My stomach had been queasy all day, and now it cramped, flipping and turning as though I had a troupe of acrobats trapped in there.

"You okay?" Finn asked after hanging up with the boys.

"Just a stomachache is all," I said. "I'm probably just nervous about flying again."

Finn nodded. "Yeah, long flight too. Phil said it was about fourteen hours. Just hope there's no turbulence; that scares the crap out of me. But we don't leave until tomorrow. No sense in getting sick now."

I smiled. My brother always made me feel safe, no matter what might be happening. I pulled him in for a hug, feeling his body stiffen in surprise before relaxing.

I buried my head in Finn's shoulder.

By the time we reached the airport the next morning, I felt much better, my stomach no longer twisting and seizing in pain.

We were shuttled to the company's private jet with "Open Borders Studio" scrolled along the side in curling black script. There were at least twenty people gathered outside of the jet, handing over their suitcases to a worker before ascending the steps.

"Welcome to my little Gulfstream," Mikael said when we reached the cabin door. "Go on through and find yourself a comfortable seat. Phil's back there somewhere."

My eyes lit up. The cabin was spacious, with comfortable sitting areas, a couple of plush-looking couches, and a large-screen television; there were even little video screens in front of the passenger seats.

Finn pointed toward the rear of the plane. "Hey, there's Phil! Let's grab a seat back there."

Phil turned around and smiled. "Glad you made it. I'll come sit by you; be back in a minute."

After we got settled and put our seat belts on, a beautiful woman with long brown hair and dressed in a dark blue suit came over.

"Welcome aboard," she said, holding out a tray filled glasses. "My name is Wendy. Would you care for some champagne?"

"Uh, sure," I said with a giggle. What if I told her my age? I'd never tasted champagne before.

The pilot's voice echoed through the overhead speakers:

"Welcome everyone. This is Captain Garcia. We'll be flying to Esquel, Argentina, today, and our total flight time is thirteen hours and twenty-two minutes. Should be a fairly smooth trip, so just relax and enjoy the ride."

A few minutes later, we were speeding down the runway and lifting off into the sky. I took it much better this time.

I sipped the champagne and wasn't sure I liked it.

Finn leaned over to Phil. "I thought we were flying to Chile."

"Ah, yes, I mentioned this at our briefing the other day, but you may have missed it. The closest airport we can land at is in Argentina; from Esquel, we'll take a van to Futaleufú. The drive is spectacular; I've gone several times in the past few months. You're gonna love it."

After food was served, Mikael asked everyone to be seated at a cluster of sitting areas toward the front of the jet.

He cleared his throat and began, "Seems like yesterday we were all gathered on our way to Mexico for our last production, and now here we are, heading off to Chile and Brazil. There are a few things I wanted to cover before you all enjoy yourselves for the remainder of the flight. First off is that our safety is priority number one. We'll have a security task force with us, as well as local guides, but it's important to stay vigilant in the more rural parts where we'll be shooting. Some of the areas—particularly in the Amazon—have reported increased illegal drug activity. I want to remind you all never to venture off on your own, to listen to our guides, and to always stay aware. Also, this is a no alcohol shoot, so enjoy your champagne now. Once we land, no more booze. Phil will be coming around with the itinerary for you."

With papers in hand, Phil stood up. "Once we get to the Futa, we'll be staying at a private lodge. The first few days will be scenes twenty through twenty-seven, and we'll also be doing a few dry runs on the river so Boyko, Tia, and Finn can get acclimated. If everything goes as planned, the actual whitewater filming will take place on days six and seven, followed by the camping scene. Then we'll come back across the border and fly to Manaus, Brazil, for the Amazon shoot."

He began handing out copies of the itinerary.

Finn and I returned to our cushioned seats, and I giggled when I discovered they turned into recliner beds with the push of a button.

Maybe it was the champagne, but I decided to take advantage of this arrangement and take a nap.

I woke up when the pilot came on the speakers, saying we were about to land.

The ground seemed to come up quickly, and after touching down with a series of bumps that made someone in the back hoot and holler, everyone filed out of the plane and onto the tarmac.

Outside, the air was thick and humid, and I already felt perspiration on my forehead. After going through customs, we loaded into waiting vans and made our way across the border into Chile.

As we neared our destination, our van driver said, "The Río Futaleufú is a beautiful river fed by the Andean glacial snow; that's what gives it such a vibrant turquoise color. *Futaleufú* means 'big river,' and the locals refer to it as *un paisaje pintado por dios*, which translates to 'a landscape painted by God.' You will soon see why."

I smiled in anticipation, despite the butterflies in my stomach.

When we finally arrived at the small lodge nestled on the bank of the river, my butterflies turned to excitement. Exotic Patagonian trees, flowering fuchsias, and white sandy beaches stretched for miles around. From a distance, I could see the towering Tres Monjas peak, little farms with paddocks of horses, and the sparkling river.

I heard a familiar voice behind me say, "You made it!"

I turned to see Boyko walking across the garden path. He was wearing a white button-down short-sleeve shirt and navy blue shorts.

I caught myself holding my breath when he flashed his smile, exposing those dimples.

God, he's sooo cute.

He planted kisses on both of my cheeks before turning to the scenery. "What do you think? Spectacular place, right?"

"Crazy gorgeous," Finn said, swinging his backpack off his shoulder and resting it on the ground.

"I'm going to run some lines right now, but I'll see you in the morning, okay?" Boyko flashed a jaunty wave before taking off in the other direction.

My pulse thudded in my ears.

What is going on with me?

I didn't know what it was about Boyko that affected me this way, but it was the same every time: my cheeks burned and my pulse raced whenever he drew near.

I just hoped I wasn't being totally obvious about it.

CHAPTER 9

Turquoise Spring

The next morning, we met up with Boyko, Mikael, Phil, and the local whitewater rafting crew at the put-in by the beach. I was able to keep my thudding heart and blushing to a minimum.

"Morning, guys," Mikael said. "Glad you wore shorts today; it'll be a warm one." He paused and studied me.

I felt a bit like a bug under a microscope as he stared.

"Get the hair and makeup crew over here," he shouted.

I laughed as I slid my fingers through my wild, curly hair, picturing what it must look like in this humidity. I noticed Mikael's graying hair was once again all brown. I hadn't noticed that on the plane yesterday. I had liked the gray streaks, as they made him look more distinguished. He was wearing a polo shirt and tan shorts, so other than his hair, he hadn't really changed.

A woman approached and led me to a chair, where she started

messing with my hair and then began putting lotion and makeup on my skin. Then she applied fake eyelashes: the first time I ever had those.

When she finished, she held up a mirror. I was a bit taken aback, as my skin was at least a shade darker, with the artificial eyelashes making my bluish-green eyes pop. My long strawberry blonde curly mass had been pulled back in a tight bun. She helped put a helmet on my head.

Finn had taken the chair next to me, and I saw he, too, was a shade darker, with a hint of blush on his cheeks.

"Looking mighty fancy, Brother," I cracked.

"Say one more word, and I'll beat the fire out of you," Finn said, putting on his helmet. "Hey, get a load of Boyko over there, staring down at them rapids. He looks as nervous as a long-tailed cat in a roomful of rocking chairs."

I couldn't help but laugh at Finn's comparison. Boyko did look apprehensive, or maybe he was contemplative.

There was no doubt these rapids were faster and more turbulent than on the New River. Beyond the water, I soaked in the sheer magnificence of the panoramic views, with lush green trees lining the steep mountain banks and a massive rock formation jetting out along the river. Turbulent whitecaps peppered the surface of the water. I could just barely hear high-pitched screeches from rafting adventurers off in the distance.

Mikael returned with a man introduced as Fabian, who was to be our master guide while Finn and I familiarized ourselves with the river. The man was tall and rugged, with leathery brown skin and muscles that bulged at the seams of his tight shirt. His brown hair was long but pulled back into a ponytail.

"It's great to meet you," he said with a slight accent that I couldn't quite place. "Today, I will be taking you down the spine of the river that flows through the glaciated Chilean Andes. I understand you are well versed in whitewater rafting, and that is definitely a bonus. We will traverse massive waves and green-blue ramps, and as I like to tell my tourists, you will plunge into many big frothy holes."

We walked up to the water's edge, and I dipped my hand in the turquoise blue water. It was crystal clear and cool.

Mikael stepped up between Finn and me.

"We'll take some practice shots cruising down the river and through a few warm-up rapids. I've got camera crews in their own rafts ahead of you, behind you, and located along the Terminator, Himalaya, and Mundaca sites. We need to make sure the cameras are positioned perfectly before the actual shoot next week."

Fabian pointed toward the farthest reaches of the river. "The final section is called *Casa de Piedra*, also known as stone house. When we get to that section, pay close attention to me. There are a lot of turbulent eddies and holes there. I will let you know when we get close."

"Freakin' awesome, Finn said, with sparkling eyes. "Let's hit the waves!" He took off his shirt and snapped the lifejacket on.

Mikael gave us a brief primer on his signals to prepare for the filming, and then the team launched the raft.

We made it through each milestone on the rushing water with

ease. The river churned and rushed all around us, and I never felt more alive than at that very moment, traversing those rapids.

I yelled, "You did fantastic, Boyko," after a particularly bumpy spot. "It's like you've done this for years."

Boyko grinned. "Thanks, Tia."

Over the next few days, the production crew filmed Boyko in other scenes of the movie while Fabian worked with Finn and me until we'd mastered the Río Futaleufú's rapids.

On the third day, Fabian asked, "Ready to go on your own?"

"Absolutely," Finn said.

We took several runs down the rapids, sometimes with a raft, and other times with a kayak. We became immersed in the exhilaration and beauty of the surroundings, as well as the barrage of rapids and monstrous standing waves.

On the first day of live filming, the weather was glorious, the sky was cloudless, the temperature was perfect, and the water was a deep turquoise. I have to say Finn, Boyko, and I masterfully navigated the river, bracing for strong uppercuts as we were tossed and turned by one high-octane rapid after another.

As we approached the final descent, the Casa de Piedra, the sound of the water barreling over the massive boulder sent chills up my spine. The ferocity of it was untamed, and every time we crossed that section of the river, I felt like a plastic toy being flushed down a toilet bowl.

Mikael and Phil were waiting for us at the lower takeout and rushed over to us the moment we appeared.

"Amazing," Mikael said. "We got it in one take! That's unheard of."

I collapsed on the beach in exhaustion next to my brother, breathing hard. I felt exhilarated.

"No time to rest now," Mikael said. "I need you to prepare for the campsite scene. Phil, check that the camera crew's ready."

Once we arrived at the campground area, we were shuffled off to a large tent for hair, makeup, and a change of clothes. When I glanced in the mirror, I had to look twice. For the first time, I thought I looked almost elegant. Something—I'm not sure what—looked different about me, and I couldn't help but smile at my reflection.

When I emerged from the tent, Boyko was standing by the campfire. He glanced up and smiled. I'm sure I blushed. I hoped he couldn't tell due to the makeup.

"Are you sure you are only sixteen?" he asked. "You always look adorable, but tonight, you are simply beautiful." He reached out and took one of my hands into his, brought it up to his lips, and kissed it.

I felt my cheeks burning; a shiver shot down my spine, and I had no idea what to say. All I could come up with was "Thank you."

Before Boyko could continue, I walked over to Finn. I thought that if Boyko said anything else, I would start babbling like an idiot.

When it was time to shoot the scene, we gathered around the campfire and, just as we'd practiced all winter and in California, said our lines a few times.

"Okay," Mikael said, "it's music time. You guys can practice a bit while we set up the cameras."

We pulled out the guitars and tuned up. I loved the song written especially for this scene, "Turquoise Spring." From what I understood, it was written by a famous composer named Jonathan. Now, after having experienced the Futaleufú River firsthand, I could truly appreciate the beautiful melody. After a few takes, it was a wrap.

Mikael embraced both of us when we were finished. "You both were brilliant. The world will come to love you."

To be honest, I was beginning to think Mikael—and Phil as well—were being overly kind because we were newbies. I mean, I doubt we were *brilliant*, but I appreciated the thought.

As the crew was packing up, Boyko looked around. "I'm really going to miss this place. There's so much to do here. We should come back on our own someday."

"Without a doubt," Finn said, nodding.

I rested the next morning, sipping fresh fruit juice as I stood on the balcony to admire the small farms and rural rolling hills. It was all so gorgeous, and everything had been perfect, but I still had a pit in my stomach, the same one I had since first boarding the plane out of LA.

Maybe I'm getting sick or something, I thought, setting the juice on the bedside table.

There was a knock at the door. "It's open," I called.

Finn stuck his head through. "Vans are here," he said. "Let's go to Brazil."

"Yeah, okay," I said, ignoring the mounting anxiety, that odd feeling in my stomach. There was something coursing through me that said something wasn't quite right.

I took a moment to reach up and touch the golden maple leaf hanging around my neck and quietly said a prayer.

There was a security team, and I had my brother. As long as I stuck close to them, everything would be fine.

The flight to Manaus went smoothly, and after dropping the suitcases off in my room at the hotel, I grabbed a free booklet from the concierge and rejoined Finn and Boyko.

"Hey, y'all." I waved the brochure. "There's so much we can do before we go on the boat tomorrow. What sounds good? We can walk through the Botanical Gardens or check out the Praia da Lua beach. There's a local market along the bank of the Amazon River. If you want to just walk around, we can do that too."

"Let's explore the market," Boyko said. "We can get a closer look at the river while we're at it and maybe grab a bite to eat."

When we got there, all I could see were hundreds of locals and tourists filling the streets and markets, peddling everything from electronics, fish, and bananas to souvenirs and toilet paper. I saw a table with different types of musical instruments, some I didn't recognize. Boyko helped negotiate the purchase of two shakers for Wes and Paddy.

Then we ventured through a huge market, where every kind

of sea creature imaginable was available. I'd never seen so many different species, dead and alive, and the strong smell of fish was undeniable. The blood and guts … it was dizzying, and I felt suddenly nauseous.

"Can we get out of here?" I said, pulling on Finn and Boyko's arms.

Thankfully, we quickly left and walked along the river, buying some coconut juice. We paused along the riverbank to stare in awe at the vast Amazon jungle, a tangle of green intermingled with a profusion of bright colors from the tropical flowers that dotted the landscape.

"It's really amazing, isn't it?" I said. "Just across the river is a wild jungle. I never thought I'd be in a place like this. It's so unlike anything I've ever seen before."

"Yeah, the closest I've come is watching *The Jungle Book*," Finn said. "No movie could ever do this place justice."

"It's crazy, right?" I said. "My stomach's doing flip-flops just looking over there. It's so dark and mysterious, kind of like when Luke Skywalker went into the creepy forest of the Dagobah system."

"What made you think of that?" Boyko asked.

"She just comes up with these things out of the blue," Finn said. "No use trying to understand."

Boyko swatted at his arm. "Let's get out of here. These damn bugs are eating me alive."

The next morning, the crew boarded a large charter boat with the words *Poderoso Jaguar* painted along the side. Unlike the Futa, the Amazon River looked thick and murky and had a dull blue hue intermixed with swirls of green and brown.

The boat's dining hall, seating areas, and kitchen were on the lower deck, with the sleeping quarters on the upper deck. There were some bedrooms, but most of the production crew members and actors were assigned to a set of hammocks that hung five rows deep on the top deck. Each hammock had a mosquito net with a zipper and a little storage compartment underneath.

As promised, Mikael had arranged for a guide and a security team to stand guard throughout the boat.

As we ventured down the river, the sounds of the jungle filled me with both excitement and intrigue. I felt like a child each time the boat rounded another bend, eagerly awaiting the terrain and animals this new part of the jungle might bring.

Finn and I stood on the deck to soak up the view. Spider monkeys jumped from one jungle vine to the next, while macaws and parrots flashed between the dense leaves, displaying their brilliant colors. Black caimans up to twenty feet long slithered alongside the boat, and every so often, we would spot a piranha feeding near the surface. I didn't want to turn away in case we missed something spectacular.

"Oh my gosh," I said, pointing. "Look over there."

A jaguar with coal-black spots was pulling a giant turtle onto the shore. In two quick movements, he had wrenched it from its shell and began eating.

I trembled, turning away. "Poor little guy," I said, my voice shaking.

Finn put an arm around my shoulders. "It's the circle of life, Sis. Animals die."

"People too. Doesn't make it any easier," I said, crossing the deck to claim my hammock.

Early the next morning, Mikael informed us that he and the crew, including Boyko, would be venturing a few miles into the jungle to begin setting up for the shoot.

"We'll see you tonight. I'm leaving a security guy here, Heraldo. Finn, don't forget your walkie-talkie, and call me if anything comes up."

"Watch out for snakes and jaguars," I teased as Boyko prepared to disembark.

He snorted and then, to my surprise, pulled me in for a hug.

"See you tonight," he whispered.

At the feeling of his arms around me, my cheeks burned. I pulled away, looking down at the floor.

We spent the morning admiring the lush green jungle from the boat's different vantage points. My senses were pleasantly overwhelmed with sweet bird melodies, fragrant perfume from brilliantly colored orchids, and the animated chattering of hundreds of monkeys. I blinked my eyes hard as if taking a photo in my mind. I never wanted to forget this magical moment. Around noon, we began packing. Our flight back home was the next day, and once we had packed, I lay in the hammock. A few minutes later, Finn got into his.

"When we get back, I want to start working on the old house," Finn said.

I adjusted the maple leaf necklace. "I can't think of anything better. I just wish Mama and Papa were around to see it. I think she'd be so happy."

"I know she would," said Finn.

We talked about the house's renovations and reminisced about our adventures.

My eyelids began to feel heavy as the warmth of the midday sun wrapped around me. The sounds of the jungle were music to my ears, but as I started to fall asleep, the jaguar's sharp teeth flashed in my mind.

I shivered, remembering the gentle turtle being torn away from its protective shell by the cat's jaw.

I sat up in the hammock and glanced over to Finn, who was sleeping like a toddler, his mouth slightly open.

I took a few deep breaths and looked out at the vast, dark jungle, listening to the rustling of the palm trees and the occasionally squawking birds. I lay back down, closing my eyes until sleep overtook me. It came in a black wave that rushed over me like water, covering me completely.

CHAPTER 10

Heitor

I slowly opened my eyes, breathing in the warm, moist air. I stretched and sat up, smiling, knowing that tomorrow, Finn and I would be flying to West Virginia. I could hardly wait to get home to surprise Wes and Paddy with their favorite meal—chili dogs and slaw—and enjoy it picnic-style down by the river.

Now to get up and check the suitcases, I thought as I unzipped the protective netting.

I swung my legs across the hammock, and a loud bang came from the lower deck.

Finn sat up in a jolt, and we stared at each other as we heard hammering footsteps, shouts, yells, and cries.

"Holy shit," Finn said as he got out of his hammock. "What the hell was that?"

I froze in place as more shouts came. Then I scrambled to slip on my shoes.

Finn held a finger to his lips and whispered, "Stay low; don't move."

"Finn, don't leave me ..."

He tiptoed to the ledge that overlooked the lower deck, and I followed close behind. We peered over the edge, and I had to cover my mouth to keep from screaming.

Heraldo, the security guard, lay facedown in a pool of blood.

Toward the front of the boat, I could see two militia-type men with guns aimed at the captain, who had his hands clasped in front of him, pleading for his life. I heard him wail, and it rattled every nerve in my body.

I crouched closer to the floor. "Oh, God, Finn, what do we do?"

"We gotta get off." His blue eyes were wide with fear. "We gotta get to shore *now*."

He took my hand and led me back to the hammocks. Then he pulled the walkie-talkie from his bag, turning down the volume. "Y'all help. Anybody! Help!" he said in a voice just above a whisper. "This is Finn. The boat's been hijacked; they killed Heraldo. They're holding the captain down. Is anyone there?"

There was a bit of static, and then a voice came through the receiver.

"Dear God; yes, we hear you. We're on our way; hide or get off that boat."

It sounded like Phil.

Finn quickly turned off the walkie-talkie and slid it in his pocket. "We'll have to swim to shore, okay?"

I quickly glanced toward the dark jungle and felt my heartbeat in my throat. The shouting below intensified as the sound of glass breaking and items being thrown across the deck echoed throughout the boat.

"We're gonna be fine," Finn said, squeezing my hand.

We snuck to the farthest end of the boat and quietly descended the steps. We stood there for a moment as I shook, almost uncontrollably.

"On three," Finn said. "One, two, three …"

We jumped and flew through the air, landing in the warm, murky water.

When I came up, I could hear yelling from the boat, followed by the sound of more gunshots.

We began swimming, not looking back. I could hear the terror behind us.

We reached the muddy bank.

"Run!" Finn yelled as he pulled on my wrist.

We stumbled our way into the dense jungle, pushing our way through the fleshy leaves and tangled undergrowth. Suddenly, Finn groaned and fell to his knees.

"Finn," I cried. "Come on. We've got to keep moving."

"I think I got hit." He pulled up his shirt to reveal a hole on his right side. As he said that, bright red blood leaked out and ran down his skin.

"No! Finn. Oh, Finn." My heart sank, and I panicked. I spun

my head around, hearing shouting and splashes coming from the river.

"Please Finn, you've got to get up. We've got to run."

Finn tried to stand, but his knees buckled, and he fell to the ground.

"Okay, okay," I said, forcing my voice to stay calm. "Everything's going to be okay." I quickly looked around and spotted a thick patch of bushes. "Let's get you over here; help me. Can you crawl over here? I'm going to hide you under those bushes."

I helped him scramble beneath the thick underbrush and took the walkie-talkie out of his pocket.

"Phil! Phil! Anyone! Are you there?" I whispered.

"I'm here. Where are you? Are you okay? Are you safe?" Phil asked in an urgent voice.

"We're in the jungle, not far from the boat. They shot Finn; they shot him. There's blood, blood spurting everywhere ..."

I thought I saw Finn's eyes roll back. I quickly turned around, pulled a long vine from a tree, and then yanked off my T-shirt, folding it in a thick square. I gently turned Finn on his side, placed my shirt against his wound, and tied it securely around his waist with the vine.

I picked up walkie-talkie. "Phil, Phil! Oh, God. I think they're coming. I can hear them coming."

My heart was racing as I imagined the footsteps getting closer and closer.

There was a crackle, and then a thin voice came through.

"We're on our way. Tia, you have to hide."

"Listen to me, damn it," I cried. "You need to help Finn.

He's tucked under some bushes. He's dying; my brother's dying. Hurry, please … hurry."

I turned the walkie-talkie off and sat as the footsteps drew closer. It sounded like they surrounded us.

Finn was ghostly white. I knew he didn't have much time.

"If they find you, play dead," I whispered.

"What? Tia, no …"

I bent down, brushed back his hair, and kissed him softly on the cheek.

His complexion was ashen, and every muscle in his face was bent and contorted, trying to stifle the pain.

"Phil and Mikael are on their way," I said. "Stay alive. Don't leave me. Please don't leave me. I love you, brother." I stood up.

He lifted his head. "What? Where are you going?"

Then I took off toward the river, racing past the armed men and screaming my head off as I did my best to lead them away from Finn.

I was tackled in seconds.

"Get off me," I screeched, swinging at the men in vain.

They seemed entertained by my attempts to resist.

I did manage to land a successful punch, hitting the shortest captor in the eye, which wiped the smile from his face.

"¡*Perra!*" he yelled, jostling me around to face him. There was nothing but malicious hatred in his eyes.

And then something solid slammed into the back of my head, and all went dark.

When I slowly came to, my head was throbbing dully, and I tasted something salty. I tried to swallow and realized I had a cloth tied around my head and inside my mouth, probably someone's dirty, perspiration-soaked bandana being used as a gag. I was wearing a stranger's shirt, camo in color.

I tried to scream, but it came out like a muffled groan. I felt the restraints around my wrists and ankles.

"Shh." A man was sitting to my left. He had dirty blond hair and large brown eyes. "Stop. Make no noise."

I heard footsteps coming down the deck and closed my eyes, pretending to be asleep.

"Vanilla, *¿Está la niña despierta?*" a voice said in Spanish.

I could quickly translate: "Hey, Vanilla, is she awake?"

Spanish had been mandatory in school since sixth grade, but I wasn't very good at it. My long nights of studying hadn't prepared me nearly well enough. I could catch enough to get the gist, but I was not comfortable at all speaking it. The words seemed to stick in my mouth, and I felt like I only mumbled.

"*No, aún no,*" the man next to me said. (No, not yet.)

"*¡Ella es una mina de oro!*" (She's a gold mine.)

My stomach turned.

Even though my eyes were shut, I could feel his gaze roving over my body.

"Cristiano, stop. She's not even awake," Vanilla said.

Then fingers squeezed my chest, and my eyes flew open.

I tried to say, "Get off me," but it came out like "Gerr aaahhh eeeee!"

My feet and legs tried to scramble away from the man's reach.

He was an ugly man who smelled as dirty as he looked. He threw his head back and laughed, and then leaned over and slapped me.

"Shut your face up!" he said in heavily accented English. "You want me to take off gag?"

I went silent.

The man leaned over and put his face an inch away. "Then do not make a fucking sound."

I nodded, even though agreeing to anything he said was against my better judgment.

Cristiano reached behind me and untied the bandana, and it fell away. My dry tongue scraped against my dry lips.

"Water, please," I croaked.

"*Escuchaste a la perra*" (You heard the bitch), Cristiano said to Vanilla. "The pretty American flower wants water."

Vanilla disappeared into the boat's cabin as Cristiano untied one of my arms, making sure his hand grazed my breasts several times.

"What is your name, little flower?" Cristiano said with a horrific, maniacal smile.

His hot, rank breath made me want to vomit. He was maybe in his early forties, at least six feet tall. His thinning dark brown hair was perfectly combed back, as if plastered to his head. It was odd; his fingernails were perfectly cleaned and groomed. He wore camouflage pants pushed into his black military-style boots and a dark-green T-shirt with a red bandana sticking out of his shirt pocket.

I turned my head from his gaze and stared blankly at the wall, ignoring his question.

Vanilla returned, handing me a paper cup. "Here."

My hand shook as I took the cup and sipped. It was warm.

"Who the hell are you?" Cristiano demanded, his pointed finger an inch away from my face.

I pushed my head deeper into the pillow. "Tia … my name is Tia."

"Who were the others on that boat?" Cristiano said as he slid his fingers through my hair.

I tried not to retch.

He grabbed a handful of hair and yanked my head around. "I ask you again: who were the others?"

I tried to swallow, which was difficult because my head was being twisted back so far. "A movie crew."

"Where are they now?"

"They had to pick up supplies in Manaus," I lied. "I'm sure they're back by now. I can talk to them for you."

Cristiano backhanded me, and my eardrums throbbed.

"Americans talk too much," he said as his cellphone began to ring. He pulled it out of his pocket. "*Hola,*" he said, followed by more in Spanish that was difficult to hear.

Cristiano hung up and smirked.

"Heitor wants to meet you."

"*No estoy seguro de que sea una buena idea,*" Vanilla said. (Not sure that's a good idea.) "*Tengo un mal presentimiento sobre este.*" (I've got a bad feeling about this one.)

I sat without expression, as if I didn't know what they were saying. I decided it was my only advantage.

Cristiano waved him off. "Enough," he said in English. "Stop being fucking spineless. Stay here and watch her."

Then he stomped off and took another phone call, while Vanilla retied both of my wrists and returned to his seat nearby.

He looked to be in his late thirties and was short and stocky. His sandy blond hair was dirty and disheveled, and he wore faded blue jeans tucked into a pair of brown hiking boots. His shirt was a plain white tee, blotched with dirt. While his face was hardened, he had soft brown eyes that seemed to reflect a look of concern, maybe even remorse. It could have been my imagination or hopefulness.

I closed my eyes again, picturing Finn's unmoving body on the jungle floor. I was unable to contain the tears any longer as I reached with my bound wrists for the golden maple leaf necklace around my neck.

Now I lay me down to sleep, I thought. *I pray the Lord my soul to keep. If I should die before I wake, I pray the Lord my soul to take.*

It was the only thing I could think of that could bring me any comfort in that moment: the thought that if I were to die soon, I would be reunited with my parents and be with my God.

With each hour that passed, my fear intensified. The sun had gone down, and the room was pitch-black, except for a small gas lantern flickering on a side table.

Suddenly, men were shouting on the upper deck. I tried in vain to release the restraints around my wrists and ankles.

Two men ran down the stairs, one of them the shifty-eyed Cristiano.

"Get her up," he ordered in Spanish, and Vanilla began untying my restraints. "Hurry!"

"Okay, okay!" Vanilla said, tugging on the strips of fabric.

As they came off, I thought about running and jumping out of the boat, but Cristiano had already grabbed ahold of my shirt and quickly pulled me out of the room; he pushed up the stairs and into a small dinghy.

As we made our way to the shoreline, I took in the jungle air. It was a humid, slightly chilly night, like a West Virginia evening right after a thunderstorm.

It was so dark, I could barely see my hands. We climbed out of the dinghy and stumbled our way into the Amazonian jungle.

Cristiano was in front, holding a flashlight that illuminated his path alone. I did my best to shield my face from the whacks of gigantic jungle leaves and razor-sharp branches, but I tripped every few feet. A few times, I fell.

In the virtual darkness, I could visualize the creatures of the night, the piercing screech of a howler monkey in distress, a coal-black jaguar lunging at me, ripping me apart. I shivered, knowing I had no protective shell to give me a chance.

After twenty or thirty minutes of slogging through the damp underbrush, flashes of light began to appear through the trees, coupled with boisterous shouts and punctuated with occasional random gunshots.

"Oh, God. Oh, God," I whispered.

"Quiet!" Cristiano hissed, spinning and raising his hand threatening to strike me.

As we entered the camp, tall, shadowy figures loomed around the high flames of a fire with their arms raised, roaring like wild beasts into the night.

I counted at least two dozen men covered head to toe in mismatched uniforms of black, green, and camo. All of them had guns either slung over their shoulders or pointed in my direction.

A dead boar dangled by its feet over a massive fire, and I saw beyond the large pit were dozens of tents. The camp reeked of burning meat, cigar smoke, and cheap alcohol. The jeers and hollers reached a deafening crescendo as more men saw me and stared.

Cristiano turned to two of his men and said in Spanish. "Tie her to Heitor's tree."

I jerked around wildly, trying to escape the men's grip on my arms. They dragged me to a tree ten yards away, one with rusted chains and handcuffs bolted into the bark. The base of the tree was darker and mangled, as if dozens of people before had bled all over it as they kicked in a futile attempt to get away.

The men shoved me forward hard, slicing my cheek open on the tree's jagged bark. They untied my wrists but then put the left in a handcuff, and the right in another. Then they forced my arms around the trunk, locking the restraints to a chain so I was hugging the tree; my backside was to the group.

I couldn't see much, except for men seeming to form a circle around the tree. A gigantic man twirling a large machete came up and pulled my hair back. He drew the blade below my ear, and I felt it scratch my skin. I could feel blood trickle out.

"Please *stop!*" I screamed.

To my surprise, Vanilla pushed through the others and shoved the huge man away.

"*¡Apártate!*" he said. (Back off!)

"Vanilla, please let me go," I pleaded, twisting to look at him.

Vanilla just frowned and shook his head before disappearing again into the unruly crowd.

The circle parted, and a squat, muscled man appeared. He had an unruly gray and black mustache, coal-black eyes, and an unnaturally long and crooked nose. He wore a bandana around his bald head and was holding a thick cigar.

"Heitor, this is Tia. Tia, Heitor," Cristiano said in a formal yet sarcastic tone.

My head was whipped back as someone yanked on my hair.

"Tia, Tia, my beautiful *bebé*," Heitor whispered in my ear as he blew gray smoke from his cigar; the stench enveloped my face and stung the inside of my nose.

The gang members cackled and began to chant my name as Heitor bent closer, forcing me to stare into his eyes.

Then, without warning, I felt my pants being yanked down to my knees, and I was smacked on my bare skin, the sound remarkably loud.

Just let me die. Lord, wrap me in your arms and take me from here.

"Let's see what you're made of, my little *bebé*."

"Stop, *please,*" I wailed, but it only seemed to egg him on.

"Only the jaguars and anacondas can hear you." He pulled my pants off completely and spread my legs farther apart.

I tried to fight him, kicking to the right, kicking to the left, but the way I was positioned made it nearly impossible to move.

And then what I feared the most:

I let out a piercing scream as I was brutally attacked in the vilest way possible, over and over. It felt like scalding hot knives ripping and tearing at me. The louder I screamed, the worse it felt.

My naiveté, my understanding, my forgiveness, my purity, all disappeared in shrieks of agony and pain.

While it was excruciating, I looked up, hoping upon hope to see a star, just one, any star. But instead there was only a faint white mist floating among the thick jungle leaves as if my purity had melted and drifted away.

Heitor grunted loudly as he finished his torture; he backed away as the other men cheered. I felt his hand between my thighs for a moment.

"Ah, *una virgen*" (Ah, a virgin), he said to the crowd. "So glad you waited for me."

Then he said what I feared, yet expected:

"*Tu turno, mi hermano, pero nadie más. No quiero matarla esta noche.*" (Your turn, my brother, but no one else. Don't want to kill her tonight.)

I braced myself against the tree as Cristiano approached. My breath was ragged and knees wobbly. My head was spinning and …

… everything went black.

I awakened to someone's fingers gently pulling up my pants and uncuffing me from the trunk.

"You be all right," a voice said. Vanilla? I wasn't sure. "Aline will fix you."

He picked me up and carried me to a small tent farther away from the others. Inside, I was laid on a small cot.

In a foggy haze, I looked around.

"Bring me a tub of warm water, towels, some medicine, and a night dress," a woman with a dark braid said in Spanish.

Vanilla slipped out of the tent.

I wrapped my arms tight around my knees, cowering from the woman's reach.

Aline was short and husky; she wore baggy khaki pants and a black T-shirt. She had deep wrinkles around her lips and eyes, and while her face was hard, her voice was soft and gentle.

"Be still. I not hurt you," she said. "My name, Aline. What is yours?"

I couldn't answer; there were no words to say.

Aline began to wash me, using special care around the many lacerations. Then I was dressed in a faded nightgown and covered with a light sheet.

Vanilla stepped in, his face passive.

"Finished," Aline said.

"Sleep in my tent tonight," Vanilla said to Aline, and she nodded, leaving the tent.

Vanilla handed me a water bottle.

"Try to sleep," he said.

I buried my head under the blanket, feeling as though the

world was crashing down upon me. Every part of my body felt unbearably heavy, wilted, dirty, weak. Broken.

How do I live after this? Why would I want to?

I was just beginning to doze off when Vanilla burst into the tent.

"Police coming," he said. "We leave now."

He grabbed a few belongings.

I sat up, pain racing through my abdomen and pelvic area.

"We go," he said, kneeling, reaching out to me.

"Don't touch me," I snarled, wincing. I knew if I left with the group and went deeper into the jungle, a rescue would be even less of a possibility.

"Listen," Vanilla said. "If you not go, Heitor will kill you." He stuffed a gun into his pants.

Then he grabbed my hand and jerked me up, pulling me out of the tent. We jogged at a fast pace through the camp.

Heitor and Cristiano appeared on the pathway and I froze. They didn't acknowledge me.

"Take the Jeep and get back to the river," Heitor said in Spanish. "Eduardo's already waiting for you. Keep heading east until I contact you. And Vanilla, don't let anything happen her."

"*¡Vámonos!*" Cristiano yelled, leading us to a dirt-covered Jeep twenty feet away.

123

Every bounce of the vehicle sent a volley of agony through my limbs. The shrieks of monkeys high in the trees had reached an ear-piercing level, adding a cacophony of fear and dread to my already high anxiety.

In the commotion, I considered jumping out and running deep into the jungle.

What are they going to do with me after we get to the boat? Will they kill me? Would I have a better chance in the jungle? Should I jump? I need to jump and run, but it's pitch-black with poisonous snakes and jaguars. I wouldn't last the night, or maybe I could.

It didn't matter. A few moments later, before I had a chance to work up the courage to jump, we were stopping next to a yacht waiting at the riverbank. We boarded and then pushed off into the murky river.

"Sorry," Vanilla said as he handcuffed my left wrist to a handle. "I talk to Eduardo, but I will be back."

How could we have been so stupid coming here? Chile was done; we could have flown home from there. For that matter, I could have said no to the whole damn thing in the first place. So close; we were almost home. Our flight was leaving in a few hours; we were almost home.

I reached for the maple leaf pendant with my free hand and clung to it as my eyes searched the skies, still hoping for that star, that sign.

CHAPTER 11

Prisoner Below

I could hear a hum, which soon became the whapping of
helicopter blades in the distance, as the yacht appeared to glide
down a remote arm of the river. We must have been about twenty
or more miles away from the camp. I doubted the helicopters
would find us, since the boat was fully covered by a blanket of
giant trees, if the helicopters were even looking for us. But I could
feel a thick tension and worry hanging over the thugs, which told
me the people in the aircraft were not their friends.

Vanilla gazed up into the leaves and then glanced at me before
looking away.

"We never should have taken her," he said to Cristiano in
Spanish.

"Damn Americans," Cristiano said, flicking his cigar so flakes of ash floated on the light breeze that hovered across the river. "They always overreact."

"They probably have the entire Brazilian Special Forces on our asses by now," Vanilla said, looking up again as the radio crackled to life.

"Cristiano, pick up!" Heitor's voice shouted through the radio in Spanish. "Pick up!"

Cristiano fumbled with the device and finally managed to unclip it from his pants. "I'm here, Heitor. What's the update?"

"Just got word the military's coming in full force. They've closed down the river; get farther downstream before the choppers spot you. Tell Eduardo. And don't use this radio for any reason; we're going on radio silence. I'll contact you when I can."

So the helicopters *were* looking for us. I could feel a little bit of hope rise from my pain.

It was pitch-black except for the faint light coming from the boat's instrument panel and strip lights on the stairway that led to the lower deck. The boat was moving at a decent speed, and the threadbare nightgown I was wearing proved useless in shielding against the cool night air, penetrating straight to the bone and adding a new misery.

The yacht twisted and turned until Eduardo finally anchored it under a canopy of trees, and the nighttime sounds of the jungle were all I could hear. The helicopters were gone.

I let out a long, slow breath, cradling my knees closer to my chest under the nightgown, trying to find warmth where I could.

"I'm taking the girl down below," Vanilla said as he walked up to me, placing a finger to his lips, reminding me to keep quiet.

He unlocked the handcuffs and placed a firm grip around my arm as he led me down the stairs.

At the end of the narrow corridor, he guided me into a back room and flipped on the light. Inside was one small porthole, two twin beds against the back wall, and a small dresser with a bottle of water on it. Each bed had a bedspread decorated with images of parrots and one large pillow.

"Go, lay down. I have a pill."

He dug a little white pill out of a mud-splotched pocket and dropped it in my palm. "Should help you sleep. I will be outside." He readjusted the rifle over his shoulder before slipping out to stand guard.

Did I see a look of concern in his eyes? Or was it my hopeful imagination again?

I crawled under the covers and wrapped myself in the blanket to stifle the deep chill. A nightlight in the shape of a wildflower illuminated the far side of the room with a gentle glow. I considered the pill and then shoved it under the mattress.

I closed my eyes, but the violence refused to stop playing over and over in my head. I couldn't get the scent of sour breath and burnt meat out of my sinuses, or the way I was smashed against the tree, again and again, pain piercing my body, and the sound of my own voice begging and praying for help that did not come.

I gave up. I reached down under the mattress, fetched the pill, and slipped it into my mouth, figuring anything was better if it could make the thoughts stop. I didn't care if the pill he gave me was poison. That might have been preferred.

I forced myself to change my thoughts, turning to the safety of Uncle's church, kneeling in prayer, the smell of incense drifting through the air. We had missed so many Sunday Masses since we left for California. I longed to see Father Harold with his white tuft of hair, wearing his long colorful robes and standing behind the altar, blessing the wine and bread, blessing those among him.

Once, I asked Uncle Harold why he became a priest. His answer was short and to the point:

"I was the oldest son, we were poor as dirt, and Mama told me to become a priest. In those days, every mouth to feed was a burden, and me entering into the priesthood, well, it took part of the burden off. Dad was sick with the cancer by that time and died shortly after I left. Your papa, my younger brother, took care of Mama until she passed away about four years later."

He looked thoughtful.

"But honestly, I wouldn't have wanted any other life, and at the risk of sounding cliché, this was indeed my calling."

Would Uncle forgive me for missing so many Sunday Masses? And could God ever forgive me for being so defiled? I knew it would be easy to say it wasn't my fault, but the truth was I put myself in harm's way out of greed. Putting myself first over my family.

I buried my face in the pillow, pain radiating through my whole being.

Eventually, the pill kicked in, and sleep—my only recourse and escape—finally found me.

The next morning, Vanilla came in and placed his hand on my forehead.

"Very hot," he said. Was that a hint of worry in his voice? "Did you take the pill?"

I opened my eyes, and it seemed like the intense pain from the night before had only grown. I grimaced.

"Did you take the pill?" he asked again.

"Yeah, I took it," I said, pulling the blanket up to my neck.

"I will get you another one," he said. "It will help the fever."

"Where are we?"

He ignored my question. "I will be back."

I sat up, wondering if I could break the small window and squeeze out. I could hear footsteps and murmurs from the top deck and decided against it. For now.

I inched my way out of bed, tiptoed to the bathroom, and closed the door behind me.

Decorated with bright orange, blue, green, and purple wallpaper, it had a good-sized sink with gold handles and a large shower.

I lowered myself to the toilet, and an intense burning sensation shot through me as if all my delicate parts had been rubbed raw with sandpaper and were now being doused in vinegar.

I bit my tongue to keep from screaming, my legs shaking uncontrollably as I tried to get to my feet, holding on to the small sink to reclaim my balance.

I looked in the mirror and almost didn't recognize the person looking back. My cheek had a three-inch gash running from under my left eye to my ear, and my right eye was bruised and swollen. The skin on my neck and chest was a patchwork of scrapes, bruises, and red insect bites.

A sudden knock on the bathroom door startled me, and I had to take a couple of deep breaths to calm down. I went to the door and opened it a crack.

"Put on this," Vanilla said, holding out a pile of clothes.

I widened the door a bit to take the clothing: a pair of tan slacks, a black shirt, socks, and tennis shoes.

"Shower. Clean the cuts before they get, uh … infection."

I shut the door and slipped off the nightgown to step into the shower. The warm spray of the water stung like a horde of bees. Red water pooled as the caked blood glued to my hair dissolved. I touched my swollen eye, removing the hardened crust of pus and dirt in my eyelashes. Though it didn't feel as wonderful as the beautiful, deep bathtub with the shooting jets in the fancy Los Angeles hotel, my body relaxed as it was cleansed.

I prayed Finn was still alive.

How would I ever live with him gone? Without him, I couldn't imagine. And Wes had warned us not to go. He'd been certain something bad would happen. I had ignored him along with the periodic bouts of mysterious fear I experienced.

Then I thought that if Finn was alive, and if we ever made it home, what would I say about the … about the rape? *Do I say anything? Do I keep it to myself?*

It was hard not to think about the loss of childhood and innocence, what had been so brutally taken from me.

Now I felt broken.

My virginity—something that had been intangible, special beyond words—was taken from me, stolen, wrenched cruelly away, leaving me feeling like nothing more than a pile of dirt, my virtue discarded in a pile of filth.

I found myself curled up in shame on the floor of the shower as the water beat upon my head, the heat soothing on my scalp, even if there was no hope of it ever washing me clean.

Again, there was a loud bang on the door.

"Just a minute," I yelled, getting up and wiping the tears from my eyes. I turned off the water, got out, dried off, and put on the oversized shirt, pants, and shoes.

I came out of the bathroom.

"Go, lay down. Brought you food," Vanilla said, handing me a plate of fruit and bread. "I be back." He walked out, leaving the door open.

I stood for a moment, listening. I went up to the doorway, staying just out of view. I could hear a conversation in Spanish.

"What's going on, man? Did Heitor call in last night?" The voice sounded like Cristiano's.

"No word. We're on radio silence," another man said. Maybe Eduardo.

"We can't just wait here like sitting ducks," Vanilla said. "Turn on the radio. Let's see if anything's on the news."

"I got it," Eduardo said, and the sound of static followed. "We're too far out."

"Go to thirteen-fifty. I always get that channel," Cristiano said.

A few moments passed, and then, a voice in English" "… are searching the area after the abduction of a young girl from West Virginia. Police believe the Black Jaguar drug cartel was behind the kidnapping. The girl, Teagan McSherry, and her twin brother, Fionn McSherry, were actors in a movie produced by Open Borders Studio when their boat was captured by the cartel. Fionn was shot, and we are awaiting updates on his condition. Teagan was taken by the cartel, and a massive manhunt is under way. All resources will be made available to rescue Miss McSherry. We will keep you updated as more information becomes available."

My heart suddenly came alive.

They're looking for me. I'll be home soon, and Finn may be alive "Awaiting updates on his condition" means they found him, right?

Thoughts spun, and I immediately started second-guessing what I thought I heard.

"Shit!" Eduardo yelled in Spanish. "They know we took her! Heitor must still be in hiding, but we need to get the hell out of here."

"We're not going anywhere," Cristiano said. "You heard Heitor; we need to stay here until he contacts us. I don't get it though; we kidnap girls all the time, and only the local police come out. Just because she was in a movie, the military is getting involved? What kind of shit did we get ourselves into?"

I heard footsteps and hurried back to the bed, putting a small piece of fruit in my mouth.

Maybe Finn did die. What's gonna happen to Wes and Paddy?

The truth was, I hated them all: Cristiano, Vanilla, Eduardo. And Heitor most of all. I hated them all. That burned in my chest, and I felt like I might catch fire from the force and depth of that hate.

I can say I had never felt this vengeful toward anyone else.

There was an overwhelming urge to kill them all, and I imagined myself digging a sharp knife into each of their hearts, one by one, the blade piercing their flesh repeatedly, until blood covered my hands.

Then, the whiplash: painful guilt for feeling so hateful. Confusion and desperation mixed and blended, and again I started to cry.

Help me, dear Lord. Help me to understand and to forgive.

That word stung. I didn't know if forgiveness was possible, but I knew it was expected.

I moaned, willing it all to go away, hoping that if I prayed hard enough, I would open my eyes and find myself back in our little house in West Virginia, the river rushing swiftly outside with its unfailing, beautiful melody.

Instead, an old devotion came to mind. I struggled to remember the words, which I had memorized, or so I thought.

It was a prayer by Saint Alphonsus and had been shared by Father Harold time and time again.

How did it start?

And then the words came.

"If the devil tempts me," I said quietly, "thy name will give me strength to resist him. Thus do I hope to live, and so do I hope to die, having thy name always on my lips."

That wasn't the full verse, but I found that, almost miraculously, the pain receded somewhat, and I no longer felt quite so alone.

"Having thy name *always* and *forever* on my lips …"

At that moment, the bed shifted; someone sat on the mattress next to me.

I opened my eyes, staring at the slightly sweaty face of Vanilla. "Get the hell off!" I shouted.

He immediately launched himself off the bed, and his somewhat passive face fell into a look of hurt.

I almost immediately regretted the words. Especially after just having to remind myself to keep Jesus's name always on my lips.

"Sorry ... you ... you just scared me." I looked away from the wounded expression on his face. I couldn't believe I actually yelled at him. *Maybe he really isn't like the others.*

Then, as if to confirm my thought, he offered a tentative smile. "Your voice is ... different."

I just stared at him blankly.

"I like watching old black-and-white TV shows," he said. "Andy Griffith. You know Andy Griffith?"

I only blinked.

"You sound like Aunt Bee on that show." He kind of smiled and then turned, pointing toward the bedside table. "I brought you more food. I leave you alone now; eat, then sleep." Vanilla nodded, still with a small smile, then quietly left the room, closing the door behind him.

CHAPTER 12

Vanilla

When I woke, the room was dark. I must have slept the entire day. On a small table, a reading lamp glowed, illuminating a small plate of food. More ominously, I could see Vanilla's dark silhouette in a chair by the door. At least I hoped it was Vanilla. He seemed to be the only one who didn't want to hurt me.

"I am glad you sleep. Try to eat," he said, pulling the chair next to my bed.

During the day, I thought he was around forty years old. Now, in the shadows of the dimly lit room, he looked twenty years older. At least he was freshly showered and smelled of soap, his sandy blond hair combed and parted on the side.

"How you feel?" he asked, placing the palm of his hand on my forehead.

I paused to consider this, taking inventory of what hurt. "I'm not sure what you want me to say. I guess I'm better."

Vanilla looked down at the floor, as if ashamed.

I reached for the plate of food and placed it on my lap. "I just want to go home. Can …" I paused again, this time to pick the words. "Can you help me get out of here?"

He shifted in his chair. "I don't know, but I promise, I will do what I can."

I cocked my head, curious. "Why are you being so nice to me?" I had to imagine that even thinking about helping me could probably get him killed.

It took him several moments to reply.

"You … you are just a girl. I had a daughter, Isabela. She would be your age now."

Had?

I ate some fruit and bread, and waited.

He looked exhausted and worn. His shoulders were slumped.

After a few minutes of awkward silence, I said, "You seem too nice to be with these guys. Why are you with them?"

Vanilla looked down and studied his hands.

"They are family. They are all I have."

"You mean that you've been with them all your life?" I asked, repositioning the pillow against my back.

"Yeah, I guess." He sighed and looked up at me. "My father was in the gang, and I followed. It was, eh, expected of me."

"Who are these people?"

Vanilla stared at me, thinking. "We are …" Then he went quiet.

"I won't tell anyone. Who would I tell?" I said, with a reassuring voice.

Vanilla took a deep breath and released it slowly. "Okay. I want you to trust me."

But why would I trust him? They're all killers. What kind of game is he playing?

After careful consideration, I decided to play along. Maybe I could find a weakness, anything to give me more of an advantage, over him and over them.

"We are the Black Jaguars," Vanilla said, looking visibly uncomfortable.

"What does that mean?" I asked, sitting cross-legged on the bed. "I've heard of gangs before, but I didn't realize they got involved in kidnappings and stuff."

"This is … this is like a, uh, cartel. Like a business. Guns and drugs, mostly." His voice bordered on emotionless.

"And the police? Don't they come after you?"

Vanilla snorted. "We have always been strong in Manaus and through Brazil since becoming, eh, partners with a powerful cartel out of Colombia. We have connections to a few police. For the most part, they leave us alone."

"Didn't you want to do something else?"

"It is all I know." He shrugged. "My father wanted me to finish school and get out, get a real job, but he disappeared in Mexico when I was twelve. Haven't seen him since."

"Oh. I'm sorry, Vanilla. How about your mom? Where does she live now?"

"I never knew her. She died after I was born. My father said it was a miracle I lived. I was born out here in the jungle ... not too far from here, actually."

I looked out the small port window into the darkness. I couldn't imagine anyone being born out in the middle of this jungle.

"So what do you do now? I'm mean ... like, what's your job in this cartel?"

Vanilla shook his head slightly, as if he wasn't going to answer. But he did.

"When I turned eleven, I smuggled drugs in a small dinghy with Cristiano. He's my cousin. Did that for about ten years."

I was shocked that he'd been running drugs since he was little, more shocked that the monster on the top deck was his cousin. "You're cousins? If you didn't tell me, I would have never guessed."

"Yeah. We were really close growing up. Not anymore. And I'm sorry what he did to you."

Remorse? He's sorry for Cristiano's actions? I nodded my head in acknowledgment.

"We would travel from one end of the Amazon River to the other, smuggling cocaine in the boat. I remember feeling important. After a while, everything changed. It got worse."

"How could things get worse? What happened?"

"When our old boss was killed by a rival gang, Heitor stepped up as the leader of the Black Jaguars. Since that time, more kidnappings, more rapes, more killings."

I remained quiet as a rush of nausea swept over me. I pictured Heitor's face looming.

Vanilla seemed to sense what I was thinking.

"To Heitor, women are a piece of property to be used, sold, to do whatever. The louder they scream, the more violent he becomes. It makes me sick, but there is nothing I can do. He's a … what you say … a monster, even to his own family. We're all his family now."

Dumbfounded, I asked, "He kills his own kin?"

Vanilla paused, frowning, as if he didn't understand what I said.

"Kin, family," I said.

He nodded. "Okay. There was one time, at a dance party. Heitor loves Latino music, all kinds: samba, *carimbó*, choro. It was at this party that Cristiano became like Heitor."

I remained quiet, not sure I wanted to hear this story.

"Everyone dancing, having a good time. There was a new kid, Heitor's runner. I think his name was Tiago. He was about my age then, eighteen. The kid got drunk, his first dance. Halfway through the samba, Tiago, eh, vomited on the floor, right in front of Heitor. Everyone froze. The music stopped. I looked over at Heitor, and his face was … evil. If I were asked to draw the devil, it would look exactly like Heitor."

He paused, frowning.

"He handed a gun to Cristiano and told him to shoot Tiago right there. Cristiano had never killed anyone, and I didn't want him to. My instincts told me to stay back, but I make mistake, telling Heitor that Tiago was just a kid who didn't know any better. I tell him I take him home. I remember his eyes grew wide, and he pulled a switchblade from his pocket, telling me to get on my knees. I couldn't believe Heitor. I kneel down, and he took me by my hair, sliding the blade down my cheek." Vanilla's eyes grew distant, his mouth twitching.

"Yeah," I said. "I can see the scar."

"He shoved me to the ground, and kicked me, and didn't stop. Then, a gunshot. Cristiano shot Tiago, and he was lying, crumpled and dead. *Dead.* For having too many beers. I couldn't believe it. Heitor clapped and laughed, forgetting all about me."

Vanilla paused again and sat back in the chair.

"As I think, Cristiano did it to save me. But he changed that day. He stopped running cocaine down the river and began working under Heitor. Now as brutal as Heitor. They call him the *Disciplinador.*"

"Do you still smuggle drugs down the river?"

Vanilla shook his head. "I stopped many years ago after my … my family was killed."

"Your wife and daughter?"

"Eighteen years. It was eighteen years when I met Camila at a Christmas dance. When I saw her, my knees, eh, my knees buckled."

Vanilla stood up and walked to the porthole.

"From that night, we were, eh, what's the word?"

"Inseparable?" I said.

He nodded. "Inseparable. We married a month after, and my Isabela was born that year. She was so beautiful."

A long, long pause.

"They were my life, the only thing I cared about."

He walked back to his chair, wiping away tears.

"You remind me of Isabela. She would have been your age."

"I'm so sorry," I said. Under normal circumstances, I might have reached out and took his hand in sympathy, in support. But I didn't move. "How did they die?"

"I was not in town. When I returned that night, I learn that my wife and daughter had been caught in a drive-by shooting. They died on the street, waiting for an ambulance." He shook his head. "Too hard to think about, too hard to talk about, just too hard." He paced back and forth. "After all this time, I still can't believe they are gone."

He sat down, wringing his hands as if he wanted to tear them off at the wrists.

"Since then, I want to die. But now *you're* here. I know that Camila and Isabela would want me to take care of you. I don't know why, and I can't really explain, but I feel, eh, responsible to protect you." Vanilla went quiet again, hunching over.

I didn't know what to say. I felt sorry for him, I guess, or at least I wanted to believe I felt sorry for him. "I can see how much you miss them and, well, thank you for wanting to protect me."

"Yeah, something snapped in me. I looked for a way out, for a reason to keep living. I been quiet for so long. I never try to stop the violence."

Vanilla paused and looked up to the ceiling, unable to face me.

"I'm guilty, guilty for not stopping them, guilty for doing *nothing*." He slumped farther down in the chair. "When I saw what they did to you, that was … I couldn't live this life anymore. This is not who I am. This is not who I was to be."

I stayed quiet, not knowing how to respond.

Vanilla leaned forward and lowered his voice to a whisper. "Listen. I think there may be a way out. It is just those two up there, and we could try to take over the boat, or sneak off and go to the next town. Give me some time to think."

I would have felt somewhat hopeful at the possibility of escape, but I could see doubt and fear in Vanilla's eyes. And I still wasn't completely convinced I could trust him. I guess if I had a choice between Cristiano, Heitor, or Vanilla, I'd choose him, but I wouldn't be very comfortable about it.

Suddenly, he stood up from the chair and turned off the light. "I'll be back."

And he was gone.

I looked out the porthole and saw the first signs of morning creeping in over the horizon, yet the thick canopy from the trees masked most of its rays.

What day is it? Thursday? Yes, it has to be Thursday.

If Vanilla could get me out of there, I could find Finn, and we could be home soon, back to the little house, back to Paddy and Wes, who were probably worried sick since they hadn't heard from us in days.

Cristiano would come down every day just to glare at me and make me feel uncomfortable. He wouldn't say anything except for a loud, annoyed grunt whenever he decided to leave.

Vanilla grew increasingly tense and cautious. He was always checking his backpack and cleaning his gun, taking it apart and rubbing it with an oiled cloth before methodically putting it back together.

Early one morning, Vanilla came into the room and urgently nudged me awake.

"Get up," he said.

"Huh?"

"If we leave, you need to be ready to run with me. Can you do it?"

I tried to blink the sleep away and nodded mutely.

He checked his handgun before reaching into his bag and pulling out another one. He removed the clip and began filling it with more bullets.

"You're scaring me," I said, watching his swift, instinctual movements.

Vanilla put the guns down on the small table and sat on the side of the bed. "I told you I would do anything to protect you. Do you remember?"

I swallowed. "Yes."

"Okay. Good. Now, you have to trust me."

"I trust you," I heard myself say, although I wasn't sure I believed it.

He told me I reminded him of his daughter, and he promised me he would do anything to protect me. I hope I wasn't wrong about this.

Vanilla packed what looked like a small tent into one backpack and filled another with snacks, water, a loaded handgun, and five boxes of ammunition. He placed his compass around his neck, shoved one of the handguns in the waistband of his pants, and took both backpacks out of the room, apparently to the upper deck.

I waited and then heard a crackle come from the boat radio. I went by the door to listen.

"Eduardo, come in. Eduardo! Do you hear me?" It was Spanish. Heitor's voice.

There were footsteps and then Eduardo's response, "I'm here, brother."

"Can't talk long. I need your coordinates. I'm sending a few guys out to bring you to where I am. We need to get the hell out of the country for a while."

Eduardo said some numbers, and the radio went silent.

Vanilla ran down the stairs and into my room. "Get ready to run," he whispered urgently.

My heart started beating fast. I reached down and tightened my shoelaces, hearing the frenzied steps of Cristiano and Eduardo echoing from the upper deck.

I stepped out of the room and walked to the bottom of the staircase, listening intently. I could hear Cristiano talking in Spanish.

"We got to get out. I am sure the military picked up that call. They're probably sending out a force right now. Let's at least hide in the jungle until the guys arrive. We can't wait out here in the open." A pause. "Where's Vanilla?"

Eduardo yelled down the staircase, "Vanilla, get the bitch ready. We're leaving."

Vanilla turned to me. "This is our chance," he said. "Stay here."

I could see determination and terror on his face as he pulled the gun from his waistband. He climbed the stairs and disappeared from view.

Within moments, there was a loud bang—a gunshot—that made me jump, followed by a muffled thump.

I scaled the steps to see Eduardo face down in a pool of blood next to the steering wheel. Vanilla was pointing a gun toward Cristiano, aimed at his head.

"What the *hell* are you doing?" Cristiano roared, looking down the barrel of Vanilla's gun before dropping to his knees. "*¡Primo, soy yo; no hagas esto!*" (Cousin, it's me; don't do this!)

I turned away just in time as another gunshot exploded. Even though I knew it was coming, I still jumped.

I looked to see Cristiano slumped in a bloody mass along the floorboards.

Vanilla dropped down to his knees. "*No eres primo mío.*" (You're no cousin of mine.)

He picked up the backpacks and handed one to me. "We have to go, now!"

Using a machete, Vanilla chopped at the thick leaves and vines in an attempt to clear a path through the Amazonian jungle. He lifted his compass from his neck and pointed. "This way."

"Why are we going deeper into the trees?" I was weak and out of breath.

"We need to stay quiet for a few days," he said as he cut another swath of foliage with the machete. "They'll look for us."

We seemed to walk for miles, taking small breaks to eat and rest along the way. After a few hours of trekking through the brush, Vanilla settled on a place to set up camp for the night, a quiet clearing nestled against a rock wall. I looked up and saw only the cover of palm fronds.

After the tent was pitched, we sat quietly against a tree. There was a sweetness in the air from the aromatic blossoms that seemed to contrast with the inherent dangers that lurked in every corner. The jungle was alive. In every direction, as far as I could see, brightly colored parrots sang and squawked, spider monkeys screamed and grunted, and the buzzing and humming of a thousand different insects engulfed my senses. In that moment, it was beautiful. I was free, and it was beautiful.

"I'm so thankful to be off that suffocating boat," I said. "It's so strange out here, in the middle of the jungle and all. Seems like so many wild things can sneak up on you. Have you ever seen a jaguar? Have you been bitten by a poisonous snake?"

Vanilla smiled. "Nothing's got me yet."

As if on cue, there was a loud rustling sound not too far from where we were sitting.

"Go in the tent and rest. I'll be in soon," Vanilla said, scanning the closest trees.

My skin crawled with the thought of Vanilla joining me, but it was the only tent.

I unzipped the front flaps and curled up on the hard ground, rubbing my swollen feet and ankles until they no longer ached.

An hour or so later, Vanilla crawled into the tent and zipped up the canvas flap.

"I don't know what animals might come, but this little tent will keep the snakes out. Keep your shoes on and sleep. We leave at dawn."

"If they catch us, you could get killed for trying to save me," I said, pointing out the obvious.

"Doesn't matter. It is the *only* way out." Vanilla paused. "You know, I dreamed of my beautiful Camila and Isabela. First time in so long. I saw them clear. They were wearing matching red and white summer dresses. I knew I was dreaming, but I felt wide awake. I walked up to them and held them in my arms. It was so real. I could actually feel the warmth of their skin against my cheek. My wife whispered in my ear, 'It will be okay; everything will be okay.' I woke up knowing what I needed to do. If I can save you, I will feel redeemed. If I die, I will be with my wife and daughter again." He lay down with his back toward me and let out a deep sigh.

I stayed silent, not knowing what to say.

I curled up in a ball, exhausted, but wishing for daylight so we could keep running, running until we found help.

Though my eyes were closed, I was wide awake with nervous anticipation as I considered different escape and rescue scenarios.

That turned to images of running into my brothers' arms, smelling the deep aroma of the pines, and lying in my own bed in the little cabin tucked deep beyond the New River.

CHAPTER 13

Masks of Deceit

"Wake up!" Vanilla said, urgently shaking my leg. I sat up, little streams of early morning light already peeking through the tent's canvas.

He pulled out his handgun and got up on his knees.

I could hear people outside the tent. My heart raced; I hoped for the best but feared the worst.

He had a look of pure terror on his face, his eyes wide with grief. He leaned over and gently kissed me on the top of my head.

"No matter what happens," Vanilla said, "always know that you saved me. You gave me a reason to hope again, a reason to finally do the right thing."

"Wait, maybe it's the police," I said in a hoarse whisper. "You don't know it's not."

"Either way, I'm a dead man," he said, as he stuffed a sheathed knife into his pants.

A moment later, the tent was unzipped from the outside, and a man commanded us to emerge.

Vanilla crawled out first. Then he stood with his hands—including the one with the gun—raised high into the air.

When I followed, a feeling of grave disappointment coupled with terror swept through me as I saw five armed guerrillas surrounding us. Two grabbed Vanilla, confiscated his gun, and were holding his arms behind his back.

The apparent leader of the group grabbed me, swinging me to the ground where I tumbled like a rag doll.

As I looked up, the man took a gun from his holster, pointing it at Vanilla.

Before I could utter a word, much less react, he pulled the trigger, shooting Vanilla in the chest.

I screamed like an animal before I covered my face with my hands. I can't honestly say if I screamed out of fear that I would be next, or over the murder of the man who was trying to save me. Probably a mix of both.

I twisted away from the gunman and fell on my knees next to Vanilla. In vain, I tried to stop the rush of blood with my hand.

"I'm sorry," was all I could say.

In Spanish, I heard someone say, "Tear down the tent and take everything else. Let's head out."

The leader—a man about fifty with jet-black hair streaked with gray on top of his head—yanked me onto my feet and then spoke in Spanish into his radio: "Andre here; we've caught the parrots."

"Copy," crackled a voice on the other side.

Andre didn't seem to have much of a chin or cheekbones. He wore camouflage from head to toe with ankle-high black boots. His voice was dry and rough, as if he'd smoked his entire life, and his beady brown eyes looked small against his bushy gray eyebrows.

"All this trouble for one little girl," Andre said in English. "By the looks of you, I wouldn't even say it has been worth it."

He jerked me by the hair, and my mind went blank, thinking of the last time I was surrounded by a group of hostile men.

After what felt like miles, I was about ready to break down, fruitlessly swatting away the insects that had been assaulting me for hours.

"I can't walk," I gasped. "My feet … can't walk."

"Keep quiet," Andre said. "We are almost there." He blew out acrid cigar smoke that made me so nauseous, I almost threw up.

After another twenty minutes or so, we had reached the shores of the river, where there were two small dinghies.

Andre pulled off his military-style camo shirt and pants, putting on ordinary clothes, plus an old fisherman's hat. Then he pushed me into one of the boats while the other four guerrillas climbed into the second.

The stench was overwhelming from a large net filled with

dead fish. He pulled the net aside to expose a small compartment in the bottom of the dinghy.

"Get inside," he said, lifting the rusted metal lid of the compartment.

It was a tiny space, about the size of a small person's coffin, a child's maybe.

I began to panic, the adrenaline rushing through me.

"I can't," I said, almost screaming. "Don't make me!"

Andre pushed me down and stuffed me inside, slamming the lid before I could try anything.

Distraught, I gagged, almost vomiting as a trickle of water from the dead fish sputtered across my face. And then I started to scream.

Andre kicked the compartment so hard, my ears rang.

"Shut the fuck up," he yelled.

I felt myself shutting down, the walls closing in, throat and chest threatening to collapse.

There is no air … no air … no air … no air.

Maybe dying would have been better. There would be less pain, less fear.

But instead of giving in to the panic, I tried to convince myself that I was okay.

"Stay strong, stay quiet. Breathe through your nose; just breathe."

"One more word from you, and it'll be your last," Andre said through the small opening in the compartment.

I could hear the other dingy going off in the opposite direction as ours pulled away from the shore.

At least ten minutes went by when I felt the boat slowing down. Then, in Spanish, the voice of a man spoke in the distance: "By order of the police, you are ordered to stop the boat. I want to see your hands; raise your hands!"

I could hear more footsteps on the small boat, and my heart began to race in my chest, skipping and stopping in an erratic dance.

"Where you going, old man? Don't you know this section of the river's been closed?" one of the voices said in Spanish.

"Didn't know," Andre said. "Just getting fish for the family."

"Let's see some identification," someone demanded.

Bright light flooded into the compartment as someone lifted the net from the lid.

"Help," I screamed, using all the air left in my lungs.

Then, the sounds of gunfire, followed by the low thud of a body collapsing.

Did they kill Andre? Is he dead?

Then, laughter.

"Elias! What took you so long? You look great in your police uniform. I almost didn't recognize you!" Andre said in Spanish.

Elias said, "I've got to check in soon. We'll have to come up with some fucking story."

Next came the sound of the body being dragged off the boat, followed by a heavy splash as the corpse hit the water.

A few minutes later, Andre lifted the compartment lid open and ordered me to get out. I almost decided to stay put, thinking it might be safer than whatever came next, but he grabbed my arm and pulled me out.

I was led to a police speedboat pulled alongside the fishing boat. I climbed aboard, studying Elias's crisp police uniform as Andre bound my hands in front, twining rope around my wrists until they felt heavy and numb.

I was confused and disoriented and stunk of fish juice and guts.

Elias and Andre jumped into the shallows and pulled the fishing boat under a canopy of trees before climbing onto the speedboat and starting it up. The engine roared.

"We're heading back about five miles," Elias said in Spanish, yelling over the noise. "Heitor arranged for a helicopter to airlift this girl out of the country. He's pissed, man."

"What the hell happened, anyway?" Andre said. "Heitor sent me out to his boat to bring this bitch back to the north side camp. When we got to the boat, Eduardo and Cristiano were dead. Heitor went crazy; had me search all night for Vanilla and the bitch."

"I don't have the details," Elias said, maneuvering the speedboat down the river. "But a week ago or so, I got a call from the police commander. All of us were deployed. Before I left my house, I was able to get word to Heitor that the police were on their way, and he needed to hightail it out of there. You should've seen it, man; it felt like I was going back to war. Commander had eight teams searching twenty miles around the camp and sent another fifty troops to the Manaus pier to secure the river. I was part of the team that initially went into the camp. Hilarious. Poked my head inside my own tent," he said, laughing.

"What the hell? You're the one who gave Heitor the warning?" Andre said, looking shocked.

"Yeah, and check this out: I even took pictures of the camp and bagged up the girl's bloody clothes. Tell you what: the spotlights are on us. Haven't you seen the news? Every day, updates that include her photo have been splattered across all the channels. That curly head of hair stands out like a sore thumb. We got politicians, activists, tourist agencies; hell, we even have movie stars sticking out their necks, calling for the end to corruption. All of a sudden, this bitch is the poster child to end sex trafficking. We gotta lay low for a while."

"Who the hell *is* she?" Andre asked, looking at me like I was a circus freak.

"Not really sure. Just know she's American. Came here with her brother. Guess they really were shooting a movie."

"Where's Heitor taking her? Why the helicopter?" Andre asked.

"Montevideo," Elias said. "You should arrive there by four or so."

Montevideo? I thought. *Where's that?*

I kept my head down and eyes focused on the bindings on my hands, trying to act as though I was completely ignorant of the men's words. At least there was some relief hearing that so many people were looking for me. I hoped they would mention Finn was alive.

Elias docked the police boat, and Andre led me to a small grassy field that appeared to have been recently cleared of all vegetation.

As we waited, Andre asked me, "Where you from?"

He removed his baseball cap. His bushy eyebrows seemed to have a mind of their own, jetting this way and that. He looked like someone's grandpa.

"West Virginia."

"I mean originally. Your heritage and shit. Where did you get those blue eyes and all that *rojo* hair?"

"Uh ... Ireland."

"Ah," he said, as if it explained everything. "I have ancestors from the land of saints and scholars on my father's side. Always wanted to see it for myself. Well, maybe one day."

I could hear the whop-whop-whop of a helicopter before it came into view and landed. Andre took me inside it, put me in a seat, and then covered my eyes with a red bandana. Then he strapped me in. A few moments later, I felt the weightless ascent as the helicopter took to the air.

I thought about what Andre said, thought of Ireland, a country I had never laid eyes on and, the way things were going, probably never would.

Every Christmas, Papa used to tell the tale of the family's last three generations, going all the way back to when the McSherry's had first come to America. Papa was proud of our heritage and often reminded us to never forget how Patrick McSherry and his wife Eliza had escaped the famine and sailed from Belfast to New York in 1880.

I felt the helicopter begin to descend, and a wave of nausea rushed over me as my stomach dropped to the floor.

Andre removed the blindfold when we landed and then

pointed me to a small car with an armed driver as I blinked to adjust my eyes.

"Get in," he ordered, guiding me into the back seat.

I rolled down the window as we went down a long dirt road. We stopped in the middle of nowhere, surrounded by a spattering of trees and overgrown bushes. There was an old farmhouse, painted bright white with firehouse red trim around the doors and windows. The white smoke coming from the chimney seemed to complement the white lace curtains adorning each window. A small gray barn stood along the side with a clucking of chickens heard just beyond the two large opened doors.

It might have looked quaint and homey, if I wasn't kidnapped.

I spotted an older woman in a calico dress and a brown, full-length apron. She was tending a small vegetable garden. She stood and waved.

"Hey boys!" she said in Spanish. "Good to see you. It's been too long."

Andre got out and gave the elderly woman a hug. Then she turned to look at me.

"This must be Teagan." Her English was surprisingly good.

I was taken aback, hearing my formal name, and suspected the woman had heard it on the radio or read it in a newspaper.

She stretched out her arms and placed her hands on my arms in a welcoming manner. At least it would have seemed welcoming if my wrists weren't bound with rope.

"Well, you're a tiny little thing. I'm not going to hurt you, child. You can call me Carolina."

I was skeptical but felt a flickering sense of hope. How could anyone who looked so grandmotherly want to hurt me?

Maybe, against all odds, I thought, *I am finally safe.*

"Let's go in the house," Carolina said. "I made something special for dinner."

Inside, the farmhouse was warm and inviting, with colorful woven blankets strewn across soft, comfortable chairs and family photos lining the small living room's mantle. I could smell something like sausage cooking with jalapenos and green peppers. My mouth began to water. I hadn't eaten a full meal in days.

I was relieved when Andre and his driver stayed outside.

"Are you hungry? I thought we'd eat something first before you get cleaned up." She motioned to a large pot bubbling away on the stovetop.

"Yes, please," I said as the woman pulled out a chair for me. Then she untied the rope from my hands.

I shook to make sure the blood was flowing as Carolina fixed me a plate. It was slid in front of me, and I almost didn't bother with the fork to shovel chicken enchiladas, tortillas, and rice into my mouth.

"Slow down, slow down," the woman said, placing a glass of water in front of me. "It's not going anywhere."

I managed to swallow. "Can I ask you a question?"

Carolina glanced at me. "I may not be able to answer."

"Do you know I've been kidnapped?"

Carolina began washing a plate at the sink, seemingly unfazed. "We all have a role to play in life, Teagan, and right now, this is my role. You sitting here and eating is your role."

I frowned. *What a strange answer.*

"But please, I think I understand that you were asked to do this, but maybe you could make an exception? Maybe that's *your* role: to help me."

Carolina continued washing dishes as if I hadn't spoken.

"Please," I said.

"My role is very clear, and I can't change it. Just enjoy your meal for now."

Maybe the old lady was senile, since she wasn't making any sense.

"How long have you lived here?" I asked, hoping that maybe if we got to know each other, I might persuade Carolina to help me escape.

"I was born in Brazil, but I met my husband in Buenos Aires, and we raised our children there until about twenty years ago, when we moved here to Uruguay. My husband died shortly after we moved into this house." Carolina held a soapy hand up and pointed around the room. "You know he built this place with just his own two hands? Well, him and our boys. My kids are all grown up now and quite successful. They live in Brazil, but they visit when they can."

I raised my eyebrows. "So … I'm in Uruguay?"

Carolina nodded, turning back to the sink.

"I love your garden. My mama had a small garden out behind our house in West Virginia, and it was hard to keep the deer and other critters out of there. We all helped out tending it, my three brothers and I." I paused. "How many children do you have?"

"Just two boys. I had a little girl, but she died when she was a baby."

"I'm sorry," I said after a long moment. "That must've been very hard."

Carolina looked up and met my eyes, and for a brief moment, I thought I saw a look of empathy there.

Maybe this is it; maybe she's going to help me get out of here.

Just then, the door flew open, and Andre walked in.

"Andre! Come on in and eat," she said in Spanish as I stood up. "I'm about to take Teagan back to get cleaned up." She headed for the hallway.

Andre flashed me a look of warning. "No funny business," he snarled, reaching for my wrist.

I dodged him, hurrying down the hallway after Carolina, my heart beating quickly.

We entered a large bathroom.

"We're going to make you look real pretty, okay? Take your clothes off and get in the shower," Carolina said as she shut the door behind us. "I'm not going to hurt you, but I need to color your hair, and I don't want this messy goo to get on my nice floor or on your clothes. Right now, that curly head of hair of yours makes you stand out like … like Rudolph," she said, laughing. "You stand out like Rudolph's red nose."

I took off my clothes and stepped into the shower with the water off, covering my breasts as Carolina drenched my hair in a dark brown dye that stunk of chemicals.

"Oh, look! This new color makes those beautiful blue eyes of yours really stand out!" she said, stepping back. "That's pretty." She pointed at the golden leaf pendant.

"Thank you," was all I said. I wondered if she was going to take it from me.

"You will want to make sure you do not lose that. Now I want you to wait in here for twenty minutes, then take a shower and wash your hair. When you're done, just come back to the kitchen."

After my shower, I dried my hair and got dressed. When I looked in the mirror, I didn't recognize the brown-haired girl staring back. My face was pale, and my once prominent freckles seemed translucent, as if hiding in horror.

I closed my eyes and felt for my golden leaf necklace. Carolina was right: I didn't want to lose my only symbol of hope.

As I made my way back to the kitchen, I stopped to look at the family photos along the hallway. I sucked in my breath as I saw the last photograph, a faded picture of Heitor, Eduardo, and Carolina smiling and sitting on a porch swing. They were noticeably younger. Heitor wasn't bald in this photo, his brown hair cut short and parted on the side. His nose was straight, not bent and distorted, but it was definitely him.

I was sickened by the realization I was in the monster's home.

I heard male voices outside and tiptoed to the window.

And there he was, dressed in full camouflage gear, with a long gun slung around his shoulder, the short, stocky, grotesque pig that had tortured me for his own pleasure and evilness.

I took a step back, shaking, and my brain on fire.

Heitor seemed to sense my gaze and looked up, right at the window, smiling; that evil smile sent chills through me.

He quickly turned and was in the house, walking right up to me, blowing a gray smoky plume from his rancid cigar directly into my eyes.

I saw a faded red scar spanning the circumference of his throat. I wished whoever did that had finished the job.

"I missed you, my little bebé," he said. "Did you miss me as well?"

I screamed, feet frozen to the spot.

Move, I told myself, but my feet remained stuck to the ground.

Carolina ran over from the kitchen, grabbing Heitor by the shirt collar. "That's enough."

Heitor scowled as his mother let go. "We're friends, this one and I. We know each other quite well. Wouldn't you say so, my little bebé?" Heitor grabbed my hair and yanked my head back. "I do not like this new hair color though. When it washes out, we'll meet under another tree together. What do you think?"

Carolina forced her way between us. "How about some dinner, Heitor? I made your favorite. Enchiladas."

"Sure, I'll take a bite," Heitor said as he released my hair and walked into the kitchen.

"Go, sit," Carolina told me, indicating a couch in a corner of the room.

The conversation turned into Spanish.

"Tell me how you've been, my son," Carolina said. "I never see much of you anymore."

"I've been busy."

"How's Eduardo doing? He hasn't called in a while. I'm still hoping you two will visit on my birthday next month."

Heitor shot me a hateful look, his expression as black as death itself.

He's blaming me for Eduardo's death.

I did my best to keep my face expressionless, so he didn't think I understood what was being said.

"He's fine," Heitor said. "Minding the boat, mostly."

He inhaled half of an enchilada in one bite.

"I'll come back after I drop the girl off and spend a few nights here, okay?" Heitor said.

"Oh, good. We can really catch up then, and maybe you can help me repair the roof," Carolina said, spooning another enchilada onto Heitor's plate. "Where are you taking her?"

Heitor shook his head. "You know better than to ask questions. Why the sudden interest? You never cared before. As long as the money keeps coming your way, you're happy, right? Let's just leave it at that."

Andre came in through the front door. "Everything's in place."

"Let's move out," Heitor said as he pushed his chair away from the table.

I tried desperately to catch Carolina's eye, but there was no reaction from the woman, who was bustling around the kitchen, putting plates in the sink, obviously ignoring me.

"See you soon, Mama," Heitor said, giving Carolina a hug before making a beeline for me. "Get up." He yanked me off the couch and led me outside to a waiting car.

It was reminiscent of a hearse, black, and long with dark tinted windows. Heitor pushed me inside and pointed toward the driver.

"My man's going to take good care of you. Keep quiet, or there'll be hell to pay." He slammed the door.

The driver was a gigantic man with an overgrown bristly beard and a large, bulbous, pock-marked nose. He pulled out a handgun, turned, and pointed it at my head.

"We've got a long drive," he snarled. "One word from you, and it will be your last."

I heard a muted click and realized he had locked the car doors. *I'm trapped.*

Hours seemed to go by; the car finally stopped, somewhere. It was pitch-black outside, but I could see a row of gas lanterns flickering in front of what appeared to be a plywood structure. There were clusters of trees just beyond the building with dark waving arms. If I was quick enough, maybe, just *maybe,* I could make a break for it.

Once I heard the muted click of the doors unlocking, I quickly pulled at the door handle, jumped out of the back seat, and sprinted in the opposite direction of the lanterns, toward the dark abyss beyond.

It was only moments until the bearded man tackled me, slamming the side of my head against the ground.

The world tilted … spun …

… then went black.

CHAPTER 14

Lidia and Marcelo

Present Day

I slowly regained consciousness realizing two things: My head was throbbing in pain, and I smelled dirt. As I carefully opened my eyes, I saw nothing but dark gloom, but I could hear moaning. I sat up slowly, trying to focus, with nothing much to see. The agony in my skull nearly made me pass out again, so I propped myself into a sitting position with my back against a wall. It was a rough wall, made of uneven wood. I could just barely see the outlines of several bodies; whether they were dead or alive was impossible to tell, but at least one was groaning.

Come on, Tia, I thought. *Focus.*

The pain in my head slowly eased, but it only made me realize how much I hurt everywhere else. I allowed my fingers to gingerly touch my throbbing scalp, and I discovered a thick patch of crusted blood at the hairline.

As my eyes adjusted to the gloom, my nose took in the stench: body odor, human waste, decay, vomit, and maybe decomposition. I shuddered.

I hoped Finn was okay. Wherever he was, I prayed he was okay.

I closed my eyes and tried to control a wave of nausea. At some point, I fell asleep sitting up.

There were four low-power lights on the low metal ceiling, and the dirt floor held darkened splotches of elongated smears that could have been grease and grime, or bloodstains, appearing fresh and wet in the dim light.

I felt dizzy and disoriented as I attempted to stand, not making it; I collapsed and nearly passed out again from the crippling pain in my skull. I placed my hands on both sides of my head and squeezed my eyes shut, hoping to quiet the relentless pounding.

I slowly opened my eyes and looked around, seeing a door at the far end of the room. I had an urge to run, make my way to it, escape, then I remembered that's how I ended up here and why I was in pain. I had tried to escape, had tried to run, and didn't get very far.

There was a tall, slender man in the corner of the room wearing a wide-brimmed cap and holding a rifle.

I took a deep breath to calm the urge to run, but the stench was overpowering. I looked around to identify the source of the foul odor and saw a swarm of flies dancing upon a pile of human waste a few feet behind me. I looked around the room, hoping to find a spot that wasn't so close.

I held a hand to my mouth, stifling the vomit that threatened.

The gun-toting man looked my way as I crawled on hands and knees to the farthest corner of room. There was a small gap between a skinny girl and a skinnier boy, and I sat.

Though the room was stuffy and hot, I couldn't stop shivering. I wrapped my arms tightly around my legs, resting my cheek against my knees, and soon the pounding in my chest slowed to a normal rate.

I looked down at the sleeping girl, judging her to be twelve or thirteen. It was one thing for me to be held captive, but another to see someone even younger held against her will. It made me want to cry.

I sat quietly, wishing the guard would find something else to look at. He was still staring.

I began studying the cuts and blood streaks on my arms. In the dim light, my normally peachy-colored skin was a golden brown. Tan? Sunburn? Dirt? Hard to tell.

I was so tired. I decided being unconscious wasn't the same as sleeping. I forced myself to stay awake, running an endless series of escapist scenarios through my mind.

I stretched out my legs, feeling my inner strength slowly draining from me, ebbing away.

Throughout the sleepless night, I kept my eyes fixated on the rickety door across the room. Finally, the first signs of daylight filtered through the narrow cracks in the plywood walls.

Two women carrying a cardboard box abruptly entered the dingy room, followed by a massive, grotesque-looking man. He was as big and broad as a mule. He wore faded jeans, black army boots, and an olive-green shirt rolled up above his elbows. There were sweat stains under his arms, and his black unkempt beard covered the better part of his face and neck, exaggerating his bulbous, pock-marked nose. A long knife was sheathed and holstered on his belt.

I realized he was the driver, the one who chased me down and knocked me out. The one who put the wound on my scalp.

He looked across at me and sneered. "*¡Levántate!*" he bellowed. (Get up!)

Everyone in the room jolted at his command, some moaning as they struggled to stand.

One boy, surely no more than fifteen, had the imprint of fingers around his upper arm, bruises that were a rainbow of colors, from darkest purple and green to a sickly looking yellow.

The bearded man pointed to two people. He said in Spanish, "You ... and you! Grab the bucket and shovel and clean this shithole up."

The pair of teens he pointed at retrieved the bucket and shovel and began scooping up the waste. When the bucket was full, the man followed them out of the building and they returned a couple of minutes later. They removed what was left of the pile and left again, returning to take their positions against the wall.

I felt slightly less vulnerable now that everyone was awake, with some moving around the room as if to stretch their legs and get in a little exercise. Others stayed where they were, looking either stunned or completely blank.

There were eight girls and three boys, ranging in years from eight to twenty. Some stood with their arms dangling, eyes fixated on the two women and their boxes. Similar to the bearded man, the two women wore jeans, army-style boots, and olive-green shirts. The older woman with short gray hair was tall and thin, perhaps too thin for her height. Looked like she was wound tighter than a three-day clock.

The other woman was short and rotund, with dark brown hair pushed back with a tight black headband, allowing her plump, red cheeks to pop out from her face like two apples. She pulled food out of the box, glanced up at the older woman, nodded, and hastily left the room.

I stared at the food, and my mouth would have watered if it weren't so dry, but my stomach did growl.

The broken children got up and turned. They marched toward the table like robots.

I managed to stand, forcing my legs to bend and move. When I reached the table, I picked up a roll, a piece of cheese, and two water bottles.

From the corner of my eye, a blurred motion came at me, but I couldn't react in time to avoid the full force of a balled-up fist connecting across my jaw.

"¡*Una botella de agua!*" the older woman yelled in Spanish as she stood over me. (One water bottle!)

I stifled a cry as a boy helped me to my feet. Then he picked up the food I'd dropped, handing me a water bottle. Dusting off the bread and cheese, I trudged to my place against the wall. I slid to the floor, twisted the cap off the bottle, and took a swig.

I jumped when I felt a hand on my arm. It was the boy, giving me a small, concerned smile.

The armed guard pulled back a piece of plywood to expose a large window, allowing some fresh air into the room, but not much. The putrid aroma was still overbearing, although I seemed to be getting used to it.

I took another sip of warm water and had some of the stale bread and cheese, but chewing sent a searing pain through my jaw. I ended up tearing the food into small pieces, placing them on my tongue, and swallowing each with a gulp of water.

Then I slouched against the wall, watching the others as they ate their modest meal. There was a myriad of splattered dirt, scrapes, bruises, dried blood, and some injuries more prominent than others. Their hair was matted and balled into tangled webs, like they hadn't seen a bath in weeks, their skin looking pallid and ashen.

The girls in the room were wearing shorts or a dress, and I was thankful to have on a button-down shirt and long tan pants covering my legs, even if they were a few sizes too big and covered in streaks of grime.

The armed man left the room; at least he kept the door open. I could see three other men sitting outside, each with guns.

To my right was the girl who'd been sleeping so restlessly. She was pretty, with long, wavy brown hair, and big brown eyes. I guessed she was around thirteen. Her cheeks were pale, smudged with dirt, and she had a long, ragged cut along her arm with pockets of bile-green pus along the edges.

I drew a big circle in the dirt, with two eyes and a wide, happy smile. This was a goofy game I used to play with Wes when he was feeling down.

The girl looked from the smiley face to me and back again. Then she reached down and added eyelashes, hair, and earrings.

We looked at each other and smiled.

I glanced at the boy on my left who helped me earlier. He was about my age, sixteen or so. I didn't know if it was a coincidence or not, but he looked very much like the girl. They must have been brother and sister.

"*Hola. Soy Tía*," I said to the girl.

The girl smiled but didn't say anything.

"Do you speak English? *¿Habla usted Inglés?*" I asked. That was the extent of Spanish I was comfortable speaking.

"I am Lidia," the girl said in broken English. She pointed. "My brother, Marcelo."

"Hi." I turned to the brother. "Thanks for helping me. I kinda thought you two might be related."

Marcelo smiled and sat up straighter.

His English was pretty good.

"We saw you come in last night. You looked like you were, eh, not awake. They threw you on the ground over there; it looked like they hit you very hard."

"Yeah, that guy tackled me and must have knocked me over the head." I nodded toward the bearded man sitting outside the open door. "Am I still bleeding?" I asked, pointing at the wound on my head.

Marcelo shifted his weight and looked, his hands gentle as he checked. "No, it stopped, but there is a … a gash. How is your face? The old woman really nailed you." He mimicked the right hook she had given me.

I wiggled my jaw, wincing. "It's okay, I guess. I should have pulled a Reagan."

"A … a ray gun?" he asked, looking confused. "What's that mean?"

I chuckled. "Oh, no, sorry. You know, President Reagan? After he was shot, he told his wife, 'Honey, I forgot to duck.' I always thought that was funny. We studied him in high school last year …"

My voice drifted off as I realized how ridiculous I must have sounded. I wasn't even sure they understood me.

"Um, okay," Marcelo said. "Maybe you got hit harder than you thought. You're talking a little loco."

I smiled and nodded. "Is there a bathroom where I can rinse the blood off?"

"Tia, is that your name?" Marcelo said. "Look around; we are pissing in the dirt here. If you think we have running water and toilets, you must have brain damage."

I nodded again, this time I felt my cheeks reddening in embarrassment. "Guess I really didn't think that through. Where are we? When I came in last night, all I could see was an open field and some trees."

"We are not sure," Lidia said. "I only go outside a few times, and all I saw was trees and the field."

I pointed at Lidia's arm. "Are you okay? That cut is really deep; looks like it needs a good stitching."

"It is, uh, getting better," Lidia said, poking at the inflamed skin around the cut. But the pain and fear in her eyes when she looked up said something else.

"What happened?" I asked as I leaned in to get a better look.

She paused as if deciding to tell me. "When they took me to the building, I got scared and twisted away from them. I lost my … my, eh, my balance and fell against the corner of a metal table. It cut my arm open."

"Did they hurt you?" I asked, hoping she knew what I meant but afraid to hear the answer.

"No, but I don't want to talk," Lidia said, staring down at the ground, her lower lip trembling.

"Okay." I felt guilty for having brought it up. "Sorry. I didn't mean to … to remind you."

"No worry about it," Marcelo said. "Where are you from? You've got a funny, eh, what to call it? Voice."

"Twang?" I said.

His eyes lit up. "Yes. A *twang*."

"I grew up in a little town in West Virginia, Fayetteville. We all have the same twang."

"I like it."

"So what is this place?" I asked, looking around, wondering how the weight of the aluminum roof didn't collapse on top of us.

"I think it is a holding cell until they move us somewhere else," Marcelo said.

"Somewhere else? Where do you think they'll take us? What have you heard?"

"We really don't know what's going on. But a few days ago, they split everyone into groups. I heard one of the men say how the ..."

His voice drifted off and his face flushed bright red; he struggled with his words. " ... how the filthy ... whores would be sold to the cartel, the virgins would go to Belgium, and other kids would be sent to labor camps. There are still some of us here, and he said we were being saved for another day." He paused, looking almost sick. "I will kill myself before I am ever sold."

"We will get out of here," Lidia said. "You can't ever say that."

"How long have you been here?" I asked.

"Ten days, I think. I'm not sure. Every day is the same. We get food twice a day, shovel out the shit, and wait for new kids to show up."

"Where are y'all from?"

"Peru," Marcelo said. "I grew up in a small fishing village. My father is a fisherman."

"Oh ... wow, Peru. It sounds so far away and mystical. I always picture llamas when I hear Peru. Is it beautiful there?" I asked.

"Yes, very beautiful," Lidia said.

"How'd you get here?" I asked, before taking a drink from the water bottle.

Marcelo looked toward his sister. "Lidia and I were waiting

for Father on the pier, and a group of kids were across the way. I knew a few from school, and they waved us over. There was a guy who said his name was Wilian; I've never seen him before. He told us they were doing a … uh … pictures, and needed extras. He said it would only take about thirty minutes and that he would give us money. It sounded okay."

Lidia frowned. "He was wearing a really nice suit and had a diamond ring on his little finger."

"We had about an hour before Father returned, so we thought why not?" Marcelo said. "We could use the extra cash. Wilian told us the location was about a half-kilometer away and we could walk there or get in the van. Everyone got in the van, ten of us. After a few minutes, the van didn't stop, and there were no windows back there. I remember we looked at each other, just staring, scared shitless. We screamed and banged on the sides of the van."

Lidia said, "We seemed to drive forever, and finally, the van stopped. Some of us had to … you know. When they opened the door, there were men pointing guns at us. They told us to get out and, eh, go potty on the side of the road. Except for the headlights, it was so dark. Then they put us back in the van, gave us some food and water, and locked the door again. After riding for … I don't know, a couple days, six of the kids were told to get out. They took me, my brother, and a two other girls to a car and drove for another day or two, until they dropped us off here."

"I feel bad for Mother and Father," Marcelo said as he stared blankly at his sister. "They always warned us. I guess I thought if someone were trying to kidnap me, they'd point a gun in my face or something." He shook his head in disgust.

I put my hand on Lidia's. "I'm so sorry this happened to you."

"Except for being hungry and dirty, we're better off than most people in here," Marcelo said.

Lidia pointed to a girl a few feet away. "That is Claudia. She said she was taken seven years ago and worked in a brothel. She's been really sick, can't … she keeps throwing up."

It was hard to guess Claudia's age, as long, greasy strands of black hair covered her face, and her limbs were stick-thin. Maybe in her early twenties?

"What about that little girl next to her?" I asked. "She can't be more than eight."

"Valeria. She's very quiet, won't say a word except for her name," Marcelo said.

Valeria reminded me of Sophie and Maddie, the two little girls I'd met during that rafting trip in West Virginia.

What if Sophie and Maddie were here?

"Has anyone tried to escape?" I asked.

Marcelo said, "About a week ago, a boy climbed through the window, but we never saw him again. The guard told us they tracked him down, tortured him, and killed him; he warned us not to try and escape. Later that day, they boarded up the window. It's only opened during the day now."

There was a long silence.

Lidia whispered, "We got to know some of the others when we first arrived, but after they were taken, we keep quiet now."

CHAPTER 15

Claudia

I glanced over to the girl with the long greasy hair. Something about the way she sat, her eyes downcast, her hair hanging in clumps around her thin face, pulled at my heart.

"I'm going to talk to Claudia for a few minutes," I said to Marcelo and Lidia. "I'll be back."

I made my way over and knelt down, speaking gently, so as not to startle the girl. Maybe there was nothing I could do for her, but I had to try.

"Hi," I said. "My name is Tia. Can I sit with you?"

There was a long pause. I wasn't sure if the girl spoke English.

I looked over at Valeria and smiled. She smiled and scooted back, making room for me to sit down.

Claudia looked up. She was sickly pale and thin. Her eyes were like a shark's: vacant and nearly black, with little to no iris.

She wore a thin, short-sleeved faded dress that fell to her knees. Her legs and arms were emaciated, void of muscle or definition, like one of the Holocaust victims I'd seen in a schoolbook. She was a walking skeleton.

I offered Claudia the remaining water in my bottle and said, "Hi, I'm Tia."

Claudia looked at me woefully but then took the bottle and unscrewed the cap.

"I'm Claudia," she said in a raspy voice before drinking what was left of the water and dropping the empty bottle in the dirt.

There were two dark gaping holes where Claudia's front teeth should've been.

"Lidia over there tells me you can't keep food down, and I have to say you're looking peaked. I'm worried about you."

"Hmm," Claudia let out a long, slow breath and stared vacantly at her hands.

I wasn't sure what to say. On one hand, I wanted to know what had happened, but at the same time, I knew I might be dredging up something Claudia was trying to forget. And I could be listening to my own fate, as well.

"Well, I'm here if you need help, or maybe if you just want to talk. I want you to know that."

"Nothing you can do," she said, glancing at me again and adding, "and by the looks of you, you're in shitty shape."

"I've been better," I said, looking away.

"I saw you come in last night. Where were you before here?"

"I was in the Amazon when they took me."

Claudia sat a bit straighter and leaned forward, pulling herself away from the wall. "The Amazon? Who took you?"

"A drug gang, I think." I didn't want to say too much. I wasn't ready to share. "How about you? Where are you from?"

"Mostly Havana."

Another long pause. Nothing more about that was coming. So I tried a different angle.

"Claudia, I know you don't know me, but I want to hear everything. I need to hear everything; I'm thinking it could prepare me for what might happen."

Claudia rolled her eyes. "Oh please," she said in nearly perfect English. "Get a fucking clue. You have no control here, you know. Nothing is in your hands now. You eat when they say, you sleep when they say, and you piss when they say. You just do what they say and live with it."

"Sorry. I just … I'm just really scared is all."

Claudia stretched out her legs and leaned back against the wall. She had a look of hopelessness written across her face. "Good. You *should* be scared. Really scared."

I waited. Several minutes later, she let out a deep, long sigh and began to whisper. I could barely make it out. Her words were slurred from her missing front teeth.

"I was taken from my family a long time ago, my whole life, it feels like. I can hardly remember what my mother looks like anymore."

"Where are you from?"

Claudia licked her pale, cracked lips. "I was born on a farm in Colombia. I was the baby of the family, with six brothers and sisters. We worked the farms since we were old enough to walk, and I guess you could say we were poor; seems like I was always hungry. But I loved my family. I miss them so much. I'm stupid for leaving."

I reached down and took her hand.

"I remember complaining about working out in the fields," she said, "not having a nice pair of shoes, and only getting one slice of bread. When I look back now, I would trade anything for that."

"When did they take you?"

"I'm twenty now, so I think I was thirteen at the time. I was in town with my two older sisters when we met a woman just outside of the marketplace. I don't remember anymore how we met her, just that she started talking to us. It was all so casual. I don't even remember what she looked like … dark brown hair; a pretty smile, and I remember she wore a bright-colored flowered dress. She said that her toy company needed people with small hands to work the assembly line at the factory in the city and that she was visiting our town to find help. She said they'd offer us good pay, clothes, a bed, and meals if we went with her.

"The lady grabbed my hand and said, 'These are perfect little fingers to assemble our toys.'

"I guess my sisters somehow knew better and started to walk away; my sister Katarina pulled my arm, telling me to go with her."

Claudia frowned.

"Why didn't I leave with my sister? I mean, I can see her so clearly, pulling at me, and me pushing her away. I should've gone with her, and my sister should have protected me. I was only thirteen; she should have protected me."

Claudia's voice broke, and she paused, looking toward the ceiling.

"At the time, I remember being excited to leave that small farm town. I just wanted to see something new. Plus, I'd be putting together toys and thought maybe I could even play with some. The lady was really nice to me. She bought me lunch, a new pair of shoes, and even a new dress. I rode with her in her car, and she kept smiling like she really liked me, like just being around me made her happy. I remember being happy too. Later that night, she gave me a brownie. And then my head began to spin. I got all dizzy and woke up the next day in Havana with a pounding headache. I never saw her again."

"I should know this, but where *is* Havana?" I asked. I'd heard of it but couldn't place it.

"Cuba." She pronounced it "Koo-bah."

"Seems so far away."

Claudia took another deep breath, pursed her lips, and slowly let the air out. "I was beaten, tortured, and raped almost every day."

"Oh, Claudia, I'm so sorry."

"The men came from everywhere, every continent, it seemed. There was a new group every night. Tourists from Europe, teenage boys, older businessmen."

"Where'd they keep you?"

"Some shitty brothel. The men would either come there, or my pimps would take me to their hotel rooms. The pimps escorted me everywhere. I was never alone, never at peace. I was always on edge, waiting for the next job. Sometimes, they'd bring us out to different hotels along the Santa Maria and Playa Jibacoa beaches. From a distance, I could see families and couples walking hand in hand, laughing, jumping through the waves, and picking up seashells. All I wanted to do was stretch out on a beach towel, feel the sand between my toes, and let the tide rush over my body.

"Weren't there any tourists around who could tell something was wrong?"

"Like I said, the pimps never let us go anywhere by ourselves." She shrugged. "Pimps loved the beach; it's where they made most of their money. I overheard one of them say how I brought in a quarter of a million dollars in the last year alone. I don't know if he was lying to impress his friend, but it could be that's how much money can be made when you're having sex with up to thirty men a day."

"Thirty men?" The nausea in my gut rolled, and I clasped a hand over my mouth in disbelief. "Oh, God. I just don't have any words. How did you survive?"

"I kept to myself, mostly, tried not to stand out."

"And what about ending up here?"

Claudia paused.

"I had one friend, we were more like sisters. We worked in the same place for the last four years. Toward the end, we even came up with a plan to escape, but I was told she was found in the gutter one morning. Maybe it was true. I lost my mind that day, went totally crazy, screaming, breaking things, and tried to run away. They beat me, knocked out a couple of my teeth, brought me here. Not sure why they kept me alive. Not sure how I *am* still alive."

"I'll pray for you," I said, clutching Claudia's bony hand.

Claudia shook her head and rolled her eyes. "Sometimes, I wonder if there really is a God. If there was, do you think this would be happening to any of us?"

She didn't finish. Tears spilled out of her eyes, and I reached over and held her. I had a feeling this was the first time she confided in anyone in such a long time.

"Claudia, I don't know why this is happening, but I just know there *is* a God, and He loves us very much."

I paused.

"When sad or horrible things happen, I think about something a holy man named St. Anselm said: 'For I do not seek to understand in order that I may believe, but I believe in order to understand.' For me, anyway, it's through faith that I can keep believing in a God who loves me, even if I don't understand the reason for any suffering I'm experiencing."

"I'd like to believe that, and deep down, I know I do," Claudia said, "but it's just hard sometimes, with everything I've been through, everything I've seen."

With nothing more to say, I just held her tight, feeling warm tears fall on my neck, my arms snugly around her shoulders.

After a few moments, Claudia looked up, smiled faintly, and nodded.

I looked to Valeria and gently placed my hand on hers. She was a frail girl with thin strands of light brown hair. She wore a flimsy light blue dress with stained white socks and a pair of sandals held together with a few strips of silver tape.

I looked at Claudia. "Do you know anything about her?"

"Her name's Valeria," she said. "That's all I know. When she first got here a few days ago, she cried all day. I'm glad she stopped. It was getting on my nerves. Now she just sits by me. God knows why. I mean, it's not like I can do anything for her."

I lowered my head toward Valeria. "Hi, little one."

The girl looked up and smiled.

"Do you want to sit with me over there?" I asked, pointing toward Marcelo. "Claudia, you can sit with us too."

Claudia nodded and spoke quietly to Valeria. Then we went to the corner where Lidia and Marcelo were waiting. Valeria sat next to me, resting her head on my arm.

"You probably already know Lidia and Marcelo," I said.

"What about your home, Tia? What is it like?" Marcelo asked, jumping back into our previous conversation as if I'd never left.

"Well, I think I told you before that I'm from Fayetteville, West Virginia. We lived in a small house." I paused and looked around. "Not much bigger than this room here. Fayetteville is such a cool old town, and back in the day, all of my kin worked in the coal mines. They're all closed down now, but people come from all over to vacation, to get out of the big city to camp, hike, and fish. It's really beautiful there. Finn and I work as whitewater rafting guides on weekends and during the summer."

"Who is Finn?" Lidia asked.

"Sorry. My twin brother."

"You have a twin?" Lidia said. "Do you look alike?"

I smiled. "Well, he's much taller than me, but we both have the same curly reddish-blond hair and the same blue eyes."

The three of them looked confused.

"Oh yeah," I said, tugging on a clump of my hair. "A woman dyed it this ugly brown color to disguise me. Anyway, on a weekend rafting trip, Finn and I met a movie producer who asked us to be in his upcoming film in South America. Everything was going great until a week or two ago. I've lost track of time. But we were attacked. That's when they took me."

I paused and lowered my head. "Like you, Claudia, I never should have left home."

"Where are your mother and father?" Lidia asked.

The question caught me by surprise; I could feel my eyes well up, picturing Mama's tiny frame with her baby blue eyes, set against her long black hair, and Papa's gentle face with his sandy blond hair and bright smile.

If only if Papa were alive, he would have found me somehow; with shotgun in hand, he would have found me. He wasn't very tall, but he was burly and fit. He smiled all the time, except in those rare moments when something really got his goat. In those moments, his face would turn bright red, and he'd hold a crooked index finger against his pursed lips. That was the sign for the kids to scatter quicker than a cat could lick its own ass. I glanced up at the door, knowing for certain that if Papa were alive, he would crash through that rickety door, his face red as a turnip, shotgun in hand …

"They died a year ago," I said.

"I'm sorry," Lidia said.

"How old are you?" Marcelo asked.

"I'm sixteen," I began. "Wait, wait. What's the date today?"

"End of May, first of June, somewhere around there, I'd guess." Marcelo said.

"Then I've had a birthday. Good Lord! I'm seventeen now."

"Me too," Marcelo said, smiling.

I could hear the sound of heavy footsteps and turned around quickly. I looked up to see the grotesque bearded man with the bulbous pock-marked nose standing in front of me.

He grabbed my arm, jerked me up on my feet, and led me outside, across a dusty path toward another small building.

There were two shacks nestled in the tree line, both haphazardly constructed with dilapidated plywood and roofs of aluminum. I looked into the forest, imagining taking off at a sprint and hiding among the highest branches of the tallest tree. I felt as small and helpless as a toddler as the bearded man's hulk-like hand wrapped easily around the thickest part of my arm, yanking me through the doorway of the adjacent building.

A woman approached, and the bearded man pushed me toward her. The woman grabbed my wrist.

"Watch her," the bearded man said in Spanish. "She tried to run last night." Then he left.

The room had a kitchenette, a foldout table with chairs, some cabinets, and one long table along the edge of the room laden with ropes, a chain, and padlocks.

The woman was about the same size as me and not much older than Mama had been when she passed away. The woman's brown hair was pinned up with a large barrette, and she had a drained, lifeless complexion.

"Take off your clothes," the woman said in a thick English accent, leading me to the table. The restraints looked menacing.

"What?"

"You hear me," the woman snapped, shouting. "Take off your clothes!"

"Please, no." I crossed my arms over my chest, but the woman reached out and yanked them away.

"I not say to you again. Take off clothes."

Slowly, I began to undress, trying my best to hide my private areas.

"Please, don't hurt me," I begged, hating for having to say the words out loud.

"You okay. I not hurt you. Okay, you get on the table."

I pushed the chains away and lay down on it, and the woman roughly spread my legs.

"Looks like you have trouble," the woman said, her tone void of emotion as she poked and prodded my genitals.

The woman cleaned me and gently applied some cream. Whatever it was, it was ice cold, and then calm and soothing.

"You can dress now. I clean that on your head before it gets trouble."

I thought—or hoped—the woman might have some compassion. "Why are you doing this to us? Why are you with these people?" I asked as I finished dressing. "You seem so nice."

The woman whipped around to face me.

"Quiet," she snapped. "You not know. I need food. I do what

they say, they give me. No more hitting. No more fucking. I can sleep."

The woman roughly dabbed at my head wound with a cotton ball and a cold liquid followed by a gooey cream. When she finished, she led me back outside to the bearded man.

"She's broken, but she's a beauty," the woman said in Spanish. "Once she heals, she should be placed with the virgins. Her beauty alone will bring a good price."

The bearded man just scowled before leading me back into the darkened cell with the others.

CHAPTER 16

The Opportunity

I t was still dark when I woke. My head still throbbed, but it was manageable. I could hear loud voices and laughter coming from outside, so I lifted Valeria into my arms. The other sleeping bodies nestled against the wall began to stir, as the voices grew louder and more disconcerting. Then, out-of-tune singing erupted, one man's shouts much louder than the others, followed by a series of bangs from what sounded like metal objects pounding against each other. When the belligerent singing stopped, an eerie silence fell over the cell.

"Marcelo, what's happening?" I asked.

"Just stay quiet," he said as he took Lidia in his arms, cradling her head.

I've got a real bad feeling, I thought.

The four walls felt like they were closing in.

"Lie back down! Lie back down," Marcelo said loud enough for everyone to hear. The bodies that had been upright melted to the ground, the children curling tightly into balls.

Two husky men barreled through the door. I recognized the bearded man, but the clean-shaven man was unfamiliar. It soon became apparent they were the raucous singers as they swayed drunkenly, muttering things I couldn't understand.

I pulled Valeria tight against me and shut my eyes, pretending to be asleep as the men drew closer. I could sense their boots were inches from my face.

I clenched my muscles and prepared to be yanked up and dragged off, but instead, the men turned and walked on by.

I dared to peek and saw them staring down, as if inspecting the line of children.

I watched as one of the men reached down. A moment later, a young girl around my age let loose piercing screams.

Scared, Valeria trembled against me, whimpering.

"Shh," I said, placing my hand against Valeria's mouth. I didn't want to do that, but we didn't need the attention.

The girl the men had selected was dragged to the door, her shrieks desperate, animalistic.

My heart raced as I tried to think of something, anything.

The girl pleaded, and I was suddenly pushing Valeria into Marcelo's hands. I scrambled to my knees, all of my instincts telling me to stay and remain timid, the way they wanted me.

But I felt a powerful surge of adrenalin; my vision became tunneled, focusing only on the wild screams of the girl being dragged away.

In a flash, Marcelo grabbed my wrist. "Don't move," he hissed.

I yanked my arm away and ran, feeling a surreal energy as I raced outside and threw myself on the back of a man. "Leave her alone," I cried.

It turned out I had landed on the ugly bearded man, so the clean-shaven man grabbed me by the hair and wrenched me off onto the ground with intense force that made me dizzy. I clamored to my feet, blindly kicking until I made contact with one of them. I'm not sure what I kicked, but the clean-shaven man howled.

Before I could make another attack, he back-handed me across the right cheek. Somehow, I stayed on my feet and turned to see if I could free the girl.

"Lay off this one," the bearded man yelled in Spanish at the other man, pointing a finger at me. "No marks. She's worth a lot."

The clean-shaven man grunted and then reached down, grabbed my wrist, and pulled me through the dirt to the entrance of the holding cell, where I was jerked over the threshold and released. The door was slammed behind me.

I lay there for a minute, cringing from the screams of the teenaged girl on the other side of the door.

"What the hell were you thinking?"

I rolled my head to the right and saw Marcelo staring at me. I didn't have an answer for him. I slowly got up with his help and made my way over to the corner. Lidia and Valeria watched me, wide-eyed.

"I had to do something," I said. "We just can't sit here."

Marcelo's eyebrows furrowed together, almost as one, making it look like a dark caterpillar had crawled across his forehead. "You wanna get your head blown off? Get us all killed?"

I opened my mouth to say something, but nothing came.

"I'm begging you," Marcelo said. "Just sit down and be quiet."

When the door opened again sometime later, the girl was dumped just inside, sobbing; the door slammed shut again.

I cautiously got up and grabbed Marcelo's arm. "We need to get her back over here. And you need to help me."

He said nothing, showed no expression, but stood and walked to the door with me. Then he lifted the girl to her feet; I pulled her dress down, which had been tangled around her neck, exposing her bruised torso and her ripped underpants.

We slowly led her back to our corner, where she collapsed, sobbing, hiding her face in her hands.

I did my best to comfort and soothe her. Eventually, she calmed down and fell asleep.

I left her and went back to my spot, leaning against the wall, feeling hazy and confused, not truly believing or comprehending what I just witnessed.

"*¡En tus pies!*" (On your feet!)

The night had gone by too quickly, and every muscle in my body was tight and sore. But I got up, stretching my hands above my head, feeling my muscles relax. The others around me also began to rise.

"Claudia, Claudia, we've gotta get up," I said, bending to brush her long hair away from her gaunt face. I had to look twice. Her blackened eyes were open and vacant.

I gasped, crouching closer and wrapping a hand around Claudia's balled fist, which was plastered against her chest. It was cold and stiff to the touch.

"Oh, God! Help! Someone *help!*" I screamed.

The armed man shouted something out the door, and seconds later, two women hurried in. Without pausing, they picked up Claudia's body by her shoulders and legs, carrying her outside as if she were one of their brown cardboard boxes and not a human being.

I had only met Claudia the day before, but I felt like I'd lost a sister. I knelt down and held Valeria, who had started to cry. "I'm so sorry," I said as I wiped away her tears.

In a small, self-consoling way, there was a sense of relief that Claudia wouldn't suffer anymore, and I hoped that she knew she was surrounded by friends who cared for her.

As if nothing had happened, the two women returned with their boxes, and like clockwork, the young captives in the room somberly made their way toward the measly morsels of food.

After we ate, the bearded man came in and said it was time to go.

I looked at Marcelo as if to say, "What's going on?"

He only shrugged, looking as puzzled as I felt.

We slowly shuffled outside; a large black van was driving into the compound.

I closed my eyes and inhaled the fresh, cool air; a weird sense of relief flooded over me. I glanced at the lush forest, realizing that in other circumstances, I would have found the surroundings serene and peaceful.

The bearded man opened the van's windowless back door and instructed us to get in and sit on the floor. Once we did, the door slammed and was locked. The vehicle sped off; we tried to brace ourselves against the relentless bumps and bangs as we hurtled down an unpaved road.

There was nowhere to look, so I stared down at my hands, which ached and stung. It was strange, really. I couldn't recall a time when my hands had throbbed in pain before. I was no stranger to hard work, but they never hurt like this in the past. I placed them between my thighs in a vain attempt to soothe the discomfort. I looked up and saw everyone's terrified expressions. Their skin was streaked in mud and cuts, and I suspected I looked equally terrible. I searched their faces, realizing the girl who'd been dragged away and raped wasn't with us.

They must've left her back at the cell.

After a few hours of driving, I could hear other sounds: motorcycles buzzing and the honking of a hundred cars.

"Where do you think they're taking us?" I asked Marcelo.

"Sounds like we are in a city," he said, stating the obvious. Maybe he thought I couldn't hear the ruckus.

"That's good, right?" I asked. "There will be a lot of people. Do you think we can make a run for it? Maybe we can just get one person to notice? I mean, look at us. We're dirty and bloody and beat up; someone's bound to notice if we can get their attention."

Marcelo glanced at his sister, his face full of trepidation, and the emotion clouding his expression.

"It would be dangerous to run. What if I get separated from Lidia?" He looked at me with pleading eyes. "She can't survive without me. And I won't let her get raped."

I understood, and nodded. "Yeah, maybe no one will care about us or how we look." I thought of Javier on the park bench in Los Angeles and how disassociated and uncaring everyone had been about his plight.

Then Marcelo's expression changed. "Okay, I think you're right. We should run," he said. "We need to be brave, or we die."

I nodded. "What about the others?"

Marcelo frowned for a few moments before he scooted to the middle of the van and squatted down.

"Listen, everyone," he said in Spanish. "This may be our only chance to escape. When the van door opens and everyone gets out, we're going to run like hell toward people on the street. Scream as loud as you can. Go in every direction. If you get away, go to the police and tell them. Tell them to come back and get the rest of us out of here. Are you with us?"

As he looked around the van, everyone just stared at him for several moments. Then they began to nod. They weren't very convincing.

"I'm scared," one girl said.

"I am too," Marcelo said. "But it will be better than going back or ending up wherever they're taking us. It could be worse."

A few minutes later, the van slowed down before rolling to a stop.

"Listen to me: we all need to work together to get out of here," Marcelo said. "This is it; get ready to run."

I looked down at Valeria. "Hold my hand and don't let go, understand?"

Valeria squeezed my hand and nodded solemnly.

The rear doors opened, and as we were led out and onto the road, doubt filled my mind. A scowling man held a military rifle in our direction. I could see we were at the dead end of a long alley, about half the length of a football field. At the opposite end, I could see people walking casually along a sidewalk. Cars lined the street as if in a traffic jam, waiting patiently to move forward. I could see two old, faded white buildings on the other side of the street.

I took a deep breath. *I can do this,* I thought. *I can do this.* My eyes darted between Valeria and the gunman, and I lightly tugged on Valeria's hand, getting her ready to sprint.

Marcelo gave the nod.

Just as I'd practiced in my head, I bolted, running as fast as I could, with Valeria behind me, struggling to keep up.

"Help! Help us," I screamed, frantically waving my arm in the direction of the people in front of us.

Marcelo and Lidia were actually ahead of me, out in front, and I saw they were the only ones to have actually run.

I was almost halfway down the narrow alley, envisioning our rescue.

Almost there. Almost there …

Suddenly, the ground appeared out of nowhere as my face smashed into it. I realized we were tackled from behind, and almost immediately, my arms were pinned to my sides. Something was jabbed into my ribs, and I knew it had to be the barrel of a gun.

I was jerked up onto my feet and dragged back down the alley. Valeria was crying, and as I looked around, all hope of being rescued was shattered; Marcelo and Lidia were in the grip of the bearded man, blood streaming from Lidia's nose.

We were forced down a concrete stairway into the basement of a skyscraper. The long corridor was musty and damp, and I heard a scuffle behind us. I turned and saw the bearded man sucker-punch Marcelo, who instantly collapsed on the ground.

"Stop! Please stop!" Lidia screamed, throwing herself on top of Marcelo.

"Get up," the bearded man yelled as he heaved Lidia away from her brother. Then the man said in Spanish, "Too bad. You could all be enjoying a hot shower and a nice meal right now. But instead, you chose to run. Now you're fucked."

The bearded man grabbed Lidia and Valeria and handed them off to one of his men.

"Take them upstairs with the others. I'm throwing these two in the hole."

"Don't take her," Marcelo shouted as Lidia was pushed into a service elevator next to Valeria.

Lidia frantically reached out. "Marcelo! *Marcelo!*"

The doors closed.

The bearded man led Marcelo and me down another corridor and into a dilapidated kitchen. There were large blackened ovens, one with the door hanging off. A gigantic sink had rusted faucets, and busted cupboards were littered with debris and animal droppings.

The bearded man stopped at the back of the kitchen and pulled back the handle of a large cooler door.

I braced myself for a rush of freezing air but was surprised to find that although the refrigerator stunk of mold and mildew, it was warm. The ceiling had an air vent with a small round light, one that flickered and doused everything in a faint yellow hue.

The bearded man towered over us; he pulled out a horsewhip and spun us to face the wall.

I hunched over, covering my head with my hands as the lash came down three times. With each, I screamed in pain and was relieved when he stopped after only three.

Marcelo was next, and he kept silent through the whipping, three blows that would have sent a weaker man to his knees.

When the bearded man was done, both of our shirts were torn, and our backs were welted and bleeding.

"Next time you run, you die. You belong to us now." Then he left, slamming the door.

"Tia, Tia," Marcelo said, making his way over. "Are you okay?"

It was hard to find my voice.

"Tia," he repeated. Then he helped me to sit on the floor.

CHAPTER 17

Oedipus Rex

At least an hour had passed before I lifted my head, feeling mostly pain from head to toe.

"What's going to happen to us?" I murmured.

Marcelo had a cut on his forehead; one end of it had bled down the side of his left temple. "I don't know," he replied. "I don't know. I just need to find Lidia."

I slowly shifted into a different position, wincing. "I've had a few whippings before, but none quite like that. I'm gonna try and stand. I'm crampin' up here."

Marcelo seemed to be heavy in thought.

I tried to lighten the mood. "You said you're seventeen? I'll be a senior this year; you too?"

Marcelo looked up at me and said slowly, "I hurt too much to talk."

"I know. Just trying to get our minds off it all. Tell me something about yourself, anything at all. Like what do you want to do after you graduate?"

Marcelo closed his eyes and rubbed his temples. "You talk too much."

I was so restless and scared. I didn't want to just sit there and mope. I walked to the cooler door and tried the push it open.

"Feels like he locked it from the outside. Won't budge."

There were four water bottles on a rusted shelf. I took two and sat next to Marcelo.

"So what about it? What do you want to do after you graduate?" I handed him a bottle.

Marcelo let out a long sigh. "What makes you think I'm going to graduate? What makes you think I'm going to get away from here?"

"Because if we don't have something, if we don't have hope, then we have nothing."

"We have nothing now."

"That's not true," I said. "We have water." I smiled, holding up my bottle.

He looked at me in what was an expression of annoyance, which turned to a slight grin. "Yes, we have water."

"So what do you want to be when you grow up?"

He sighed again and looked away. "I wanted to go to the university. My father has been saving his whole life. He wanted me to be the first in the family to get a degree. I was supposed to be an engineer. I always wanted to build bridges, dams, skyscrapers."

"It can still happen. You can be an engineer someday and build beautiful things."

Marcelo tilted his head back against the wall of the cooler and closed his eyes. "I used to build model bridges and small cities from toothpicks, Popsicle sticks, cardboard. I had a friend who worked at the market selling ice cream, and he would save the sticks for me. Sometimes when my father got home from fishing, he would help me. Other times, we would go downtown and watch the construction. It was amazing to watch a building being built, floor by floor."

"I'd kill for a scoop of ice cream right now."

Marcelo looked at me like I had lost my mind.

"At home, we always went to the soda shop every Friday after school," I said. "They had the best cream soda in those old glass bottles. You know which ones I mean?"

Marcelo raised his eyebrows and shook his head.

"Well, anyway, I'd always have a bottle of cream soda with my ice cream. My favorite was their banana split covered in hot fudge, nuts, whipped cream, and a cherry on top, but I always asked for two. God, that sounds so good right now."

Marcel stood up slowly and stretched his legs. "I have never had a banana split, but it sounds good. My favorite is *queso helado* flavored with coconut, or *dulce de leche* stuffed in a doughnut or scooped on ice cream. Especially on hot days."

"I've got to try that some time," I said. "It sounds delicious. I also just love saying 'dulce de leche'; it has kind of a magical ring to it."

"I promise I will make it for you if we ever get out of this place," Marcelo said as he sat down next to me.

"Deal."

"What do you want to do after high school?" he asked.

I leaned my head against the wall and stared up at the light bulb.

"Papa wanted all the kids to finish high school and go on to college, if we could. He and Mama never graduated. We had to get good grades or Papa wouldn't let us ride down the river. We lived in a log cabin on the side of a mountain; it was nestled near a big river. All Finn and I wanted to do is start our own whitewater rafting company. One of the reasons Finn and I agreed to go on this trip was for the money. It would have paid for our little brothers to go to college, fix up our cabin, and maybe even start our own business."

Marcelo looked thoughtful. "I have been out on the water many times with my father. I went fishing with him, but I have never gone whitewater rafting."

"It's an adrenaline rush. Plus, it's so beautiful with all the mountains, trees, and wildlife. You'll have to come to West Virginia."

We fell silent for a while until I stood up again; fighting the throbbing pain that mainly resonated from my back. I paced, trying to walk it off. It only took six steps from one side of the cooler to the other.

"It feels better to stand up."

"I don't want to move right now," Marcelo said. "I just want to sleep." He rolled to his left and lay on his side.

I stood, staring at him. I didn't want to be alone. "What's your best guess on where we are?"

Marcelo opened his eyes and looked at me sideways. "Please, just let me sleep."

"We need to stay alert and active," I said, not really believing it. I didn't want to sit there and be consumed by my thoughts.

"You are not going to stop talking, are you?" he said as he got back into a sitting position.

"I'm usually quite shy."

He snorted. "I don't believe that."

"No, really. I keep to myself mostly. It's just that … I guess I'm really scared."

He nodded thoughtfully. "Yes. I know."

"I guess people worry differently," I said. "You want to sleep; I want to talk."

"Can we have a deal?" he asked. "If I let you talk for a while, will you let me sleep?"

I smirked and then nodded. "Deal. So where do you think we are?"

He paused to think. "I'm not certain. We could still be in Peru. Maybe Bolivia, Chile, Brazil, Colombia, even Argentina. I don't know which direction we drove. Does it really matter? We're still screwed."

"Yeah, I guess it doesn't matter." I sat down cross-legged directly in front of Marcelo.

"Tell me more about what happened in the Amazon," he said.

"It's really hard to think about. Maybe later."

"That is not fair," he said. "You want to talk, and now you don't want to talk?"

"I just … I'm not ready to get into that."

Marcelo blinked and then nodded.

I was quiet for several moments. "Why do you think we're here?"

"I don't understand," Marcelo said, uncapping the water bottle. He took a drink.

"Have you ever read *Oedipus Rex*? By Sophocles? It's Greek literature. We read it in my English class last year."

"You are a little strange, but go on," he said with a smile.

"It explores fate versus free will. It says that a long time ago, there was a king and queen. They heard a prophecy that their son, Oedipus, would kill his father and marry his mother. To prevent the prophecy from coming true, the king and queen left their son out in the elements to die, but he was found by a shepherd, who brought the infant to a different king, King Polybus,- who raised Oedipus as his own son. When Oedipus became an adult, he discovered that he might be adopted, so he went to an oracle who repeated the exact same prophecy: that he would kill his biological father and marry his mother. Oedipus thought he was smarter than any prophecy and believed he could use reason and free will to avoid fate. But no matter how carefully Oedipus planned, his fate ruled over free will. The choices he made eventually led him to do those *exact* two things. He was blinded to the truth by his pride."

Marcelo frowned. "What does that have to do with where we are right now?"

I sat pensively for a moment. "When we talked about it in class, I remember not saying a thing. I just sat there, listening to everyone else. We even had to write a paper on fate versus free will. I really didn't understand it all at the time, but I think I'm beginning to get it. Being here and all, trapped in this place, the question just seems to make sense now." I rested my head on my knees, looking vacantly at the floor. "I'm just trying to figure out why this is happening. Is this my fate? Is it part of God's plan? Or did I bring this all upon myself with the choices I made?"

Marcelo covered his ears with his hands. "You need to stop; you're making my head hurt."

"Sorry, I'm just …"

"As my father would say, 'You're chasing chickens that aren't there.' But you keep me on my toes. Tell you what: If we ever do make it out of here, we can talk about this some more. But now, my eyes are burning. I need to close them for a while." He leaned his head back against the wall of the cooler.

I scooted next to Marcelo and laid my head on his shoulder. But I kept my eyes open. I was too afraid to close them. I was too afraid of not seeing what horrible thing might come through the door.

It actually didn't take very long.

The cooler door opened, and the bearded man filled the doorway. "Let's go," he growled.

Marcelo was on his feet in a split-second. "What did you do with my sister?" he demanded. "Where's Lidia?"

The man ignored him as he led us to the service elevator.

We went up a couple floors, and when the door opened, the bearded man grabbed us each by an arm and took us to the end of a corridor. We walked into a large, empty bathroom with six open shower stalls. It reminded me of the gymnasium locker room at school, except this one was considerably worn.

"There are clothes and hairbrushes over there. Take a shower and put the clothes on."

The bearded man pushed both of us toward the stalls before sitting down on one of the paint-chipped benches.

I stood for several moments, terrified. I didn't want to take off my clothes in front of Marcelo, much less the barbarian who had raped a young girl last night.

I saw Marcelo had gone into one of the stalls and then cocked his head at me as if to say, "Get in the stall."

I understood. I stepped into the stall and removed my clothes; first reaching into the pocket of the pants I was wearing and taking the golden leaf pendant, sliding it under a towel.

I turned on the water, shivering and cringing as the tepid spray washed over my open wounds. I glanced at Marcelo in the stall next to me. He was rinsing his head under the water. The wall between was about shoulder high and kept us modest, but the bearded man had a full open view. He didn't take his eyes off me.

I did my best to ignore him, trying to pretend he wasn't there.

I used both small bottles of shampoo to wash the blood and dirt away. I rinsed off and took the small towel to dry off before getting into the clothes. They were used but looked clean.

I slid the golden leaf into my underwear. I then quickly put on the simple blue dress and sandals left on one of the benches. I brushed my tangled hair, scanning the walls in search of a mirror. I was somewhat relieved that there wasn't one.

Marcelo stayed in his stall as he got dressed: a pair of slacks and a men's ribbed-knit undershirt. It reminded me of what Papa used to wear on hot, muggy days. Mama would always laugh when he'd strike his best Hulk Hogan pose, striding around the tiny living room and shouting, "Well, let me tell you something, brother!" over and over.

Marcelo's thin, pale bruised arms drooped by his sides as he donned the shirt, and my happy memory quickly faded as I saw his mottled skin, purple and blue with bruises, some fading to yellow.

The bearded man took us back to the service elevator, and after going up at least twenty floors, we were led to a large ballroom. Four crystal chandeliers hung from the ceiling, illuminating the blue and gold carpet. It looked like a room that originally was for music, dancing, and laughter.

And then I noticed the left side of the room; armed thugs were lined up behind a dozen elegantly dressed girls sitting in high-backed chairs.

There was a door next to the last chair in the row, and when it opened, an armed man led another girl through. Along the right side of the ballroom, there was another set of young adults and children sitting motionless in a row of metal folding chairs. There were about thirty in all.

I recognized a few from the dirt cell. The grime and blood had been washed away, and they wore nice clothes and sandals.

But I noticed the outline of the breasts of the girls protruding through sheer linen gowns, dark nipples poking through the thin fabric.

I saw Lidia and Valeria, who were sitting side by side on the high-backed chairs, and my heart was filled with both relief and fear.

Marcelo saw his sister and immediately sprinted to her, bending down and taking her hands in his as he tried to persuade her to stand.

The bearded man ran over and grabbed Marcelo by the arm, swinging him to the floor before kicking him in the ribs.

As Marcelo writhed in pain, I expected Lidia to jump up and defend her brother. But she didn't move; she didn't even turn her head.

I thought it peculiar that no one looked at Marcelo, who was now curled in a ball.

I watched the long line of passive girls, whose heads were bobbing. They seemed to be struggling to stay upright as they stared ahead with glassy, lost eyes. I subtly tried to get the attention of Lidia and then Valeria.

They didn't respond, as if I weren't there. They were staring blankly into space, hypnotized.

The side door opened again, and an armed guard led the next girl through the door.

"Over there," the bearded man yelled at me. "Sit over there." He pointed.

I helped Marcelo up and over to the opposite side of the room, and we sat down with the other group. Everyone on this side was dressed the same, the girls in their simple blue dresses and the boys in slacks and a white-ribbed muscle shirts.

"Why are they separating us?" I whispered to Marcelo. "We're dressed differently than the others."

"My guess is they are all the virgins," he said. "They are drugged up. Lidia didn't even recognize me. I'm surprised they haven't drugged us."

"What's going to happen?"

Marcelo didn't answer.

I wondered about his suggestion that one side of the room had the virgins, and we were on the other side. Did that mean … I knew what happened to me; did it also happen to him?

I shook my head, trying to keep the thought away.

"Did you notice that every time the door opens," I whispered, "it sounds like someone is speaking in the other room? Listen. They're taking that girl from the other group."

The girl was led to the door, and it opened. I could distinctly make out the words while the door was open.

"And this beautiful young lady has been sold to number fifty-four. Please bring in our next darling!" A pause. "Oh yes! This little beauty is eleven years old. She comes to us from a village just beyond the snow-capped mountains. Let's start the bidding off at …"

The door closed, and the sound stopped.

"Tia, they are auctioning everyone off."

"Yes," I said, feeling sick.

One by one, children were sent to the other room. When it became Valeria's and then Lidia's turn, the bearded man came up and stood near us, with his gun pointed so we wouldn't try anything. Over the next several minutes, one girl, then the other, was led away and sold to the highest bidder.

Marcelo sat quietly in his chair and cried.

The door opened, and three men approached our group. They split the boys and girls into smaller sets of five; I let out a sigh of relief when Marcelo and I were placed in the same group. We were led through the connecting door and onto a large stage. I had to squint, shielding my eyes from the blinding lights. Rows of shadowy figures jeered and catcalled at us, and my breathing sped up to the point of hyperventilation.

"Calm down. Just calm down," Marcelo said.

A man's voice came through the speakers: "Behold, my friends, a group of strong, beautiful, and willing beauties. They've all been nicely broken in and are eager to do as you command. Let's start the bidding …"

I stopped listening and closed my eyes, praying that God would protect me and every other child here.

Next thing I knew, I was being pulled off the stage; Marcelo tried to twist out of a man's grip.

We were squished into the service elevator and led out of the building the same way we came in.

Standing in the alley, a rusty, dented white van pulled up, and we were shoved into the back compartment. Across from me, Marcelo was sandwiched between two unshaven thugs. He was sitting with his head lowered, as if in shame. I wished he'd look up; I needed some reassurance in his eyes, but he stared at his feet.

There were three other girls with us in the van, but I hadn't seen them before. Their eyes were glazed over in a distant stare.

A short time later, the van parked, and as I stepped out, I was surprised to see what looked like an ordinary street with a small bakery, tobacco shop, and convenience store. Wedged between two men, I could feel a gun pressed up against my ribs.

Why am I out in the open? If someone would just look at us, they'd have to know we're prisoners.

The stores were rundown but looked operational, although some appeared closed. I guessed it was late at night, yet there were people walking around.

I saw a poster on one of the buildings showing a half-dressed girl with her legs wrapped around a pole. Next to it was a three-story windowless structure with red lettering. "Emanuel's Auto Repair and Body Shop," it said in Spanish.

When we entered the building, colored disco lights flashed to the beat of loud dance music. We came into a large room with scantily clad young women entangled around grisly-looking men. Thick smoke filled the room from cigars and cigarettes.

The grip around my arm was tightened as I was pulled through the horde. Toward the back of the room was a narrow, darkened staircase just wide enough for one person to ascend at a time. As we climbed it, I reached up and held Marcelo's hand. The stairs buckled and squeaked with each step, and I felt sickly and weak by the time we reached the third floor. Back home, I could have dashed upstairs like that in a breeze, but now it was a struggle just to keep moving.

We found ourselves in a hallway reminiscent of an old rundown motel, with small, gloomy rooms on both sides. Halfway down the hall, one of the men shoved me in a room and slammed the door closed.

I spun around and banged against it, tugging at the locked handle, screaming to be let out. Someone unlocked the door and pushed it open, sending me backwards. Full of rage, a man lunged forward and pushed me to the floor.

"That's your first warning. Sit down and shut up," he said in Spanish. Then he backed out and slammed the door shut.

I pulled myself up and scanned the room, half-expecting to see someone else in there. But I was alone.

The twin bed had a simple sheet with a threadbare blanket strewn across it. I felt like an animal that had been trapped in a cage. I went over to the boarded-up window and tried to yank off the planks of wood. I would need a screwdriver or some kind of metal object to pull them back. I checked the room for something I could use but found only undergarments, a dress, a sheet, and blankets crumpled in a small dresser drawer. The room reeked of something unrecognizable: a putrid, sour smell that turned my stomach. I would have thought I'd get used to filthy smells, but no luck so far.

I went to the opposite side of the bed, where there was a small lamp on a round end table. Next to the lamp was a plate holding a sandwich and a bottle of water.

I was starving and tore the white sandwich bread into pieces before putting them in my mouth. I didn't even care that blue circles of mold dotted the crusts or that the bread was so stale it tasted like cardboard. Nausea came as I swallowed the last bite, a clump of vomit forming at the back of my throat.

Oh, God. I lay down on the bed and wrapped the worn blanket tightly around my body. *What's going to happen to me?* I closed my eyes and tried to picture home, but my visions were blurred. *How long had I been gone? Was anyone searching for me?*

The seconds ticked by in that small, desolate room, the walls slowly closing in around me. I curled into a ball, and buried my head under the blanket, wishing somehow, someway, this was all just a sick joke or a terrible nightmare.

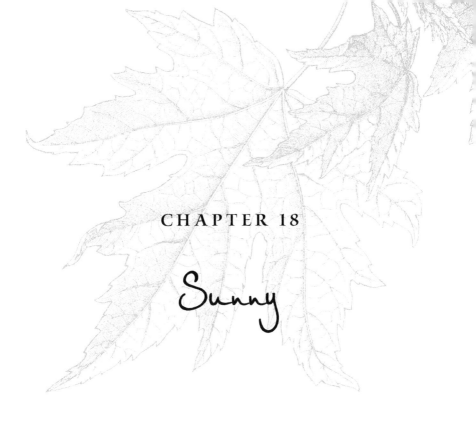

CHAPTER 18

Sunny

*W*hat if I rushed the bearded man the moment he opened the door, before he had a chance to protect himself? What if it isn't the bearded man, but two or three men? What if I fell on the ground, pretending to be sick, refusing to get up? They would just drag me out, probably by my hair. What if I tripped my captor once we got outside? I still wouldn't get very far.

I shifted around on the rickety bed, listening to the muted conversations through the room's paper-thin walls.

I was certain this place was a brothel, just like the one Claudia had described. A few days ago, I could hardly imagine something like this, but now, being trapped in this dingy room, and from what I'd been through, I not only feared the worst, I knew it was coming.

Yesterday, I sat in a dirt cell somewhere in a distant country, but it felt like it was years ago.

If there was just a window, I could escape, or yell, or get someone's attention. Someone who was dropping their car off at Emanuel's Auto Repair or picking up some milk at the little grocery store. Maybe they'll just leave me alone. Cristiano said I was worth a lot; maybe they'll trade me for money and let me go home.

I knew those scenarios were long shots, but it was all I had to hold onto for now.

A boy's scream came from the room next to mine and startled me, his voice high and wailing.

I got up from the bed, realizing it may be Marcelo. I prayed he didn't do anything stupid, but even when we did what they said, we'd get anyway punished. So maybe it didn't matter.

A dull thud pounded against the wall, followed by a gunshot and a low groan. There was a dragging noise as if someone was pulling a body along the floor.

Was it Marcelo? Are they dragging Marcelo?

Footsteps, garbled voices, doors opening, doors closing.

I watched the door, knowing it would open soon, and I would be next. I realized I may have to get naked, and I didn't know how to preserve my golden leaf pendant so it wouldn't be confiscated. I decided to slide it between the fitted sheet and the mattress on the bed. It wasn't a very good hiding place, but it was the quickest. I'm glad I did it because a moment later, the doorknob turned.

I ran to the far end of the room and sat in the corner, wrapping my arms around my knees.

Two husky men with unshaven faces walked in and shut the door. I recognized them as the guards who'd brought me here.

I was quickly yanked up and thrown on the bed, facedown.

I kept my eyes closed and felt something cold and metal pressed firmly against my temple; *the muzzle of a gun?*

A set of hands lifted my dress up and began ripping off my underwear.

"No," I said, barely above a whisper. "Please, no."

The man's rough hands on my skin was unbearable.

"Don't scream!" he said in Spanish as he wrapped a filthy palm around my mouth.

I squirmed as he put his full weight on me. He was too strong; his body pinned me to the bed.

"*Stop,*" I wailed as I felt him force his way into me.

"What did I say about screaming?" he said, his mouth next to my ear, breathing heavily. He wrapped a calloused hand around my neck and shoved my face into the scratchy cheap blanket.

The pain was … I couldn't even describe it.

"Oh, you are good," he said, his stinking breath going quicker.

"Kill me, just kill me," I said as he thrust himself into me over and over, each time a little less painful, but I still prayed for unconsciousness to take it all away.

"*¡Suficiente! Mi turno,*" the other man said. (Enough! My turn!)

The first man got off me. The second man seemed to not stink as much, but his thrusting was more aggressive.

Screech, bang, screech, bang, screech, bang. The rickety bed complained loudly.

I stopped trying to scream, just praying that it would stop.

"*¿Te gusta?*" the man asked in my ear. (You like?)

I just kept my eyes closed.

The man groaned and then stopped.

I don't know how long it took, but when they left the room, I rolled up in a ball and cried. I was bleeding and swollen.

My nightmare became a living hell as every few hours; different men with guns came in to repeat the terror over, and over again: a jumble of sounds and floods of pain, pain, pain. When they made me lie on my back, I wouldn't look any of them in the eye, even when they tried to force me. Sometime during it all, my wish was granted, and I did lose consciousness, blissfully floating away, where they couldn't touch me, much less hurt me anymore.

I woke up in excruciating pain and pulled away the thin blanket to find streaks of dried blood down my thighs. I cried, and cried, not knowing what to do. The tears became deep, loud sobs, almost animalistic; they sounded as if they were coming from the darkest place outside of my soul.

The door swung open, and a woman came inside.

"*¿De qué se trata todo esto?*" she yelled, her hands on her hips. (What's this all about?)

I sobbed even harder, cowering in the bed.

"I'm not going to hurt you, but you need to stop screaming," the woman said in Spanish, sounding more kindly.

She was older, at least fifty, with short brown hair cut into a bob. She was taller than most women, about the height of Finn.

She wore baggy blue jeans, a black T-shirt, and a yellow and red bandana around her neck. She was also holding a baseball bat, which made me want to hide under the bed immediately.

"You are white," she said, again in Spanish. "*¿Hablas español?*"

I just stared at her.

"Okay, I try English, but I, eh, not good. I know you had, eh, rough. I know," the woman said. "But this is life. Now, for you. Take the linens off, and, eh, we'll take to the bathroom." She pointed at the small ancient dresser. "There, clean clothes in the drawer." She pulled out a fresh dress and swung it across her shoulder. "Come, I show you where to wash. I am Berta."

I gathered the bloody linens from the bed, making sure the golden leaf pendant wasn't included, and then followed Berta down the narrow hallway to the shower room. Every step was painful and tender, small agonies from the repeated attacks.

The bathroom was large with an old vinyl floor that was yellowed and stained. There were three faded pinkish-colored sinks, two toilets, and two shower stalls. I avoided glancing in the mirrors above the sinks as I tossed the dirty sheets and bloody clothes into a bin. I took a shower and got dressed.

"Help me, dear Lord, please help me, dear Lord," I whispered over and over as I followed the woman back to the bedroom. I sat on the foot of the bed and lowered my head in submission.

"Now I tell you the rules," Berta said. "You … now Sunny. Your name. Sunny. Men will call you Sunny, and you will say yourself is Sunny."

I heard the words but didn't comprehend them. Didn't try.

"You owe three hundred thousand pesos. That is we paid for

you. Every day, customers pay us to be with you. If they like you, they might … what is the word? Tip. They might tip you. You give us the tip. When you work three hundred thousand pesos from tip, you will get your freedom. It is fair, as you see. Please them and do well. The more they like, the more tip. The more tip, the faster you go home."

Now the words were sinking in. I was sickened.

"You need shower every day, and you find clean dresses and nightgowns in dresser. You also have chores. Kitchen, bathroom, bedrooms, laundry, hallways. You have easy today; you rest. Tomorrow you work. The pills—eh, birth control pills—are in the top drawer of the dresser, and you need to take one every day. No pregnant here. Just no."

If I had anything in my stomach, I might have vomited.

"The door's unlocked," Berta continued. "But one, eh, mistake, and we'll lock you in room. No leave building without *escolta* … eh, *acompañamiento*. And no tell customer anything. Nothing. No real name, no where you from, no how you got here. Nothing. If we find out you say, you beaten. Probably killed."

I just wanted to curl up on the bed and shut out the world. What there was of it.

"You do what they say. If they want between your legs, you let them. If they want your mouth or your hand, you let them. You get more, eh, tips if you pretend to like. Pretend they special. You will have customers any time. You eat and sleep between." She paused and stared at me. "What's your name?"

"Uh … Tia."

Berta swung the bat, narrowly missing my face.

"Sunny! Your name is Sunny!" She paused again. "We'll be friends if you listen to me and do the rules. If not …" Berta waved the bat around. "Problem. Understand?"

I pointed at the wall. "What happened to the boy in the next room?"

Berta shrugged. "He didn't want to do what they say." She held up the bat. "They had problem. Shoot him in arm, just a little. They move him. Better to think of yourself now, Sunny." Berta turned to leave. "If you have questions, later. Eat and sleep; you'll be busy soon."

Berta left, keeping the door open.

I lay there, not sleeping, trying not to cry, and failing. I had to be smart. I had to think things through.

I heard a soft knock.

I looked up, wondering what evil was at the door.

Instead, a girl stood in the doorway. She was about my age, maybe a little older, and wore a similar dress.

I sat up, and the girl came over and sat on the side of the bed. Tattoos covered her arms, and a small rose was inked along the side of her neck.

"What's with all the tears?" the girl asked in Spanish.

I didn't say anything, though I wanted to.

Just look around, I thought. *Everyone should be crying.*

"Ah." She nodded and then said in English, "You need to toughen up."

"But they …"

"Yeah, every day and every night. The first night is always the hardest," the girl said, her face impassive. "But if you resist, it will be worse. You have to learn to accept it. If you are helpful to the man, he will be happy. More tips, and they, um, leave quicker. And chances are you'll live longer. I'm Phoenix. That's what they call me here."

"I can't … I can't do what they want. I would rather die." Emotions overwhelmed me, and I buried my face in my hands, hot tears flowing like a water hose.

Phoenix came closer and put her arm around my shoulder. "I get it, okay? I tell myself I'm going to get out of here one day. I need to be alive to do that. Just something to think about."

I took a minute to calm down, raised my head, and sniffled. "How long have you been here?"

"I don't know; a couple of years, I think."

"A couple of years? Are you kidding? I'm not even sure I can do this a couple of days. Isn't there any way out? Have you tried to escape?"

"No. Every window is boarded up, and every door is locked. And if it's not, someone stands guard in front of it. There's no way out."

"How much longer do you have until your debt is paid off?"

"Oh, yeah. You never pay off your debt. They tell you that so you try to make the customers happy."

"So how do we get out?"

Phoenix shrugged. "I guess when we get too old, and they

don't want us anymore. Probably, they'll just put us in a van and dump us somewhere."

I shivered. I wasn't sure if she meant they drop us off somewhere or dumped our bodies.

There was a long silence as comprehension escaped me.

"How did you get here?" Phoenix asked.

"I was kidnapped and sold in an auction yesterday."

"Oh, yeah. I've heard about that. Did they make you get naked and dance?"

"No. No, not that."

"Oh, good. One girl here said they made her do that."

"So you weren't auctioned off?" I asked.

"No. Not like that. A few years ago, I met this guy at a party. We started dating. I thought he really liked me, always taking me to nice restaurants, and he even bought me jewelry. Sounds crazy now, but I was falling for him. After a couple of weeks, he called me, said he had a surprise for me. When I met with him that night, he told me that a friend of his could get him a good-paying job in the United States. He told me he loved me and asked me to come with him. He said he could get me a job too."

Phoenix paused for a few minutes and looked down at her hands. "I always wanted to go to America and thought this was my chance. A few weeks later, he got me a green card and a plane ticket. When we landed, a driver met us at the airport. I didn't suspect anything until they drove me here."

I nodded. I know how stupid or blindsided one can feel.

Phoenix shook her head. "I was in shock, scared to death. I remember staring at my boyfriend in disbelief. He told me that I owed him for the green card, the visa, and the plane ticket. I had to pay off my debt. I know now it was all a scam."

"That's bullshit," I said. I don't use that word and felt bad it came out of my mouth, but it was the only word that fit.

Phoenix stood up and smoothed out her dress. Her frown had been replaced with a half-smile and a hint of optimism in her voice. "Anyway, that's my story. I know you just got here, but a bit of advice. See this?" She pointed to little round brown spots on her arms. "Cigarette burns." She held up her hands. "See how my fingers are all messed up? That's because someone broke them when I didn't follow the rules. It will happen to you too if you don't get along."

I leaned my against the wall and tilted my head. "Why are you telling me all of this?"

"And look here," Phoenix said, lifting up the bottom of her dress. She pointed at a scar on her upper thigh, just below the seam of her underwear. "This is from one of the pimps who stabbed me with a knife because I didn't do what he wanted. I wish someone had told me what to look out for when I first got here." She lowered her dress, covering the jagged scar. "Now when new girls come in, it makes me feel better to warn them. So now I'm telling you: get along, stay quiet, and maybe one day, we'll get out of here."

I let out a heavy sigh. "Thanks. Thanks for helping."

Phoenix flashed a quick smile. It was then I noticed her dark eyes were hard and empty in her soft, brown face.

"Okay, I better go. I'll try to stop by later to see how you're doing."

"Thank you. I hope to see you again."

The girl left, shutting the door behind her.

I fell in and out of a restless sleep, occasionally awakened from stabbing pains in my groin. No matter how I lay, it hurt. I tried to find a way that didn't hurt as much.

I could hear muted music filtering through the door; the thumping of bass along with the sounds of escalated voices and raucous laughter, intermixed with random screams. The disco must be open.

I lay underneath the thin scratchy blanket and listened intently for approaching footsteps, watching for the door handle to turn. Hours went by, and no one came.

I needed to use the bathroom, but I didn't want anyone to see me. I went to the door and poked my head out. The music was louder, but I saw no one. I slipped out and headed for the bathroom. Everything smelled of sex and other filthy body odors. If it came out of a body, it seemed to linger in the air, in the carpet, in the paint.

When I returned, I lay back down and drifted off at some point. Next thing I knew, Berta was shaking my shoulder and holding a tray of eggs, bread, and juice.

"Hope you sleep good," Berta said. "You have a busy night tonight. Eat. I come back soon. You clean kitchen today."

CHAPTER 19

Glimmer of Hope

A fter I showered and dressed, Berta took me to the kitchen on the first floor, where three other girls were already cleaning: one wiping the counters, another scrubbing a pan, the third washing out glasses.

I looked around, taking it in. The kitchen was noticeably old with yellowed vinyl floors, cracked along the edges, exposing patches of dirt in the crevasses. There was a large red double-door refrigerator, two ovens, and a large stovetop along the far wall of the room, with a silver double sink on the opposite side. Rows of mismatched dishes and cups were neatly stacked inside the opened white cabinets. There was a strong odor of bleach, which was much better than the smells upstairs.

"You use rags by sink," Berta said. "Go and help. You start on oven, and when girls done, you sweep and mop."

I went to work on the oven and then made my way to the refrigerator. There was a girl about my age finishing up a pile of dishes. She had dark skin, light brown eyes, and neatly braided black hair that hung across her shoulders.

"Do you want me to help dry the dishes?" I asked, trying out my Spanish (although I think it came out as "Want dry help me dishes?")

The girl looked at me with a smirk. "Sure, grab a towel over there," she said in English.

"Sorry," I said. "I thought ..."

"*No problema*," she said and then giggled.

I had to stifle a laugh. It felt good to be a little light-hearted.

I took a glass and a small tea towel and began drying. "How do you do this day after day? I don't mean the cleaning; I mean the men. How do you get up the next day, knowing it'll happen again in a few hours?"

"You must be new. When I first got here, I couldn't imagine doing this every day, either. But we don't have a choice, do we?" The girl's face hardened, as if slammed back down to earth unexpectedly. I guess that was my fault.

"How many are here?"

"Hard to say. People come and go. I don't keep track anymore. There's no point in making friends. They could be gone the next day."

I put the glass down. "I came here with a boy. His name is Marcelo, and he was shot in the arm. Berta said he was taken to the second floor. Have you been to the second floor?"

The girl shrugged and plunged another cup into the soapy water. "It's the same as the third floor, pretty much."

"How long have you been here?"

"Lost track. At least a year. Does it really matter?"

I paused. "Honestly, I don't know if I'll last until morning if the same thing happens to me again tonight."

"It gets better. Well, easier. Sometimes, they give drugs, and that helps. You can float away and just pretend you're not there. That's what I do. If you resist, they will beat you. I was beaten a lot the first few months. I learned how to give in. The guards don't beat me anymore."

"Have you tried to escape?"

The girl looked at me as if I was incredibly stupid. "There is no escape. The windows are all boarded, and there are guards at every door."

"My name's Tia, by the way."

"Is that your real name?"

"My real name."

"Then shh!" the girl hissed. "You can't say your real name. You will be beaten for that."

I nodded. "Can you take me to the second floor and help me look for Marcelo?"

"Look," the girl said, leaning closer so that her head was almost pressed against mine. "We're not supposed to talk to anyone on a separate floor, but maybe you will be assigned to clean there."

I shook my head. "I can't wait for maybe. I've got to find him today."

"Your funeral," the girl shrugged, turning back to the dishes in the sink. "Grab a bucket over there and fill it up. I would try to look like you are cleaning something, if I were you."

After the kitchen was clean, the others girls left, and I stayed behind, filling up a small bucket and grabbing a rag. I cautiously made my way to the second floor, passing a few guards who watched me carefully.

The girl in the kitchen was right; the second floor looked the same as the third: a poorly lit narrow hallway with rooms on each side.

Where is he? Where is he?

I hurried down the hallway, feeling the carpet squish under my feet. After I'd checked most of the rooms and began losing hope, I spotted Marcelo lying facedown on a bed at the very last room. He was naked except for a bloody towel wrapped around his right arm.

I quickly shut the door and went to his side; I found a blanket in the top dresser drawer and covered his body, smoothing the blanket around his shoulders.

I shook him lightly. "Marcelo … Marcelo." Then, louder, "*Marcelo!*"

He opened his eyes, widening as they focused on my face.

"Hey, you okay?" I asked.

Marcelo rolled onto his back. He looked exhausted. "No, not really," he said softly.

"So the bullet didn't go in?"

"No, it just grazed the skin. Luckily."

"There's always your other arm," I said with a grin.

"Why do you always try to make me laugh during times like this?"

"It's either laugh or cry." I paused to listen. "I shouldn't stay; they might be looking for me. I'll check on you tomorrow. No matter what comes next, you need to stay strong for Lidia. You need to find her. Don't forget that."

"I'm not sure if I can make it another night," Marcelo said, his face ashen. "My arm hurts all the time. And they ..."

He paused, looking away.

"... they did things."

"I know." I paused. "Me too."

He looked back at me warily.

"Every day is gonna suck," I said. "Yesterday I thought would be my last, but I'm still alive, and so are you. But we need to stay together. You need to pray; ask God for His guidance, love, and protection. You, we, both of us need to have faith. Promise me you'll try?"

A lone tear streamed down Marcelo's cheek as he nodded and pulled the blankets up to his neck. He looked like a little boy, scared and far from home.

I gave him a hug before sneaking out the door, bucket in hand.

As I stepped into the hallway, a guard from the other end of the hallway pointed at me. "You!" he said in Spanish. "What are you doing down there?"

"I'm mopping up a spill," I said in English as I approached.

I slid by him and hurried upstairs, making my way back to the bedroom, leaving the rag and bucket in the corner.

I crawled into bed, staring mindlessly at the door. The sounds of music and men's voices began to rise, making my skin crawl. It was just a matter of time before the door handle would turn. My eyes were locked on it. One simple door handle, one rickety door provided a false sense of safety, eventually betraying me.

I took in a deep breath and squeezed my eyes shut. I forced myself to think of the people I knew, not the ones I didn't. I concentrated on the memories of the faces of Finn, Wes, Paddy, Mama, Papa, and Uncle Harold.

I recalled the last time at the old house, when we had eaten pizza and sat together in front of the fireplace, reading old letters our ancestors had written. One in particular came to mind:

> My appetite has been very poor, and can't keep a
> bite down. I've worked on until yesterday but I
> had to give up; could not go any more. I lost over
> forty pounds in flesh. You asked how the water
> was, and it is not good and very scarce.

There was more, but I can't remember it, other than the last line:

God will bless her all the days of her life.

"And God will bless her all the days of her life," I said aloud as the door handle turned, and two men entered the room.

My stomach lurched when I saw one of them was Heitor.

"Get up," he growled with a sneer while exhaling a gray cloud of cigar smoke from his thin lips.

I didn't say anything; I just sat up and began to put on my shoes. When Heitor turned to talk to the other man, I reached between the sheet and mattress and pulled out the golden leaf pendant, clutching it in a closed fist.

"Come on," he barked. "Let's go."

"Wait," I said, following him out of the room. "We need to bring Marcelo with us."

Heitor turned on me. "Who the hell is Marcelo?"

"He's downstairs. I won't go without him." I felt both brave and crazy saying that. But I didn't know any other way.

Heitor scowled, wrapped a hand around the back of my neck, and pushed me toward the staircase.

When we got to the second floor, I twisted out of his grip and sprinted down the hallway. I got to Marcelo's room, pushed the door open, and saw a man on top of Marcelo, writhing.

"Get off! Get off him!" I screamed, coming at the man with my hands like claws.

"Get the fuck out of here," the man shouted, shoving me with one hand so roughly that it knocked the wind out of me. The naked man stood and made a move toward me.

I rose to my feet, gasping for air and feeling dizzy as Heitor entered.

"Enough," he shouted, pulling out a gun and aiming it at the man's head. "Touch her again, and I'll shoot." There was a sharp click as Heitor cocked the trigger, and the man reluctantly put his hands up, moving into the corner.

I went to Marcelo, who had tears streaming down his face. His bandages were drenched in fresh red blood. I placed the golden leaf pendant in his palm, just as Heitor jerked me onto my feet.

"I'll come back for you," I said.

"What?" Marcelo said, looking at the pendant.

I was yanked out into the hallway.

"You are the biggest pain in the ass," Heitor said.

As I slid into the back seat of a car, I noticed the grisly bearded man sitting in the passenger seat.

"I've got to find better friends," I muttered sarcastically.

"What?" Heitor said in that voice that was half a growl.

I shook my head. "Where are you taking me?"

"Shut up," he said. "You'll be heading home soon. I didn't know you're a movie star. Why didn't you tell me?" He let out a short, mirthless laugh.

"I'm a what?"

"Some guy in Hollywood is offering a million-dollar reward for your safe return."

Safe return.

He paused and then laughed. "Yeah, I'll make sure you get back in one piece, as long as I get that money. In the meantime, while I work out the details, I'm taking you to a little place not far from here. If you play your cards right, you'll be home before the end of the month."

Could it really be true? Was I going home?

"If you don't annoy me so much that I kill you first," he said. "I swear you've fucked up more stuff than a sane person would

231

put up with. But if you just do what I fucking say, you'll be going home, my little bebé."

I stared at him to see if he was joking.

He had a wicked smile, as if imagining counting stacks of money. He lit up a thick cigar, turned to me, and blew a thick plume of gray smoke in my direction. I held my breath and quickly turned away as the car sped down the road and into the night.

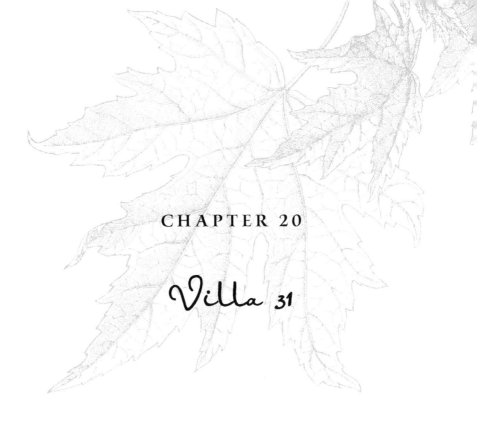

CHAPTER 20

Villa 31

I leaned forward, pressing my forehead against the window. The clock on the dashboard said it was near midnight, but the streets were as noisy and chaotic as if it were noon. The endless stream of cars, motorcycles, and bikes—missing each other by mere inches—kept me on the edge of my seat. I could see them, they could see me, but just as I knew nothing about their lives, they knew nothing about mine.

Wherever we were, it was a very old city, like the ones I saw in an art book at the school library. There were large monuments displaying proud men in uniform, old stone structures with intricate carvings, marble buildings with rows of brightly colored flags, and gothic-looking cathedrals with spires that reached high into the sky.

We went through a few roundabouts and crossed over a

bridge. Down below and in the distance, I could see a very large neighborhood, so vast, it was like a city within a city. But it appeared to be gutted-out. Even from a distance, it reminded me of pictures I saw of Chicago's ghetto areas during a sociology course, but a hundred times worse. The structures were oddly stacked and in various colors, like Legos. The homes, if that's what they were, appeared to be a mixture of faded red brick, aluminum siding, and tarps. Some of the units were missing windows or whole walls, exposing the sparsely furnished interiors.

"Where are you taking me?" I asked again as we drove closer to this odd area of the city.

Heitor ignored me and instead turned the radio up, filling the van with salsa music.

Eventually, we stopped on the outskirts of this poor neighborhood, and Heitor tossed a navy baseball cap at me. "Put it on and get out."

He was out of the car and outside my door before I could tuck my hair inside the hat and clamber out.

I followed Heitor along a darkened alleyway, while the bearded man was behind me. Ahead, I could see a woman holding a small lantern beside a small, rusted structure that looked sort of like an old storage container.

We passed her and continued through a maze of alleys, illuminated by lanterns or single bulbs hanging on thin wires. Small groups of men huddled in the shadows, and we walked passed discarded beer bottles and cigarette butts. An old man was squatting by a doorway, barbequing a small piece of meat using a rolled up newspaper and splintered wood. The putrid fumes hung like paste in the back of my throat.

Finally, Heitor stopped in front of a large brick apartment building and knocked on the door. I saw the ugly bearded man plop down on a wooden plank on the opposite side of the dirt road. An older lady with thinning white hair opened the door and greeted Heitor with a wide smile. She was short and plump, with round pink cheeks.

"Hello, Glaucia. Good to see you," Heitor said in Spanish, giving her a hug and a kiss on both cheeks.

"It's good to see you too," Glaucia said as she led us inside to a long table. "Please sit down and tell me how you've been. How's your mama? I haven't seen her in years."

"Funny you should ask. I just left her home, and she's doing great. Maybe when things quiet down a bit, you can visit with her."

I sat there pretending I didn't know what they were saying, but it was difficult since I had a hard time hearing Heitor speaking such pleasantries.

Was he human after all?

"How long will she be staying?" Glaucia asked, eyeing me up and down.

"Just a couple of days," Heitor said, resting his palm on my shoulder. "This is Tia."

Every ounce of my willpower kept me from slapping his hand away.

Glaucia nodded, hemming and hawing as she took in my appearance. She wrapped her hand around my arm and poked at my ribs. "Heitor, she's so skinny; look here, her bones are poking out. Oh, and thanks again for your gift of money last week. Honestly, I don't know what we'd do without you."

"You're part of my family," Heitor said, sounding oddly embarrassed. "Just keep this girl quiet and don't let her leave. I'll have a man outside. If you need anything, just let him know."

Heitor stood and pulled me up, turning me so I was facing him.

"Remember what I said, my little bebé," he said in English. "You try anything or if the deal falls through, you won't live to see another day."

He smiled, but it wasn't pleasant. Then he left.

I felt relief so intense, it almost brought me to my knees. I was shaking.

"Let me look," Glaucia said in English, holding my upper arms. "You've been through hell and back, eh? Let me clean you up."

I was led to a back room. Apparently, there were no windows in this structure except for the small one near the front door.

"This is the bathroom. Over there the toilet."

The room was bathed in yellow light from lanterns, and three large metal tin tubs were nearby for bathing. Steam rose in curls from the largest one, and I almost moaned aloud thinking of being immersed in the hot water.

"Wash up. When you finish, put on the dress." She pointed at cloth on a chair.

I turned to the woman with tears in my eyes.

"We can talk in the morning." Glaucia patted my arm gently. "Go on. I will make some food."

Glaucia left, and I took off my clothes and sank into the hot water, submerging my head. I came up and took the little shampoo bottle. "Four Seasons Hotel Buenos Aires."

So, maybe I'm in Argentina. I knew I could be anywhere in South America or even deep within Central America, but it was something to hold onto.

After the bath, I dressed and walked back into the main room, where Glaucia was putting food onto a plate.

"Come sit down. You need to eat," Glaucia said.

The little rolls of ham and cheese atop salted crackers were, to me, a delicacy, as if from the finest restaurant.

"Thank you. It's really good."

For some reason, and for the first time in a long time, I felt safe and somewhat hopeful. My stomach was happy, my body clean, and all I wanted was to sink into the oblivion of sleep.

As if reading my mind, Glaucia said, "Go sleep now. The little ones will be up in a few hours, and once they awake, no more sleep for anyone." She pointed to the other room and followed me in.

There were several mats on the floor with children sleeping on them. I went over to an empty blue mat and turned to Glaucia. "Thank you," I said. "Thank you for everything."

The old woman gave me a sad smile, nodded, and handed me a blanket before disappearing back through the doorway.

I lay down and covered myself.

Thank you, dear Lord, for protecting me and getting me out of that place.

A moment later, I was out like a light.

I woke to a melody of high-pitched voices and children scurrying.

I opened my eyes and squinted, watching them bounce, skip, and dart about. I guessed they ranged in ages from two to ten years old or so.

I stood, trying to ignore my body's aches and pains.

"Ah, you are awake," Glaucia said as I entered the kitchen. She was setting glasses of juice and plates of eggs on the tables. "I thought you might sleep longer. Come, have some breakfast."

Then she turned toward the room I just came from and yelled, "*¡Hora del desayuno!*"

There was a flurry of excitement as the kids came running in and took their seats, diving into the eggs with gusto and chewing heartily.

"*Buenos días, esta es* Tia," Glaucia said, wiping her hands on her apron. (Good morning, this is Tia.)

"*¡Hola*, Tia!*"

Everyone waved and smiled, except for one little girl, who rose from her seat and came over to me.

"*¡Mamá! ¡Mamá!*" she cried, wrapping her skinny arms around my knees. She couldn't have been more than three years old.

I knelt down to her level.

"*¿Por qué me dejas durante tanto tiempo?*" the little girl said. (Why are you leaving me for so long?)

Glaucia came over and pulled the girl away from me, asking her to stop. I stood up again.

"*¡No! ¡No! Por favor no me tome*," the little girl cried out (No! No! Please do not take me.)

She reached out to grab at my dress, pulling at the fabric so hard, I thought it might rip.

"She thinks you're her mama," Glaucia explained, not knowing I could understand. "You *do* look a little bit like her. She was short, skinny, and had a, eh, light-skin face, like you. Her mama died a year ago. Melina wants to know why you left her for so long."

I wanted to cry. I was both honored and saddened. Her mother had passed away. She was all alone and so very young. Her tiny soft cheeks and big brown eyes pulled at my heart.

I looked at Glaucia. "It's okay," I said softly. "She can stay by me."

I took Melina by the hand, sat down at the table, and pulled the little girl onto my lap.

"Hi, Melina. I'm Tia."

"*¿Mamá?*"

I didn't know what to say. I just hugged her and placed my cheek next to hers. I felt her little arms hugging me back, and for the first time in weeks, I felt warm and loved.

"Now that it is daytime, I can show you," Glaucia said when everyone was done eating and had run off to get cleaned up.

"What is this place?" I asked as we left the table.

"An orphanage. Not much, but the children have a place to sleep, desks for their homework, and I try to cook one hot meal a day. We are lucky. While most in the, eh, slums have no electricity or, eh, plumbing, the church run some cables and pipes. They help pay the bills. So does Heitor."

Glaucia got up and walked over to a cabinet, then brought over some pills and handed a bottle to me.

"To help with the pain. Aspirin, but it will help."

"Don't they have school?" I asked, washing three aspirin down with orange juice.

"Saturday, no. The church brought over toys yesterday, should keep them busy," Glaucia said, pointing to a large cardboard box.

I drew closer to Glaucia, keeping my voice low.

"Am I in Buenos Aires?" I asked.

"Yes." Glaucia said this simply, her expression neutral.

"How do you know Heitor?"

"We all grew up together, not too far from here. He went away. I stayed. But he would, eh, visit."

"And do you know how he knows me?" I asked, purposely being provocative.

"All I know is if I watch you, he will buy a real house for the orphanage." Glaucia gave a long sigh. "The only reason I agreed. I know he is … a dangerous man. A bad man. I heard stories. But he is like family and looks after me and the children."

"Do you know that he also sells children for sex? Do you know he sold me?"

Glaucia put her hands over her ears. "*No!* I don't want to hear. He's never hurt these children. Without his help, we would not survive."

I paused, thinking. I may have overstepped. She cares about the children and will take what she can get. That means he raped me and sold me, and as long as it helped the children, she doesn't want to know. Not that she didn't care, but she had to choose sides. If someone like me was sacrificed to help a dozen two to ten-year-olds, it was an easy choice.

"I'm sorry, Glaucia, I'm sorry," I said, raising both of my hands. "I shouldn't have mentioned it. I can see how much you love these children and are trying to find a way to help them."

After a few silent moments, I thought it best to change the subject.

"How long have you been taking care of them?" I hoped Glaucia would accept my apology and continue talking.

Glaucia sighed. "They've been with me for about four years. The pastor at church asked if I could watch some orphans for a few weeks. Weeks turned into months, then years, and now I've got all these children to watch. The church donates all the food, the mats, and school supplies. Heitor helps out a couple times a year. Once in a while, a miracle, and one of them will get adopted."

I nodded. "I'm really glad to hear that. I think if people knew they were here, without a family, without a home … I mean, just look at them, how beautiful and sweet they are. If people knew, I just know they would be adopted."

"There are so many more living on streets without family," Glaucia said.

I paused in disbelief. "I can't imagine any child living out on the streets, all alone. It's too hard to even think about."

"Many of the homeless children go to the city and beg for food or money and come back here to the slums at night to sleep.

A lot of them join gangs for protection. You hear about them getting killed or dying from a sickness."

"What happened to the parents?" I asked.

"Some on drugs, some dead, some have no money and cannot take care of them. I'm just guessing." Glaucia shook her head and frowned.

I glanced across the room and saw Melina was playing with her new baby doll. "What about Melina's parents?"

"The church told me they die of tuberculosis." Glaucia shook her head. "I remember seeing them at Mass. They moved here from somewhere else, not sure. From what I heard, they were going to America but got stuck here. They didn't, eh, adapt well. When the church brought Melina, she was too weak, and I had to hand-feed her for weeks." She paused. "This is the longest I've ever seen her play." For the first time, Glaucia smiled, her face lighting up.

"How many people live in this neighborhood?" I asked.

"Hard to know; maybe thirty thousand. They call this Villa 31. It's the oldest around, started in the 1930s. We're right next to the wealthiest area of Buenos Aires, just blocks away from the Recoleta neighborhood."

"And what does Recoleta stand for?"

"Ah, you have not heard? People from all over the world visit the famous Recoleta; it is known for luxury hotels and high clothes, eh, fashion. The wealthiest people in all of Buenos Aires live there. They see us every day yet close their eyes to us every day. We don't even have mailboxes. All my mail goes to the church. If someone needs the police or an ambulance, it can take more than an hour to arrive." Glaucia's smile faded as she stood up, putting her hands to her waist, and looked around. "But at least we have some electricity and running water. Most people don't even have that."

I shook my head in disbelief. "Wow. I had no idea there were places like this in the world. I really appreciate what you said, though, about how they see you every day but close their eyes to you. I saw homeless people in Los Angeles and, now that I'm thinking about it, even in my hometown of Fayetteville. But here, it's seems so much worse."

"Yeah, there is poverty everywhere. Different, but people suffer all the same."

"Why isn't the government helping?"

"Some work is being done, but slow. More and more people come to the slums every day, it seems. No other place to live, but we try the best we can." Glaucia walked around the table, her hands still firmly planted on her hips.

"It's bad, but we are a strong people," Glaucia said. "We have to be, or we would not have survived. Our people are proud, loving, and determined. We want our kids going to school every day, hope that they make a better life, more opportunity. Many of the kids outside of this orphanage won't graduate. I read that only 30 percent from Villa 31 will get their high school diploma. The biggest problem is that everything is expensive. The inflation is high, and not enough jobs." Glaucia sat back down and faced me, her expression exhausted but still fiery.

I nodded and smiled. But I thought about what Heitor said.

Heitor told me he was going to let me go, but what if he changes his mind? What if he takes the money and still kills me?

I took a deep breath and decided to see if Glaucia was willing to help.

"I'm from America," I tell her. "I have wealthy friends. If you help me escape, I promise they'll provide you with enough money to buy a nice house and take care of all these children, but you have to help me now. Heitor says he will help, but has he? I promise I will."

Glaucia backed away, covering her ears and shaking her head. "Enough! Please, I cannot. I can't say no to Heitor. Now go away. You go away."

"All right, okay, I won't bring it up again," I said, giving Glaucia some space by standing near the window.

CHAPTER 21

Hummingbird Wings

Weeks went by, and I began to think Heitor's reward story was just a story. There was no ransom money. There would be no rescue. It became clear that my only chance to get out of this situation was to escape.

I looked out the front window, the only window in the house. A guard was always there. When it wasn't the bearded man, it was another equally ugly guy. When either one would see me, he'd either snarl like a dog or point the gun in my direction. Maybe I'd be in a bad mood too if I had to stand outside a building and guard some teenager day after day.

On this particular day, after the children had gone to school, I went to sit at the table with Glaucia.

"It's really nice that Heitor sends you money each month for the children. It seems like he can be a good man, when he wants to be."

"He is a good man," Glaucia said without hesitation.

I nodded, picking my words carefully so I didn't upset her. "Why do you think he got into drugs and kidnapping?"

Glaucia was quiet for several moments. I didn't think she was going to answer.

"We grew up together, dirt poor, no school. We took care of each other. No one else would. We dreamed to live in a nice place and raising families, no worrying about the next meal or whether we would be killed in the night. We had to grow tough, or we wouldn't survive. I have seen others take drugs and do crime when they feel there is no other way to live. Many here do the same to make quick money. If Heitor does that stuff, which I think he doesn't, it would be so he can take care of his mama and give money to me and others like me. Like, eh, what is he called? Robin Hood? Yes, giving us things we couldn't have."

Either Glaucia was delusional or in full denial. I decided I wouldn't say anything. It wouldn't do any good for me to challenge her about her benefactor.

"Heitor told me I'd be home two or three weeks ago. Do you think something went wrong? Have you heard anything?"

Glaucia folded her hands, avoiding my eyes. "I haven't heard from him, but I wish you were gone. I can't sleep. I can't eat. These little ones depend on me. You're putting us all at risk."

"I don't want to be here either," I said. "If you'd just help me get past that guy out there, I'd be gone for good."

Glaucia's cheeks turned red. "We talked about this. No more. I won't tell you again."

"I'm just saying, maybe you can create a diversion or distract him somehow. I can sneak out the door, and he'll never know I've gone."

Glaucia pursed her lips. "I'm losing patience with you. Bring it up again and ..." She stopped and shook her head. "If you leave, I die. Heitor will know I helped you, and he will kill anyone who betrays him."

I took a few moments before I nodded, stood up, and retreated to my blue mat, racking my brain on how I might get through to her.

I had been exercising every day, in little ways, and felt much better than when I arrived. The lacerations had turned to scars, and the deep, black bruises had all but disappeared.

My love for Melina had grown so much, and I spent practically every hour of the day and night next to her, playing, reading, and laughing. We had become inseparable, and I couldn't imagine life without her in it.

One afternoon when Glaucia had stepped outside, I rummaged through the desk drawers to see what I could find. My heart raced when I uncovered an article with my picture on the front page, which I quickly folded and tucked inside the front of my dress before speed-walking to the bathroom. I pulled out the clipping and tried my best to translate the words:

The search continues for Teagan McSherry, the seventeen-year-old girl who was abducted by the Black Jaguar gang in the Amazon rain forest. Miss McSherry and her brother Fionn had been filming a movie when she was kidnapped. Fionn survived a gunshot wound and returned home. Brazilian authorities are working in partnership with U.S. officials to conduct the search and have asked for the public's help in locating Miss McSherry.

The abduction has made international headlines, highlighting the exploitation and violence toward young children, affecting every region of the world. Authorities believe Miss McSherry may have been taken out of Brazil and have expanded their search across Latin America. A million-dollar reward is being offered for information leading to Miss McSherry's safe return. Anyone with information on her whereabouts is asked to contact Brazilian authorities or the U.S. Embassy.

I burst into tears of joy. They hadn't given up on me. The reward Heitor had mentioned was real, and best of all: Finn survived and made it home safely. I wiped at my wet cheeks and flushed, quickly returning to the sleeping mat, tucking the paper under it before Glaucia could see.

To pass the time, I asked Glaucia if I could teach the kids English after their regular school. Glaucia agreed and gave me a stack of big picture books she'd received from the church. So each afternoon, I would sit and read to them aloud in English, even teaching them some old camp songs I used to sing along the river. I could even hear Glaucia whistling along sometimes. Then the boys and girls would sit in a circle and take turns dancing and clapping in the middle.

Over the passing weeks, I fell in love with the little ones, and Melina began to feel like a daughter to me. I didn't even bat an eyelash when she called me Mamá.

Each night after Glaucia fell asleep, I would sneak to the window. I had begun to keep track of when Heitor's man left his position, going around the corner. There was the mean man during the day, and a slightly less mean-looking man at night. Maybe he left his post to relieve himself or have a smoke.

I was trying to see if there were a pattern, thinking this knowledge would help me to sneak out of the house if I timed it right. My biggest concern was Melina. I had grown so close to her that leaving her behind was almost unthinkable, but I wasn't sure I could orchestrate an escape for both of us. The dilemma tore me up.

One day after I had prepared the children's lunches, I sat and watched the orphans as they ate. Although I'd had them wash their hands, there were still streaks of dirt on their faces, arms, legs, and feet.

What future do they have here? It was not their choice to be born under these dire circumstances. Will they be disadvantaged and oppressed their entire lives? What will happen to their children, should they have any? They were so young, so precious, so innocent.

When the children were finished, I had them run off to play, and the overwhelming sadness and helplessness came back again, but this time, it wasn't just sadness for myself.

I got a piece of paper and a pencil, sat down at the table, and began to write.

If I could fly on a hummingbird's wings,
darting in and out, what joy this would bring.
But alas, here I am in Buenos Aires' famous slum.
No walls, no water, no power, just love.
My "improvised" shelter, the best a mom can do.
30 percent inflation, little education, and food.
Just across the concrete, the wealthy are alive and well,
the gloating, the cameras, the sound of cemetery bells.
Please look at my home, thin roof, and no wall.
You can easily see me, but not see me at all.
They call us transients as we "chose" this life.
How convenient for you to wash us with spite.
You have made me so small, for this I am thankful,
to fly on hummingbird's wings, so safe, so tranquil.

I set the pencil down knowing I'd need the wings of a thousand hummingbirds to rescue all of the children.

I had grown up in poverty, but poverty took on a whole different meaning in this place. It's as if nobody knew this place existed.

How ignorant I've been about the world, I thought. *Why is everyone silent? Do people of means know about this place? If they do, where are they? No one—no human being—could stand idly by, live day in and day out without helping in some measure.*

Could they?

CHAPTER 22

The Rooftop

I had worked it all out in my head. The guard left his chair shortly after midnight every morning. He was gone between ten and fifteen minutes: plenty of time to sneak out. I decided that night would be the night. Waiting wasn't going to make it better.

But I was anxious, pacing back and forth in the kitchen with Melina snuggled against my hip, my only comfort.

"What is it? What's wrong with you today?" Glaucia asked as she sliced vegetables for dinner.

I glanced over to her and tried to arrange my face into something like nonchalance, trying to act calm. I guess I would make a horrible criminal.

"Oh, nothing … just bored."

"Hmm," Glaucia said.

Perhaps it was my heightened senses, but it sounded like she was suspicious.

"Take a nap or read a book to the children or something. All the walking around is getting on my nerves."

Just then, there was a banging on the door. It wasn't a knock, it was a pounding, and there was only one person who did that.

Before I could react—and I'm not even sure what I would have done—Glaucia walked over and opened the door.

Heitor barreled in, brushing past the old woman, not bothering to hug her, much less say hi. He pointed a fat finger at me.

"Get over here, bitch. It's time I get my fucking money."

"What happened?" Glaucia asked, wringing her hands. "Did the deal fall through?"

Heitor turned toward her, his face angry, which wasn't much different than his normal face. "The deal's gone to shit. My cousin Lucia went to relay information on the drop-off point where they could find this bitch and collect the reward money, but the damn police and some US officials detained her as soon as she got there. Yes, the deal's gone to shit."

Glaucia placed her hand over her mouth and slumped on a kitchen chair. "It can't be; it just can't be so. Tell me you are joking."

Heitor looked at me with pure hatred. "Elias, my man on the inside, called me from Brazil; he found out from another insider that Lucia told them where Tia is located. They could be here any minute."

"What about my new orphanage? Are you still going to help

me?" Glaucia asked, pleading, pressing her hands together as if in prayer.

"Just keep your fuckin' mouth shut. I've got another plan to collect that million. It will take another few weeks."

Another few weeks? I thought. *No!*

As Heitor approached me, Melina started to scream, tightening her arms around my neck in terror.

"Drop the kid," Heitor yelled. "Let's go."

I panicked. I didn't know what to do, so I yelled back. "I'm not leaving without her. You can't make me; kill me now if you have to, but I'm not leaving without Melina."

On one hand, I knew it was a stupid thing to demand, but deep down, I also knew it was the only chance to stay together.

Glaucia rushed over and tried to take Melina away. "No! You cannot take her," she screamed.

She tore at my arms, almost causing me to drop the child.

"I'm not leaving without her," I screamed as loud as I could, jerking away in the opposite direction.

"Fine! I don't care. Let's go," Heitor said, latching onto my arm and yanking the two of us out the door.

I held onto Melina as best I could as we were pulled into the sunshine. I turned to see Glaucia in tears, arms outstretched, begging us to return.

Heitor stuck his hand out, holding something. "Put this on," he said.

I took the baseball cap and did my best to pull it over my hair with one hand.

Melina had stopped screaming, down to a low whimper.

The bearded man was gone.

I looked down different alleys as we passed, hoping to see a rescue team or the police.

"Don't look at anyone," Heitor said. "Don't talk to anyone."

We walked through back alleys, one after another, crisscrossing dirt paths littered with garbage. Brick, tin, cardboard, and plywood shacks surrounded us on all sides. Every so often, a motorcycle would zoom by. Dogs so skinny that their bones protruded from their bodies trotted through the streets. Occasionally, children ran by, their faces smudged with dirt and their bare feet caked with mud that would never quite wash completely off.

Teenagers lined the corner of the street, one of them wearing a faded Bruce Springsteen T-shirt. He turned on a small radio; cumbia music filled the air, and several kids immediately began to dance. We passed a pregnant woman hanging clothes on a rope that was stretched across two old pipes before stopping at a two-story structure with red paint streaked across the front. Along the side of the building was a makeshift ladder made from old plywood and rusty nails.

Heitor gestured at it with his gun, signaling for us to climb it.

It wasn't easy. As I made my way up the rickety ladder, I placed my hands on Melina's back to steady her, concentrating on one step at a time. Finally, I got to the top. I was kind of surprised Heitor didn't yell at me to hurry up, but I guess he didn't want me to fall on his head.

On the roof, Heitor led us inside the small structure; it was like a shed. A blast of humid air saturated with stale cigarette smoke and the yeasty musk of old beer fumes hit me. The room was lit by one bare bulb dangling a few inches below the low ceiling. An old man with a few strands of gray hair plastered across his head jumped up from a small chair.

"Heitor!"

"Here's the girl, Julio; she wouldn't leave without this other one."

Julio had stained and broken teeth, his cheeks scarred with deep pockmarks. He looked to be about seventy, but I suspected he was actually much younger.

"They're raiding Glaucia's. You need to keep them here until I can come up with another plan to get that money."

Great. Just another holding place.

There was a worn mattress with random splotches of yellow and brown that looked even dirtier than the ones discarded on the side of the road. A lopsided foldout table had been set up in the middle of the room, with a cooler and small grill propped on top. A mass of dirty blankets were strewn across the wooden floor, and there was an open door to the left that led to what looked like another small room.

Julio pointed to a makeshift kitchen table and motioned for us to sit down and eat. Rolls, cheese, salami, and a few olives were set out on a chipped square plate. I was a bit nauseated from the smells but tried to eat some of the stale bread and cheese. I encouraged Melina to take a few bites, but she refused.

Instead of eating, she started to cry. I lifted her up onto my lap and cradled her. "It's okay, honey. We're gonna be okay."

Heitor bent down. "Do you *ever* shut up?" he growled at Melina. Then he stood and handed Julio a wad of rolled-up bills.

Frustrated, I got up, lifting Melina up.

"I need to use the bathroom," I said.

Julio took a small flashlight from the corner.

"Come with me," he said.

I followed Julio to a windowless room in the back. He turned on the flashlight and handed it to me.

"Here," Julio said, kicking a piece of plywood to the side to expose a small hole. The room instantly filled with the fumes of bodily waste. I fought back a gag.

"You'll get used to it," Julio said with a grin. Then he left.

When we returned, Julio pointed to the blankets in the corner and motioned for us to sit down. We walked over, and I set Melina down. I saw a pair of handcuffs attached to the wall.

I turned and looked at Heitor. "Don't leave us here. Please," I said in a flat voice. "They're not going to give you a dime if I'm dead."

In a flash, he came at me, grabbing at the nape of my neck, the feeling of his thick fingers causing me to recoil.

"Oh, believe me, my little bebé; I'll get that money. You may not be in good shape by the time they find you, but they'll find you, and I'll get my money."

Coughing, I returned to the blankets and sat down beside Melina, trying to keep her calm.

"*¿Agua?*" Melina asked as Julio bent to handcuff one of my wrists to the wall.

Once he was done shackling me, he returned with a crumpled

plastic bottle filled halfway with brownish water that I didn't want to touch, much less drink.

Heitor went to the door. "Don't let her leave," he told Julio, "and don't touch her. She needs to be alive if we're going to see any money. I'll be back when I can." And he left.

Was I relieved or worried?

The next morning, my body was stiff and sore from sleeping on the ragged plywood floor. Melina was confused and wanted to go home, crying inconsolably while sitting on my lap.

"We'll be leaving soon," I whispered. "But you need to be a good girl until then and stay quiet, okay?"

Melina pulled back and looked me in the face, her dark eyes huge and solemn as she nodded.

Julio released me from the handcuff so I could eat and use the bathroom, bringing over stale rolls, jam, and coffee. The room was dark, with just a sliver of faint light coming in from the small open window.

Julio was quiet. He just sat in a chair, staring at us, scowling.

The coffee tasted sour, and I wondered whether it was even coffee or just hot water boiled with a tangle of rotting leaves. After breakfast, Julio ordered us to our blankets and secured the handcuff around my wrist again.

Days turned into nights, and nights into days. I lost track of time but guessed we had been prisoners in that tiny room for at least two weeks. Maybe longer.

I felt guilty. I shouldn't have brought Melina. It didn't make anything better, and it made Melina worse. The little one was disappearing right in front of my eyes.

We both had severe diarrhea, and our appetites disappeared. Julio seemed to know we were in trouble and brought a fresh bakery roll and some good meat, but nausea set in, and we had to push the food away.

My prayers became more and more frequent, more fervent. I prayed for just about everybody I ever met, and I began to realize my words, no matter how sincere, sometimes didn't make much sense.

Finally, Heitor came through the door. I didn't know how much time had passed. I wasn't sure if it was daytime or night, and I wasn't sure if I should have been happy or scared he was there.

He spoke with Julio, and by the tone, it didn't sound good. He walked over to us and lifted our chins, one in his left hand, one in his right.

"What is this?" Heitor shouted, leaving us to smack Julio upside his head with an open palm. "You tell me how I can sell girls that look like *shit!*" Heitor took the key from the table, unlocked my handcuffs, and sat me up. "Walk over here to the light."

I got up on shaky legs and followed Heitor to the lantern. He lifted up my shirt and felt my ribs. I didn't even care. He put his meaty palm on my forehead.

"Go lay down," Heitor said.

"I have to use the bathroom first," I said, retrieving the flashlight and walking around him, avoiding all eye contact.

"I'll be back tomorrow," I heard Heitor say in Spanish. "Think you can keep them alive until then?"

I kept the bathroom door cracked open, listening to the men's hushed conversation.

"Did the deal go through?" Julio asked. "Are they making the trade?"

Heitor grunted. "It's taking too long, and they're asking too many fucking questions. I'm taking them to another place in the meantime."

No. Not another brothel. I'd rather die before I went back, and I won't let anything happen to Melina.

But you can't do both. You can't die and save Melina.

I inched as far as I could by the bathroom door without being seen.

"What's taking so long in there?" Julio bellowed.

"I need time," I called. "I've got the runs."

I waited for Heitor to leave.

Once he had, I went to Melina on the blankets.

"Lock it," Julio said.

I slipped my wrist into the handcuff but didn't latch it all the way.

Julio gave me a vague glance, grunted, then grabbed a bottle of tequila and ambled outside.

I waited a couple of minutes.

Melina laid her head down on the blanket and closed her eyes. There wasn't anything else to do.

I removed the handcuff and went over to the grill in the corner that hadn't been used while we were there. I picked it up and went to the wall by the front door. On the other nights, Julio would take his time. I could be standing there a while.

CHAPTER 23

The Lighted Path

When the door finally opened and Julio entered, he was drunker than a skunk, mumbling incoherently. He didn't see me. I didn't give him the chance, lifting the grill and swinging it as hard as I could into the back of his head. There was a loud cracking noise, not unlike breaking dry twigs over a knee. Julio dropped like a sack of mud. With the little strength I had left, I dragged him to the blanket and handcuffed his wrist to the wall.

My arms were shaking uncontrollably as I scooped up Melina, whose eyes were wide with fright. I headed for the door, picking up the flashlight on the way out. I got to the rickety ladder, peering over the edge to make sure no one was coming up. I carefully stepped down, rung by rung. When we made it to the bottom, I could feel my heart pounding. I ran down the pitch-black dirt path with Melina's little legs wrapped around my hip. My legs burned as I tried to head in the direction of the skyscrapers, but I couldn't see past the rows and rows of ramshackle buildings.

Dogs barked, howling into the night, and I heard occasional cries from babies as we ran past darkened dwellings.

At one point, I thought I heard footsteps behind us, so I ducked behind a brick wall and held Melina closely, breathing hard. I tried to listen over the sound of my heart beating heavily in my ears.

Minutes later, when all was quiet, I cautiously stepped out from behind the wall and jogged, twisting and angling down the endless maze of alleyways that made up this part of Buenos Aires.

After running nonstop for about half an hour, with no noticeable progress, I sat Melina down along the dusty path and cried desperate tears. My emotions and body were spent. *I can't do this alone, dear Lord. Please show me the way.*

At that moment, Melina's head jerked up, and her body pulled away from mine. "Look, Mama, look," she said, tugging on the hem of my shirt and pointing down the dark path.

I wiped away tears with the back of my hand and looked up. At first, I didn't see anything. It was pitch-black in all directions, except for a faint light swaying back and forth and back and forth in a distant doorway.

I stood, feeling a warm breeze and a sense of resounding peace that almost sent me to my knees.

The swaying light was gentle, yet mesmerizing, and for a brief instant, I could have sworn I heard a faint melody, a chiming of bells that was perfectly aligned with the back and forth motion of the light. Maybe I was delusional from fever.

In another sign, the clouds above parted to unveil a full moon, its soft white light beaming down to illuminate the path.

I stood and took Melina's hand. Then we walked, my heart no longer pounding, my arms and legs no longer trembling from fatigue.

We approached slowly and got close enough to see two older men dressed in white tank tops and a young boy in a Spider-man T-shirt sitting at a small table a few feet from the entrance.

We stopped just outside the doorway.

"*Niños, vengan,*" one of the men said. (Children, come in.)

I realized this was a home, about the size of a small trailer and sparsely furnished, and a darkened room that jutted off toward the back.

I picked Melina up and walked across the threshold, not wanting to go too far in case my instincts had betrayed me.

One of the men cocked his head. "*¿Qué pasa?*" he asked.

"*¿Inglés?*" I asked.

He smiled, but it was a careful smile. "A leetle."

"We need help, and I'm not sure where to begin," I said, feeling faint.

"Come," the man said in a gentle voice. "Tell me."

"We were kidnapped and held prisoner; we escaped." I paused, trying to focus on what was important. "This little one ... has a fever. We need, please, we desperately need your help."

The man stood, bumping his head on the low-hanging light fixture that hung from the ceiling. It began to swing back and forth.

"Ouch," he said, grabbing his head with one hand and rubbing it with his palm.

I turned my head toward the outside and saw how the light swayed back and forth, illuminating the path I had just walked.

"Keep banging my head on that damn thing," he said with a smile. "Come sit by me. Let me take a look at you."

He was a giant, six and a half, seven feet tall, and there was something familiar about him. And I noticed how his accent had mostly slipped away, still there, but not as pronounced.

I know him, I thought.

His face was pock-marked, and his straight brown hair was cropped and tidy. He had large, gentle eyes.

I have seen those eyes before.

I searched my memory. Could he have been one of Heitor's men? One who watched while I was raped? Someone who worked for Cristiano?

"Please, have a seat," he said, pointing to empty chairs beside the table. "This is my brother and his son. And who are you?" the man asked as he opened a cooler and pulled out a pair of water bottles.

I took the bottles, and we sat. I placed Melina in my lap. My heart picked up speed as I wracked my brain to remember this man. Did I just put us back into danger?

"I'm Tia, and this is my daughter, Melina." I twisted the cap from one of the bottles and offered it to Melina, who quickly began to drink.

The man's eyes twinkled. "You look too young to have a child."

"Well …" I paused. "I adopted her. But that's not important. She's really sick and desperately needs to see a doctor."

The man was staring at me. I wasn't sure if he was deciding to help, if he was thinking I was too much trouble, if I could put them into danger, or if he could make some money off me. Whatever he was thinking, it was obvious he was sizing me up.

I waited. He continued to stare and then he frowned.

"You look so familiar to me. You have such unique eyes. I feel like I've seen them before."

"I have a feeling that I've seen you before too." I knew that was a risky thing to say, but one way or the other, he probably saw me on the news.

I looked over at the other man. He was a little older, and his eyes were tired and distant, as if he didn't understand a word we were saying. The boy in the Spider-man shirt had laid his head on the table.

The big man squinted, and then his eyes widened.

"You were with two other people, but not this little one. It was a young man and a young woman, both your age."

He closed his eyes, as if going into a trance to focus his memory.

"I was laying down; you came up and scared me. I sat up and scared you. Yes, I remember." His eyes were lit up. "Yes, I remember now. You were the girl who helped me in California."

I gasped. *It couldn't be … was it?*

"Yes," I said, excitement growing. "I remember. Javier."

"Javier! That's right," he said, bellowing with laughter. The boy lifted his head from the table and looked around, confused.

"I can't believe it's you," I said. "I just can't believe it's you."

I felt tears well up in my eyes as I reached over and hugged his neck. I stayed there in the warmth of his neck until he gently pulled me back.

"Who kidnapped you?" Javier asked with a serious look in his eyes.

It took me several seconds for me to catch my breath and be able to talk.

"It was a man named Heitor."

Javier and the other man glanced at each other. The boy's head came up, and he gasped.

"Do you know him?"

"Yes, unfortunately." Javier slapped his big hand on the table and then snapped his fingers. "You're the girl we've been reading about. On TV. Were you in Brazil? Was your brother shot?"

"Yes, yes. That's me."

"Okay, okay." He stood up, looking nervous. "Excuse me, let me make a phone call. I'll be back."

He went outside. I could hear him talking, but I couldn't make out the words.

I drank water, feeling like it cleansed me. I closed my eyes and took deep breaths.

Could it be over? Could it?

I'd had my hopes raised so many times, in big and little ways, that I couldn't trust that feeling. But it was the only thing I had at the moment.

Javier returned. He looked concerned. He closed the door and sat down.

"It will be soon," he said.

"What will be soon?" I asked.

"They will come to get you."

I tensed. People coming to get me had not turned out well.

Javier sensed my tension and smiled gently. "These are good people. They are my friends. They will be your friends."

It wasn't long before I could hear the sound of motorcycles growing louder, and in seconds, they were pulling up beside the house.

"Let's get you out of here," Javier said as he helped us to our feet, leading us to the door.

We walked outside, and I scanned the street, expecting Heitor to pull up.

"Where are we going?" I asked, wanting to trust Javier but having learned the hard way that people's intentions weren't always reflected in the words they said.

Javier squeezed my shoulder gently. "We're going to the US Embassy. You'll be safe there."

The motorcycle ride was almost as scary as running blindly through the streets. But we managed to hang on: Javier in front, Melina in the middle, and me on the back.

When I caught sight of the American flag waving outside a big white building, I began to realize I was truly being led to safety.

Javier parked the motorcycle along the side of the road and walked us to the small security kiosk out front.

"We need to talk with someone," Javier said. "This is the girl in the news who was kidnapped."

"Teagan McSherry," I said.

We were taken inside and led into a small conference room. A man in a crisp uniform came in with blankets, hot tea, water, and cookies studded with chocolate chips.

"I will stay with you," Javier said, taking a seat across the table. "You helped me. I will help you."

"Thank you," was all I could say.

At least thirty minutes had passed before a group of people entered the room. A tall older woman with brown hair in a bun came up to me and crouched down to meet my eyes. She wore a gray business suit with a white-collared shirt and short high heels. Her face was pale, and the lines around her eyes gave her the appearance she hadn't slept for days.

"Miss McSherry, I'm US Ambassador Spiegel, and this is Commander Souza," she said nodding to a shorter dark-haired man wearing a crisp khaki police uniform and combat boots. "We've been searching for you for a long time. You're safe now, and we're going to get you home as soon as possible."

I leaned my forehead against the top of Melina's head, sighing in audible relief, now believing we were finally safe.

"But I must tell you, Miss McSherry," Commander Souza said, "that time is critical to catching those who took you. I need as many details as you can recall about where you were last and who held you captive."

I took a deep breath and closed my eyes.

"A man named Heitor kidnapped me from the Amazon and took me to a lot of different places, including a brothel about thirty minutes from here. I only stayed there for a few nights before he came back. He heard about the million-dollar reward and wanted to keep me safe until he could get that money. So he took me to an orphanage run by a woman named Glaucia. That's where I came across this little one," I said, kissing Melina on the cheek.

I took another deep breath and sighed.

"Then about two or three weeks ago, he found out that the police were going to raid the orphanage to rescue me, so he took us to Julio's. The last place I was held, the place we escaped from, was Julio's, on a rooftop."

"So we were right about Glaucia after all. Sounds like we missed you by just a few minutes," the commander said with a frown.

"Yeah, he dragged us out of there quickly. There's a guy named Elias who works for Heitor and also for the Brazilian police, I think. But he's the guy who warned Heitor about his camp being raided the night I was kidnapped, the same guy who warned Heitor that the police were on their way to the orphanage. He had to be one of the reasons you never found me."

The commander's face turned bright red, and he turned to one of his men, whispering something in his ear. The man then turned and rushed out of the door.

"We know Heitor but haven't seen him in months." He turned to Javier. "Do you know this guy, Julio?"

Javier took a few moments to answer. "Yes, I know Julio. I can take you there if you like."

"Let's go," Commander Souza said. "Maybe we can catch Heitor."

"Wait," I cut in, raising a hand in the air. "I need to tell you something else."

"We're listening," the commander said.

"After I was kidnapped, I was taken to an old hotel somewhere in this city. Heitor put me and other kidnapped boys and girls up for auction. My friend Marcelo and I were sold to a brothel. Marcelo is still there. It's about thirty minutes away, best I could tell. It's a three-story building, and I remember a sign in the front that read 'Emanuel's Auto Repair and Body Shop,' but in Spanish. The letters were bright red, and there was a strip club next to it, with a picture of a half-naked woman dancing on a pole."

The ambassador turned to the commander. "This is happening in your backyard, Commander. You need to get them out tonight."

"If Marcelo's still alive … well, he won't be for long. You have to promise me you will go tonight. *Promise* me it will be tonight," I said urgently.

"We'll do everything we can," the commander said in a confident voice.

I turned to Javier and took his hand. "I'll never forget what you did for me," I said. "There are no words to express how thankful I am. You saved us."

He let go of my hand and opened his arms wide, taking me in, hugging me.

"Little angel, *you* saved me," Javier said, "and I will never forget that." He broke away and disappeared through the door.

Ambassador Spiegel touched my arm. "Let's get you two cleaned up and fed. I've sent for a doctor to take a look at you."

CHAPTER 24

floating on Clouds

I held Melina as we went up the elevator with the ambassador to the second floor of the US Embassy. We walked down a long carpeted corridor and took a left into what appeared to be a clinic of sorts. The room had four twin beds with silver guard rails on the sides, and each bed had a stool beside it with rollers on the feet. A beige curtain was pulled closed across a long window that spanned the width of the far wall.

We were greeted by a lady in her late twenties, wearing light green scrubs and white sneakers. Her blonde hair was pulled back tightly in a bow, highlighting her freckled face and wide smile.

"May I?" she asked me, holding her arms out for Melina. "We're all ready for you, sweetie."

I held Melina out, and the nurse lifted her away.

"Mama! Mama!"

I reached over to reassure her, and Melina settled down.

"I'm Nurse Terri," she said to Melina. "What's your name?"

Of course, Melina only looked at me and remained silent.

"You're in good hands," the ambassador said. "I've sent for a doctor, and he should be in soon. I'll be back in a little while."

"While I check out this sweet one, do you want to take a shower?" Terri asked.

"Do I?" I replied. "I'd love it."

She pointed at a side room. "There's a nightgown and robe on the wall," the nurse said.

I walked into a gleaming bathroom, smelling of bleach. Compared to everything else I'd encountered, it was like the most charming perfume.

✺

I admit I probably took a much longer shower than I should have, but it was so soothing. When I came out, Nurse Terri took Melina into the room, giving her a bath in a narrow tub.

I sat in one of the side chairs, feeling clean and safe for the first time in … I don't know how long.

This can't possibly be real.

I nearly fell asleep. Maybe I dozed off, until the nurse returned with Melina all fresh and clean in her little nightgown and robe. She laid Melina in a bed and then pointed at the one next to it.

"This one's yours. I'll be starting IVs because you're so dehydrated. I'll also need to draw some blood. I'll do Melina's first; would you like to help?"

I went on the other side of the bed and smoothed Melina's

hair back while the nurse inserted the needle. I expected her to cry, but she barely made a sound. That made me worry a little.

When Melina was set, I climbed into the next bed. Nurse Terri took blood and inserted the IV. After taking my temperature and blood pressure, she left, and this time I dozed off.

Sometime later, an older man wearing white scrubs with a badge—Doctor Bradley, MD—was touching my shoulder. I jerked awake.

"Sorry," he said. "How are you feeling?"

He was a tall, slender man with salt-and-pepper crew cut hair. He had a fatherly smile.

Nurse Terri handed him a chart. "They both have very high fevers and are dehydrated and malnourished. I've rushed the blood samples to the lab."

After Dr. Bradley checked us, he said, "I'll be back in the morning. Try to eat something and get some sleep, ladies. You're both going to be as good as new."

After having bowls of soup and saltine crackers, the nurse dimmed the lights and turned on a small radio playing soft music intermixed with the sound of waves and light raindrops.

"I'll be sitting over here. If you need anything, just let me know," the nurse said in a gentle voice.

I got out of bed and kissed Melina. "God has blessed us tonight, baby girl," I said softly. "Sleep well."

Melina wrapped her arms around my neck and smiled, her first real smile in so many weeks.

I slid between the sheets once more and felt like I was floating on clouds. It was all just too good to be true. I felt a rush of uncontrollable emotions bubble up inside of me like waves crashing upon the shore of my heart. I buried my face in the pillow and cried until no more tears could be found. It was over. It was finally over, and we were alive.

"Dear Lord, thank you. Thank you for taking care of us," I whispered and then succumbed to exhaustion like never before, sinking beneath the comforting blackness that overtook me.

I woke to the smell of oatmeal and toast, and was pleasantly surprised that my stomach didn't clench in nausea the way it had when we were captive at Julio's. I glanced over to see Melina curled up in bed, her thumb nestled in her mouth as if she were an infant again.

"Good morning, Tia," the ambassador said as she walked through the doorway. "You look better than last night. Did you sleep okay?"

"Yeah, I did. Thank you."

"This is Casey," the ambassador said, indicating the woman standing next to her.

Casey appeared to be in her late forties, with short brown hair cut in a bob. Her face was lightly powered and absent of color, compared to the ambassador's rosy cheeks and matted red lipstick. She wore slacks, a button-up white shirt, and a small navy scarf tied around her neck.

"She's my second in command," Ambassador Spiegel said,

"and will be flying back with you to Washington in a few hours. She'll take good care of you and make sure you have everything you need."

"Hi, nice to meet you," I said. "So we're going home today?"

"Well, to Washington DC. From there, we'll get you home," Ambassador Spiegel said with a smile. "But you'll be staying in Washington for a bit while you recover. We need to monitor you."

Dr. Bradley knocked on the door and walked over to my bedside.

"How are you doing this morning?" he asked as he placed a palm over my forehead.

"Better, thanks."

"You're both still very weak. I'm concerned you might have parasitic viruses as well. I've already talked to the doctor where you will be staying in Washington. Her name is Dr. Patel. When you get there, she'll do a full physical checkup on you. In the meantime, I want you to both continue drinking as much water as possible and to eat when you feel able."

"Is Melina going to be okay?" I asked, concerned by the lack of color in her face.

"Yes, you'll both get better once you start your treatment. It's going to be a lengthy process though," Dr. Bradley said.

I nodded. "Okay. Thank you."

After the doctor left the room, the ambassador said, "Tia, there is something I need to tell you. It won't be easy. Once you are settled in the hospital, a team of investigators will be interviewing you. They need to record everything you remember from the time you were kidnapped to the time you were rescued. Like you, many people, young adults and children, in particular, have been abducted and sold into slavery. It's called human trafficking."

"Oh … okay," I said, rubbing my temples. I was getting a headache and didn't like where this conversation was going. All at once, I wanted nothing more than to fall back into the oblivion of sleep, the darkness closing over me. I wanted that darkness. It became important.

"I realize it will be difficult for you to tell and retell your story, but it's critical for us to learn as much as we can about the people who did this to you. Once we collect the information, we'll work with the appropriate South American agencies and try to arrest those who've hurt you and so many others. And hopefully rescue them."

"Of course. Yes, I'll try to remember and help as much as I can. And what about Marcelo? Have you heard anything? Heitor? I'm afraid he'll come looking for me."

"I have a meeting with the commander in a few hours, so I should hear more about Marcelo. And Heitor …" She waved her hand dismissively. "Don't worry about him anymore. You're safe now. We'll keep you updated as soon as we learn anything."

"Please just find Marcelo."

"We're doing everything we can, I promise. Let's talk about Melina for a minute."

"Okay. What about her?"

"We need to get her back to her family now, yes? She's not exactly yours, is she?"

Panic roared through me. I threw the blankets back and tried to climb out of bed.

Nurse Terri gently took my shoulder and pressed me back down onto the mattress.

I screamed, "No. No. You can't take her away from me. I'm the only one she has. I'm her mama now."

I lost control, the emotion bubbling up beneath the surface threatening to overflow. My eyes blazed with anger, and I simultaneously began to cry.

"Okay, all right," the ambassador said. "It's all right. Please, just explain what's going on."

Eventually, I felt calm enough to talk.

"I told you a little bit yesterday, but Heitor took me from the brothel to an orphanage run by a woman named Glaucia. She was taking care of about fifteen kids. None of them had families. When I first got there, Melina ran up to me. She thought I was her mama. Since then, she's been with me day and night. Glaucia told me that her parents died of tuberculosis, that she had no other family members. I'm her family now."

I looked from Ambassador Spiegel to Nurse Terri and back again. "It's real simple," I stated. "I'm not leaving without her."

The ambassador stood up and stared quietly at Melina. "Okay, Tia, we have time to sort this out. You understand that this woman may have been mistaken? We don't know."

She turned to Casey. "In the meantime, let's pull together the asylum refugee protection paperwork so that Tia can take Melina back with her. Tia, I can't make any promises, but because we are dealing with a dangerous cartel that will be searching for you and the child, I can make the argument to get her out of the country with you. We will have to do a thorough background check on Melina and ensure she doesn't have any living family members, that we can locate anyway. It will take about a month if we expedite the process, but you should hear something by the time you leave for West Virginia."

"Thank you so much," I said, falling back on the pillow in relief.

"Go ahead and get dressed. We need to leave for the airport now," the ambassador said. "Ready to get back to the States?"

"Yes," I said. "More than ready."

CHAPTER 25

DC

We slept most of the way on the flight to Washington on the ambassador's plane, landing at what appeared to be a military base. When we exited the plane, I had Melina on my hip, walking slowly down the jetway and onto the tarmac. I froze in denial or disbelief. *I was finally home.*

Standing in a semicircle, they were all there—all of them—and I could hardly believe it. Wes was waving, Paddy wearing the widest grin I had ever seen, and next to him was Finn, looking just the same. And there was Uncle Harold, eyes filled with tears.

"Tia!" someone shouted, followed by a chorus of people calling out my name. I looked around to see what must have been hundreds of people gathered behind a rope, some holding signs that said "Welcome Home" or "We Love You!"

I just stood there, mesmerized. Tears burst from my eyes like a fountain.

Finn rushed up and put his arms around me. "I'm so sorry," he said. I'm so sorry I left you. I missed you so much."

And with that, Wes and Paddy were running up, Father Harold just behind.

"God has brought you home to us," Father Harold said, tears streaming down his face.

We finally broke up our group hug, though I didn't want it to end.

"And who's this little one?" Father Harold asked.

I noticed Father Harold was noticeably thinner than when we had left for California. His bright blue eyes seemed to have faded a bit, but his smile was still bright.

"This is Melina, everyone," I said as the little girl stared at them shyly. "She's an orphan I met in Buenos Aires, but she's going to be a part of our family now."

"Hi there, Miss Melina," Finn said, reaching out to shake her hand.

Melina hid her face against my neck.

"She'll warm up to you," I said.

"We've got plenty of time for that," Finn said. "I missed you so much, Sis."

"Good Lord, turn around," I said. "I wanna get a look at your back, where you were shot. You look fantastic, but are you okay?"

"Fit as a fiddle," he said, "just plumb worried 'bout you is all."

I pointed to the crowd gathered behind the fence. "What's all this about?"

"I'll tell you all 'bout it after you rest up a while," Finn said, as we headed for the parking lot.

"Look," Wes said, pointing toward the east.

I turned and saw off in the distance a magnificent rainbow spanning from one end of the earth to the other. I'd never seen a rainbow so complete or so brilliantly colored.

When we arrived at the hospital, more nurses were waiting with wheelchairs to bring Melina and me up to our room. It was filled with baskets of flowers and balloons.

"This is all too much," I said, feeling overwhelmed by the cards and gifts. "I don't know how I can thank everyone."

One of the nurses said, "This is just a fraction of what you received. Your uncle asked us to donate the majority of them to other patients and to the hospital chapels. We kept all the cards though. I put them in your drawer next to your bed."

"Thank you," I said. "What's the third bed for?"

"Your brother's idea," Casey said as she glanced up and smiled at Finn. "He said he wasn't going to leave your side."

"I'm so glad," I said as I laid Melina in her bed.

Casey stepped closer, and I noticed she was holding a stack of paperwork. "Tomorrow morning, we want you to talk to our investigators. It's important they speak with you as soon as possible, while everything is still fresh in your memory."

I swallowed, glancing at Finn, who winked and gave me an encouraging nod.

"Yeah. I want to help any way I can," I said.

"Do you want your uncle or Finn to come with you?"

I thought of the shame and humiliation during the horrific events I'd experienced, and my cheeks burned. I wondered whether I could describe such things in front of my family, or if I could even say them out loud at all.

"Um, I'll let you know," I said, looking away.

There was a knock on the door, and a petite lady in her forties with large brown eyes, soft pink cheeks, and clear lip gloss on her thin lips came through the door. Her long black hair was pulled back tightly in a ponytail.

"Hi, Tia, I'm Dr. Patel. I'll be taking care of you over the next few weeks," she said as she shook my hand. She turned and laid her hand on Melina's hand. "Hi, sweet girl. We're going to get you all better."

I liked her immediately.

"Today, our nurses will be taking some blood samples and will be putting you and Melina back on an IV for a day or two. I understand from Dr. Bradley that you may have a virus, so after we run some tests, we'll be giving you some medication."

"Okay, that all sounds great. I just want Melina to get better. She just has to …"

"She's in good hands," Dr. Patel said. "Also, starting tomorrow, you and Melina will be seeing a therapist who specializes in trauma and grief. You two have been through a lot, from what I understand, and your mental and emotional health are equally important as your physical health.

I nodded, not wanting to remember how broken I felt every day since I'd been raped.

Dr. Patel said, "Now, let's take a look at you both. Gentleman, can we have the room for a few minutes?"

My brothers and uncle decided to head down to the cafeteria.

I was relieved when the examination was over and my family returned. Melina was sound asleep.

Wes came forward, holding a brown paper bag. "Here, Tia. I made this for you."

"Look at you and how tall you grew this summer," I said. "And look at all this crazy blond hair of yours; it's getting really long. I bet Father Harold's been on you about that."

Uncle winked and nodded in agreement.

"I guess I missed your birthday," I said. "Twelve already, practically a young man. We'll have to have a party when I'm home and settled."

I reached into the paper bag, feeling something cool and smooth. I pulled out a wooden doe, beautifully carved in intricate detail, with his head held high. "This is stunning, Wes. You carved this all by yourself?"

Wes grinned shyly. "Yeah, I started whittling right after you went missing. It helped pass the time."

"Kept him out of my hair, that's for sure," Paddy said.

"I absolutely love it," I said. "Thank you, Wes."

"I made you something too," Paddy said, brimming with pride.

"It looks like you shot up a few inches, and I missed your birthday too," I added. "I'm going to have to make up for that. So, I'm excited to see: what did you make me?"

"Well, I don't have it here because it was too big to bring, but remember Mama's old rocking chair? I resurfaced it for you and placed it in your bedroom; it's good as new now."

"Fantastic," I said, my eyes filling up with tears. "You two are the best brothers I could ever have. Thank you both. I love you so much."

For the remainder of the day, I visited with my brothers and listened to all the things they'd been up to while I was away. It was nice to hear about their school, friends, and hobbies, and for a little while, I was able to pretend that nothing out of the ordinary had happened.

I was glad they didn't ask about what had happened while I was gone, but I supposed Uncle Harold had told them not to ask unless I brought it up. I wouldn't have known what to say, anyway.

Melina slept for most of the day, holding tightly to a new baby doll Finn had gone out and bought her.

Wes and Paddy were getting noticeably fidgety and hungry, so they said their goodbyes and left with Father Harold for the night. Finn was sitting on the bed next to mine.

"I want to know what happened after we got separated in the jungle," I said. "You know, after you were shot. Do you remember much of it?"

Finn shrugged, and I worried for a moment that I was bringing up his own trauma.

"If you don't want to talk about it," I said, "I understand."

"At first, I didn't remember too much, but Mikael, Phil, and Boyko helped me put the pieces together. From what I understand, by the time they found me, you'd already been taken. I'd lost a lot of blood, and they rushed me by helicopter to the Manaus hospital. Wish I would've been awake for that. I've always wanted to ride in a helicopter."

I laughed and said, "Me too." I wasn't ready yet to tell him I had, while kidnapped and blindfolded.

"I was told they didn't think I'd make it through the night, but the hospital had great doctors. They removed the bullet from my lower back but were still worried about internal bleeding." He lifted the back of his shirt and smiled. "Got me a real-life war wound."

"Yeah, you do. How long were you in for?"

"Two and a half weeks. It felt like ten years though; I was going crazy in there by the end of it. All I wanted to do was look for you. Mikael, Phil, and even Boyko stayed at a hotel close by and visited every day. They had a guard outside my door. I'm not sure if it was to protect me or keep me from escaping to come lookin' for you."

"Well, what happened to the movie?"

"They stopped filming. They blamed themselves for your abduction. Mikael, in particular, was really upset. He'd be so optimistic every morning after speaking with the police and then frustrated every night when they still hadn't located you. A week or so after your disappearance, he came in my room and was *pissed*. He'd just finished talking to the cops again, who said they had no promising leads. Mikael took out his phone and called like a dozen people. By that afternoon, every newspaper, Internet news site, and TV channel had information about you and what happened."

"So that explains the crowd and all the flowers and cards."

"Your kidnapping went viral. The headlines were saying stuff like 'Tango Foxtrot: one shot, one kidnapped and tortured." There were press conferences and a million-dollar reward. I thought for sure someone would turn you in right away."

He paused for a few moments.

"Anyway," Finn said, "since this happened, I've definitely noticed a lot more people talking about human trafficking; never paid any attention to it before."

"That's a good thing, right? I mean, I'm not the first victim. I won't be the last, but maybe some good can come out of it. Out of everything that ..." My voice trailed off.

"Yeah, Mikael and Phil kept it in the spotlight, for sure. They've really done a lot."

"Do you think I'll see them? I want to thank them."

"They said they'd come to West Virginia in about a month or so. They want you to have a chance to get settled. You know, they even paid us the four hundred thousand, even though the movie wasn't completed."

"Wow. That's so ... wow."

"It's very generous of them," Finn said.

I closed my eyes and gently shook my head. I was home now, and everything was the same—except me. "You know, all those years ..."

"What about all them?" Finn quietly asked.

"All those years, for as long as I can remember, all I wanted was more money for the family. I prayed and prayed for so long. So many hiking trips, praying for just one golden ticket, money to help us all out. And now, hearing about us getting four hundred thousand dollars …"

I paused and let out a deep sigh.

"You would think I'd be elated. It was everything I ever wanted, all of those years."

Finn narrowed his eyes in confusion. "Well, that's a good thing, right?"

"Yes, of course. It will help us out tremendously. But I can't help but think about all of Glaucia's children, all of the people who barely survive in the slums, in such terrible conditions. So much worse than you can ever imagine. So much worse than what we experienced growing up. You just can't imagine until seeing it yourself."

I reached out and took one of Finn's hands.

"I feel so blessed to receive all of that money, but at the same time, knowing what I know now … Well, the money just seems so inconsequential."

Finn squeezed my hand in understanding. "Well, maybe just think of it this way. To help other people who need help, you need to have money, right? After we get home and after you recover, let's talk about it some more. Maybe there is something we can do."

I smiled, thankful that he seemed to understand the conflict flowing through me.

CHAPTER 26

Dulce de Leche

The next morning came quickly, and Casey led me down to the conference room. I was wheeled in wearing the hospital pants and a shirt with a long white robe. Father Harold held my hand on the right side of the chair and Finn on my left.

In the room, I immediately felt out of place. Special agents sat around the long table, and I have to admit, it was quite intimidating. The five men and three women, including Casey, were wearing military uniforms or business suits. As I was wheeled into place, each introduced themselves to me. They all seemed very nice, but it was quite daunting.

They explained who they were, what they were doing there, and why they needed my help. The session seemed to last forever, and I broke down in tears several times. I had to recount every scratch, slap, rape, face, smell, vehicle, man, woman, and child: basically every moment since I jumped off the boat with Finn.

Heitor was brought up far too many times for my liking, but I knew how important it was for me to help catch him. What made it even harder, though, was knowing Father Harold and Finn were listening to every detail. I felt so dirty, so dirty all over again. But every so often, I would feel my uncle's or my brother's hand patting my back or smoothing the top of my hand, and it made those dirty feelings recede, if only for a moment.

There came a point when I could no longer continue. I put my hands over my ears and screamed, "Stop! No more."

I pushed the wheelchair away from the table and stood up. I tried to walk, but my legs gave out, and I collapsed.

∞

I woke up later that evening with Finn and Melina by my side. I felt better, but I knew I would never feel normal again.

Over the next few days, I was watched closely and met with a crisis counselor twice a day, which I hated. The more I talked about the horrible events, the more stressed out and agitated it made me. I woke up nightly after a series of unnervingly realistic nightmares, covered in a cold sweat and shaking all over, Heitor's face swimming in front of my eyes.

"The truth shall set you free," one of the counselors said, apparently trying to tap into my faith.

It took all my strength to not throw something at her.

∞

A few days later, Dr. Patel came in with a worried look on her face. "Hi, Tia," she said. "I wanted to talk with you and your family about how you're doing and how they can help your recovery. Will that be okay?"

I liked her soft Indian accent, which was full of care and concern.

"Sure," I said. It wasn't like I had much of a choice before, but I sensed this was all coming to a close.

Dr. Patel went to the door and gestured with her hand, and my family filed in, huddling close.

I sat up straight, suddenly uncertain of where this was going.

"Do you remember when you first got here?" Dr. Patel asked. "You talked about your stress and anxiety from the trauma you went through. You and Melina have been meeting with a therapist every day since your arrival, and I wanted to check in with you to see how these sessions have been going so far."

I paused, glanced at my brothers, and gave them a reassuring smile. "I think okay. It's hard to talk about, but it seems like I'm working through some things. I think Melina is recovering. I still have a lot of work to do. I still have flashbacks. They're so real sometimes, as if I'm reliving things over and over again."

Heitor's angry face seemed to float before my eyes, his mouth twisted into a cruel grin.

Leave me alone. You have no place here.

Dr. Patel nodded. "I had the chance to talk with your therapist this morning, and while you are making good progress, you have a way to go in your recovery."

"Yeah," I said. "She explained everything to me. She told

me that is was common to have nightmares, flashbacks, anxiety, and trouble with sleep. It does explain the flashbacks I seem to get, especially when I'm alone or if it's quiet, like right before I go to sleep."

"Flashbacks are common, along with everything else you described," she said, "so I'm glad you can recognize them when they occur. Your therapist is arranging for you to continue your sessions after you return home. Remember, Tia, it will take some time to recover; someone who's gone through what you have is bound to have residual emotional and mental effects, and it's very important to address them every day. Your family is here to support you each and every step along the way."

"Okay. I understand," I said. All I saw now were expressions of love and concern.

Dr. Patel stood up and placed her hand on my arm, patting it gently. "I'm glad. Let's concentrate on getting you physically and emotionally stronger over the next week or two."

After Dr. Patel left the room, Father Harold stood up after a minute and cleared his throat.

"Finn, I'd like to talk with your sister before we leave this evening. Can you take Wes and Paddy out? Maybe go and explore the city a bit?"

"Sure. We'll see you in a little while." Finn put on his jacket and led his brothers out the door.

Father Harold sat in the chair next to the bed and gently placed his hands on mine. "Hi, little one. So tell me the truth. How are you feeling today?"

I looked into his sparkling eyes. His smile warmed me through and through.

"As I lay here, not moving, I feel fine," I said. "So you're leaving tonight?"

"Yes. This week flew by, but I've got to get back. And you need to get stronger. Do you want to talk to me about anything before I go?" he asked.

I knew what he meant, and I loved him for it. To add to the effect, he looked so pure and holy in his black clerical clothing with the white Roman collar. He was first and foremost a guardian angel sent down to take care of us.

"Do you think I could say Confession and receive Communion?" I asked.

"Yes, of course, Tia," he said with a smile, reaching out a hand and helping me to my feet. "Why don't we go to the chapel for a little while?"

We took our time making our way down to the Catholic chapel. The small dimly lit room had an aroma of incense. Smooth hardwood flooring, cream-colored walls, and statues of the Virgin Mary on the left of the pulpit and Saint Joseph right of the altar made me feel safe.

There were two baskets of flowers sitting on each side of the altar filled with large white, yellow, and purple flowers. In place of a large wooden crucifix, there was a painting of Jesus sitting down on a large boulder, holding two small children in his lap, with another group of children sitting in a semicircle on the grass, looking up toward him.

I knelt down on the cushioned pedestal in front of the statue of the Virgin Mary, lit a votive candle, lowered my head, and prayed. After a few minutes, Father Harold knelt down next to me, and without thinking twice about it, I laid my head on his shoulder and wept.

"How can I ever be forgiven?" I whispered. "I feel I will never be forgiven."

"Come with me," Father Harold said, helping me up again and leading me to the confessional.

We talked for over two hours, and when we came out, Father Harold blessed me and offered me Communion.

While I knew I'd never forget the horror, in that moment, I felt clean, like a pelican that had been drenched in thick, black oil and then gently cleansed and dried, one feather at a time, until I was able to fly once again.

"I need to ask you, well, I need to tell you something before you leave," I said as we sat down in the back pew. "When I was hiking during the rafting trip—where I met Mikael and Phil—I asked the Lord to help me find a golden ticket. It was my way, I guess, of asking for help. But something happened that day, something unexpected. Like a miracle. A gush of wind swept through the trees, and a thousand golden maple leaves fell, with one floating *straight* into my hand. It was at that moment that I felt the presence of God more strongly than ever before."

Father Harold nodded and smiled. "You had been looking down, when you only needed to look up."

"Yes, exactly." I paused and took a deep breath. "Later, after

Finn found that old tin behind the bricks in the fireplace, there was a golden maple leaf pressed between two sheets of wax paper. It was so uncanny, so strange, I … I still don't know what to make of it. Do you recall your parents or grandparents ever mentioning a golden maple leaf?"

Father Harold smiled again. He pulled up his sleeve and pointed to his forearm. "You just gave me goose bumps. Not easy to do!" Then he looked at the painting of Jesus with his children. "You know, now that you mention it, talk of a golden maple leaf does sound remotely familiar. When I get back, I'll rummage through some old trunks and see if I can find anything."

We sat in silence for a few moments.

"The other thing that I wanted to talk to you about was Javier. Isn't it strange how I met him in California, gave him money to get back home, and he ended up being the one to save me when I followed a strange light in the slums of Buenos Aires?"

Father Harold turned toward me and clasped my hand in his.

"Remember Psalm 119:105: 'Thy word is a lamp unto my feet, and a light unto my path.'"

It was another week before I was told I'd be going home. Finn had arranged for me to visit a local salon, where the hairdresser returned my hair to its strawberry blonde color. I looked a lot like the Tia from Fayetteville, West Virginia. The cuts had healed, though there were still scars. The bruises faded, and I had regained some of the weight I'd lost.

But when I looked in the eyes of the version of Tia who stared at me from the mirror, I saw someone else: someone who was at once tortured, yet stronger, someone who had seen brutality and cruelty, and also beauty and humanity, someone who had stared into the depths of the human soul and felt grateful she hadn't seen the bottom.

I glanced over at Melina and was overtaken by feelings of warmth and profound love. The three-year-old's bright eyes and rosy cheeks reflected the innocence and hope of all that is good in this world. As I looked into her eyes, I made a promise to speak frequently about her parents, how much they loved her, how much they sacrificed for her as they journeyed to find a better life. I prayed she was old enough to remember her parents yet young enough to forget what she didn't need to remember.

There was a soft knock on the door, and Finn and I looked up.

Casey poked her head in, smiling. "Hey, you two," she said. "Got a minute? I want to give you some updates. I would've told you sooner, but we needed to confirm everything firsthand."

"I hope it's good news," I said.

She stepped into the room, not losing the smile. "It is good news. Because of your information, the Argentina police tracked down Emanuel's Auto Repair and Body Shop. You were right that it was thirty minutes from the city, and it was exactly as you described. They raided the place, arrested the people who were running the operation, and rescued over forty boys and girls. They are now safe and have either been reunited with their families or placed in foster care until a relative can be located."

"Oh, wow," I exclaimed. "That's fantastic news. I can't believe it."

Casey held out a box and handed it to me. It was like a jeweler's box.

"A present?" I asked, confused. "Who? Why?" I lifted the lid and saw nestled inside was my golden maple leaf pendant. All breath seemed to escape me.

"He said this belonged to you," Casey said, still with that smile. "Marcelo wanted me to tell you that he's having his mom teach him how to make dulce de leche and that when you come to visit, he'll make it for you."

I finally was able to breathe. "What about Lidia, his sister?" I said as I clasped the necklace around my neck.

Casey said, "Here's more great news. The police interrogated the owners of the brothel and discovered the name of the hotel where you'd been auctioned. When they arrived, another auction was under way, and everyone involved was arrested. After questioning, Lidia and the other girls were found at the locations where they'd been sold. They've all been returned to their families now and are reportedly healthy, or getting there."

I held the maple leaf in disbelief. "I'm so happy. Thank you so much. It's a miracle they were found."

"Because of your help, they were able to put a huge dent in the overall operation. Most of the leaders and their gang members were arrested and are being held in custody."

"What about Heitor?"

"No word on him yet, but we believe he's hiding out somewhere until things quiet down. The authorities have pretty much wiped out his entire cartel. His men have either been killed or incarcerated, and I did confirm this morning that all his assets have been frozen."

My body tensed. "Does he know I had something to do with this? Oh ... stupid, of course he does. He must. I mean, who else would've been able to provide that kind of information? Do you think he'll try and come after me?"

Casey shook her head. "Don't worry Tia, truly. You have nothing to worry about. It's nearly impossible for him to cross any border right now without getting caught. They'll catch up to him. It may take a while longer, but they'll catch him."

"But what if he finds me? What if one of his men comes after me? What if he has someone kill my whole family?"

I was suddenly in full panic mode. Nothing was good; nothing made sense. *They weren't going to kill me; they would go after people around me. They'd sneak in and ...*

I jumped, thinking I saw a shadow in the doorway.

"Whoa, Sis, it's okay," Finn said, getting up and putting both hands on my shoulders, forcing me to stop to look him in the eye. "Just breathe. You remember what the doctor said; you need to focus on your breathing when this happens."

"Yes, focus. Breathe," I said, doing just that. "No, it's fine." I started counting to ten silently and drinking water. "I've gotta work through this. It's just going to take some time."

"All right," Casey said slowly. "Well, you should rest, and I'll be back in the morning to take you to the airport. Talk soon," she said, flashing a reassuring smile.

Finn studied me, his eyes filled with concern. "I think I'll take Melina down to the play area when she's done napping so you can get some rest."

"Sure, all right," I said, climbing into bed.

The next morning couldn't come soon enough.

Finn and me said goodbye to Dr. Patel and the staff before we clambered into the car.

I wrapped an arm around Melina. "We're going home," I said. "We're finally going home."

Casey joined us in the back seat, handing me some paperwork for Father Harold to sign for Melina's temporary visa in the United States, with my uncle being the official foster parent for now.

"We'll get things expedited for her citizenship, and I don't anticipate any issues," Casey said. "When you turn twenty-one, you'll be eligible to officially adopt her."

"I don't know how to thank you enough," I said, sighing as we pulled out of the hospital parking lot and onto the street. "Have you heard anything about the orphanage and Glaucia?"

"I do have some information," Casey said. "She's being held on conspiracy charges. I think her trial's in a month or so."

"What about the orphans? Are they okay?"

"I think so. The last I heard, the church brought in another lady to watch over them. I'll put a call in and see if I can find out more."

"For what it's worth, Glaucia's a good woman," I said. "She loved those kids and was only hiding me so she could get money for them. She was always good to me."

"I'll be sure to pass that along," Casey said, not sounding very convincing.

"And what about Javier?" Finn asked. "How's he doing?"

"Well, he's doing quite well, I think. I suppose your Hollywood friends haven't told you yet?"

We shook our heads.

"Because he was the one who played the largest role in your safe return, Javier received the million-dollar reward."

"Amazing!" Finn said. "Talk about things going full circle from a park bench in LA."

I simply smiled and rested my head against the window's glass, staring out at the world passing by. An overwhelming feeling of freedom and hope filled my heart.

CHAPTER 27

Cabin in the Pines

A few hours later, we were met at the airport by Father Harold, Wes, and Paddy, who cheered and acted as if it was the first time we'd seen each other.

"Okay, okay, pipe down," I said. "You're gonna give the wrong impression to your new sister."

"It's better she know the truth now, than when it's too late," Paddy joked, wiggling his eyebrows.

I carried Melina to Father Harold's station wagon, and we piled in with the rest of the brood.

Instead of going home as I so wanted—needed—to do, we went to the church, where there was a small celebratory dinner with a few members of Father Harold's parish. I did enjoy it, catching up with the home folk, but it didn't take long for me to begin to drag. Melina was worse, with her head bobbing against my shoulder, not even pretending to be awake.

"I gotta get her home and put her to bed," I said.

"Wait," Finn said. "There's one other thing I wanna show you. We all do."

I sighed but reluctantly nodded my head. "Okay, but just for a bit."

We said goodbye to Father Harold, climbed into the truck, and made our way down the curvy roads until we reached what appeared to be a newly paved road.

"Are we going the right way? Where y'all taking me?"

"You'll see," Wes said. Then he lowered his voice to a whisper. "Don't tell Tia; it's a surprise."

"Okay, I promise."

I did realize we were heading in the same direction as the old house. Then I saw an unfamiliar structure rising up out of the trees.

"Good Lord," I cried. "Someone staked their claim in the wrong spot. Whose house is on our property?"

As Finn pulled to a stop, Wes and Paddy leapt out, with Wes pulling Melina from her car seat. Then they ran inside the house.

I climbed out and stared in wonder. It was a beautiful, two-story log cabin with a porch wrapping around the front of the house, and two inviting double-seated porch swings. The cabin had a high ceiling and large windows spanning every wall. It was spectacular.

"I don't understand," I said. "What happened?"

"It's our home, Tia," Finn said, placing his hands on her

shoulders. "When you were taken from us, I couldn't eat. I couldn't sleep. I couldn't work. All I wanted was to get back, somehow, someway, to the Amazon and search for you. But it was impossible. They took my passport and told me I couldn't leave. I was a freakin' mess."

"Why didn't you tell me this before?"

"Didn't want to worry you. We need to focus on your recovery. To be honest, I went downhill quickly. It got so bad that Paddy found me passed out along the riverbank. Father Harold brought me to the rectory and prayed beside my bed, and he convinced me I needed to find something to occupy my time until we found you. I took the money that was given to us by Mikael and decided to start fresh, build a new home. Wish you could've been here. Hell, the whole town joined in, built this place in a little over two months. We still have a few things to do, but it's pretty much complete."

He paused, still looking up at it before turning to me.

"Please tell me you love it," he said. His eyes were pleading. That sad ol' moon pie face that we rarely got to see, and for good reason.

I turned to him and said, "Yes, of course I love it. It's beautiful. More than I could have ever hoped for." I paused. "I'm just so sorry for what I put you through." I gave him a tight hug before we walked up the porch stairs. "Mama and Papa would've been so happy here."

I looked up, and my eyes filled with tears. Mounted above the door was an exact replica of the golden maple leaf pendant.

"I knew you'd like that detail," Finn said. "Mr. Milano made it especially for you. And check this out: It's pretty unbelievable, but the day it was delivered, I received a call from Ambassador Spiegel, saying they'd found you. The coincidence is crazy."

I stood there, still a bit stunned, and felt a warmth blooming in my heart.

I followed Finn inside, oohing and ahhing at the rustic decor. "Just like you promised," I said, running my fingers along the soft leather sofa.

"Wait till you see your bedroom."

He led me upstairs to the far end of the hallway. As I walked through the doorway, I threw my hand over my mouth in total disbelief. Finn had arranged it to emulate the style of the hotel room we had in Los Angeles, complete with a large white comforter and a jetted tub. It was the most beautiful bedroom I had ever seen.

I reached over and hugged my brother with all the strength I could muster. "Thank you, Finn," I said. "It's the most beautiful house, the most beautiful room I could ever imagine."

"I'm so glad you like it," he said, smiling ear to ear.

"Oh, look! Mama's rocking chair." Paddy's renovation was spectacular; the dark wood was shining and rubbed with oil.

"Everything's so perfect." I sighed and turned to look outside my new bedroom window. I gasped. "You didn't tear it down: our old house. It's still there."

"Couldn't do it. When it came down to it, I just couldn't see the ol' place fall. When you get up the strength, that renovation will be your project. We're just happy you're home. I had almost given up hope. Having you back … well …" Finn said, his voice drifting off.

"Hey, remember when you discovered that hole behind the fireplace? Where the tin was?" I asked.

"Yeah?"

"Did you ever look inside? Did you find anything?"

Finn smirked. "Maybe."

"What do you mean, maybe? Either you did or you didn't."

"Maybe. Maybe I'm saving that for another time."

The sounds of high-pitched squeals and giggling echoed down the hallway. It felt good to hear Melina laugh, knowing she was safe and carefree, playing silly games with Paddy and Wes.

I looked outside, admiring our family's old home nestled between the tall maples. My mind drifted back to the orphaned children with their big bright eyes, skinny bodies, and dirty bare feet.

One day, one day, I'll return to Glaucia's orphanage and rescue every last one of them.

The sky was turning a magnificent orange and red hue as the sun settled behind the mountains.

Something caught my eye.

I looked toward the right side of the cabin, where my parent's bedroom used to be.

I was certain I saw a shadow.

It was a shadow … a man's shadow.

I looked up at Finn, but he was just smiling off into the distance, unaware of what I saw. When I looked back, the shadow was gone.

Of course it was.

I squeezed my eyes shut and wrapped my hand around my golden maple leaf.

It had only been a flashback, one of many that I had experienced over the last few weeks: ghosts from the past, coming back to haunt me, ghosts I knew I must banish and send away if I ever wanted to be whole again.

I sighed again, deciding I should go check on Melina and her precocious brothers, but before I turned, I caught sight of a gray smoky plume of mist where the shadow had just stood.

AUTHOR'S NOTE

The Girl and the Golden Leaf touches upon a wide variety of complex issues our global society faces today. I would like to specifically address two critical areas of concern: human trafficking and poverty.

On January 11, 2018, Senator John McCain (R-AZ) published a statement during National Slavery and Human Trafficking Awareness Month. These quotes address the current crisis and the need to continue the fight to end human trafficking:

> We must reaffirm our commitment to eliminating all forms of modern day slavery and human trafficking. These are horrific crimes that undermine the most basic human rights, and target the most vulnerable and at-risk individuals in our society. ...

> It is our duty to not only raise awareness, but to stop the victimization of all men, women and children.

An estimated forty million people are enslaved across the world, with profits exceeding $150 billion every year.[1] Evil traffickers prey upon the weakest, most vulnerable, and most isolated: those who are desperately seeking a better life, as they try to escape dire poverty, oppression, war, and conflict.

According to David M. Luna, former Senior Director for National Security and Diplomacy, International Narcotics and Law Enforcement, US Department of State, women, children, and migrants are particularly at risk as they fall victim to the hands of criminal traffickers through fraud, lured by false promises, coercion, violence, extortion, kidnapping, and eventual enslavement. Luna, who is now the President and CEO of Luna Global Networks, captured so beautifully the conviction we must all hold and act upon to end human trafficking:

> No person should ever have a price tag attached
> to their heart and soul nor be restricted, abused,
> and violated against their physical integrity and
> free will.[2]

According to the United Nations,[3] globally, more than eight hundred million people are still living in extreme poverty. *The*

---

[1] International Labour Organization (ILO), Global Estimates of Modern Slavery, 2018.

[2] David M. Luna, "Ending Human Trafficking: Building a Better World and Partnerships for Sustainable Security and Human Dignity," OECD-APEC Roundtable on Combating Corruption Related to Human Trafficking, Cebu, Philippines, August 27, 2015.

[3] United Nations, "The Millennium Development Goals Report 2015."

Girl and the Golden Leaf takes Tia to the heart-wrenching slums of Villa 31 in Buenos Aires. There, she witnesses extreme poverty and hardship suffered by those who happened to be born at this time, in this place.

Anthony Lake, Executive Director for United Nations Children's Fund (UNICEF), spoke on the impact of poverty on children:[4]

> As we look around the world today, we're confronted with an uncomfortable but undeniable truth: Millions of children's lives are blighted, for no other reason than the country, the community, the gender or the circumstances into which they are born.
>
> Before they draw their first breath, the life chances of poor and excluded children are often being shaped by inequities. Disadvantage and discrimination against their communities and families will help determine whether they live or die, whether they have a chance to learn and later earn a decent living. Conflicts, crises and climate-related disasters deepen their deprivation and diminish their potential.

Millions of people continue to suffer from poverty, a lack of clean food and water, and brutality at the hands of those who

---

[4] United Nations Children's Fund (UNICEF), "The State of the World's Children 2016, A Fair Chance for Every Child," June 2016.

exploit them for personal gain. In every corner of the globe, poverty exists, and it's up to those of us who are fortunate to be born under favorable circumstances to lend a helping hand as often as possible. Whether it's financially sponsoring a child, assembling care packages and nutritious meals, or finding new ways to raise awareness, there are countless opportunities to get involved. I have made a commitment to help; will you please join me? It is now our time to make a difference.

CPSIA information can be obtained
at www.ICGtesting.com
Printed in the USA
LVHW091430060219
606604LV00007B/91/P